A Memory of Fire

A Memory of Fire

The Dragon War, Book Three

Daniel Arenson

This novel is a work of fiction. Names, characters, places and incidents are either the product of the author's imagination, or, if real, used fictitiously.

ISBN: 978-1-927601-11-2

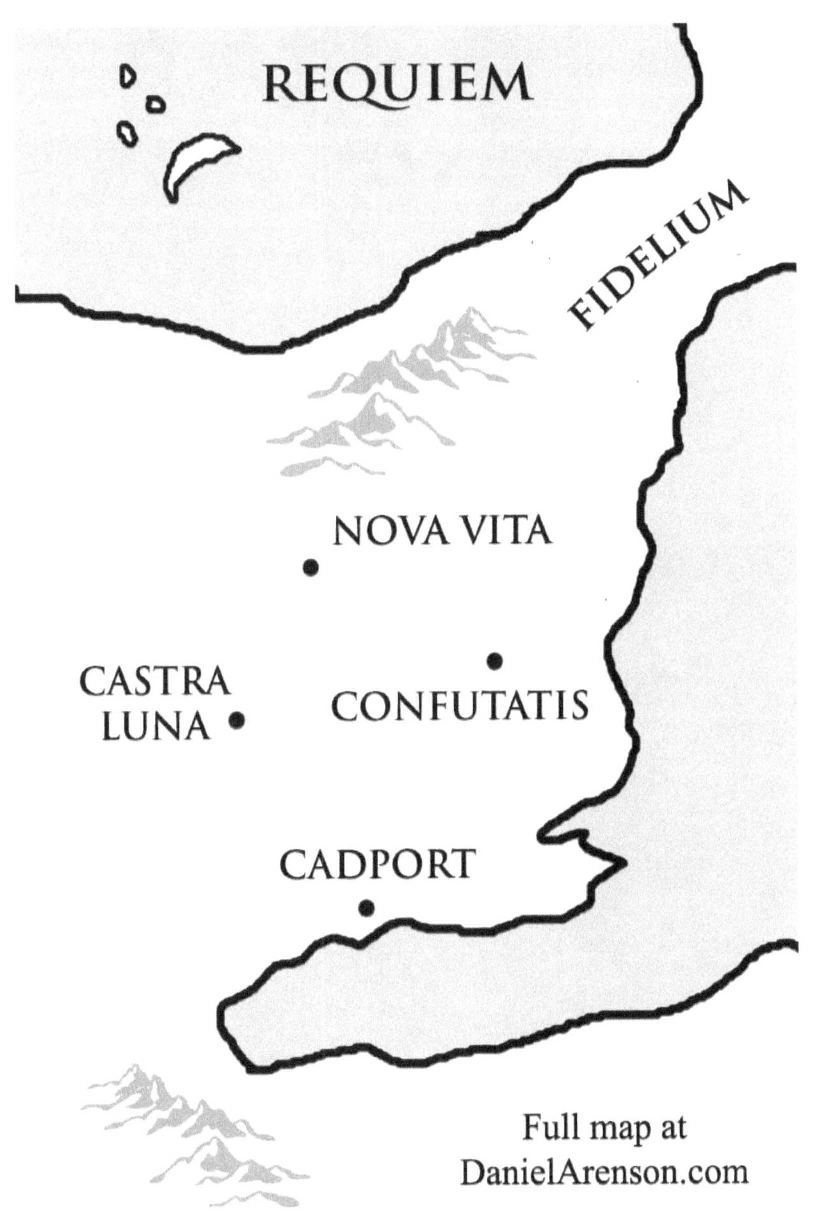

Full map at
DanielArenson.com

KAELYN

Kaelyn was scouting the islet when fire blazed, rocks flew, and she met the crazy old man who changed her life.

Many islands dotted this sea, rising in a ridge like the spine of some sunken, ancient sea god. This islet rose leagues away from the others, barely larger than a rock. When Kaelyn first saw it from above, she was going to keep flying. Valien had sent her to find new bases for their Resistance, and this place looked too small to even host a single fighter. A carob tree crested its peak, and two palm trees swayed across its shore. The cay seemed no larger than Kaelyn's old bedroom back at the capital.

A green dragon on the wind, Kaelyn was gliding directly above the islet, heading farther south, when the explosion rocked the sea.

The sound roared in her ears, loud as cannon fire. The shock wave tossed her into a spin and cracked two scales. Before she could right herself, a cloud of dust burst from below, enveloping her. Rocks pummeled her stomach and she yelped. The skin on her belly was thick, but those rocks jabbed her like arrows.

A volcano? she wondered. No. The smell of gunpowder flared here. After fighting the Regime for three years, Kaelyn would recognize that smell anywhere.

Blinded, she beat her wings mightily, churning the dust and ash. She rose higher, grimacing. Fire blazed below and smoke twisted around her like demons. She flew, not even knowing what direction she headed, until she emerged back into blue sky.

"What in the Abyss?" she said, coughing, and looked behind her.

Dust still plumed from the islet, trailing north with the wind like a rising serpent. Kaelyn hovered in place, whipping her head from side to side. Was somebody attacking her? Did imperial ships sail here armed with cannons? Had her father found her?

That was when she heard laughter and saw the old loon.

He burst out from the smoke below, racing across the islet. He wore only a loincloth, and his long, white hair hung wild about his sooty face. He ran down the islet's slope, laughing, and danced a jig.

"Fire!" He jumped and snapped his ankles together. "Explosion! *Boom!*"

Kaelyn squinted, hovering above. The man seemed unharmed, if blackened with soot. This was no enemy. This was... who was he? Kaelyn dived a hundred yards lower, heading down to the islet.

When the old man saw her, he waved enthusiastically, his whole body swaying with the gesture, and grinned.

"Hello, pretty green bird!" he said. "Caw! *Caw!* Are you a bird or a dragon? Bantis kills dragons. Bantis booms them away. Go, dragon, go!"

Kaelyn kept diving. She circled above the islet, taking a closer look. The man was still dancing, waving his arms, and cackling. His left arm ended at the elbow, she noticed. He wore a prosthetic topped with a blade.

Kaelyn gasped.

"An exiled axehand?" she whispered. She squinted, bringing him into clearer focus.

No, she decided. The Axehand Order, a fanatical priesthood whose warriors wore axes upon their stumps, had been founded fifteen years ago. The elder below, even back then, would have been too old to join.

She filled her wings with air, descended, and landed upon the shore. The old man cawed before her, waving his arms and kicking sand as if trying to scare her off. Kaelyn released her magic, returning to human form.

"Caw!" the old man said, standing on one scrawny leg and flapping his arms like wings. "Go, dragon! Leave. No dragons allowed on Genesis Isle."

Kaelyn stared at him, head tilted. The air still smelled of gunpowder and smoke, though the dust was settling, revealing a hole upon the islet's hillside. When Kaelyn looked back at the old man, she saw that he wasn't wearing an axe upon his stump after all--it was a hammer. Several other prosthetic arms hung from his belt; one ended with a shovel, another with a knife, and a third with a hook.

"Are you hurt?" Kaelyn asked him.

The man stopped jumping and waving his arms. He hunched forward, tilted his head too, and squinted at her. He was rail-thin; Kaelyn could see his ribs pushing against his sooty skin.

"Is Bantis hurt?" he asked, voice high and quavering like a taut lute string. "No. Well, yes. Some hurts run deep. Some hurts are... inside. My heart." He slammed his prosthetic hammer-hand against his chest, then yelped. "Hurts! Heart hurts! Wait. No. That's just my hammer. Wrong hand."

He danced another jig, pulled off his hammer prosthetic, and tossed it aside. He grabbed a different prosthetic from his belt--this one shaped as a shovel--and attached it to his stump.

"Better," he said and grinned. "See? Right hand. Bantis is a digger. Bantis digs! Bantis digs for a big, big weapon. Kills dragons! Come, come, Bantis show you."

With that, he spun around, darted across the sand, and began to climb the island's hillside.

Kaelyn followed, waving aside the last plumes of dust. Despite his scrawny frame and advanced years, Bantis scuttled up the hill like a spider, scampering over boulders and bushes. Even Kaelyn, slim and young and light on her feet, struggled to keep up. Soot darkened her long yellow hair, and her bow and quiver swung across her back.

As she climbed and the dust cleared, she saw many strange items strewn across the hillside. Some she recognized: barrels of gunpowder, a cannon, and tinderboxes. Other items were foreign to her: iron spheres that looked like cannonballs but were topped with fuses; shafts of wood topped with metal pipes, possibly miniature cannons; and larger pipes--these ones made of leather and wood--with glass circles filling each end.

"Did you invent these things?" Kaelyn said, treading carefully between them, unsure if they'd explode under her feet.

The old man hopped ahead. "Invent them? Yes, yes. Bantis is the inventor. Bantis deals with booms. But now Bantis digs for greatest weapon. Here, come!" He leaped onto a boulder, turned toward her, and gestured her onward. "Come, see it, see it!"

She followed, climbing over the boulder, and beheld a cave upon the hillside. Smoke still rose from it, and the smell of gunpowder invaded her nostrils.

"Bantis made this hole," the elder said, nodded, and scuttled down into the darkness. "Bantis boomed it. Bantis digs! Come, see. Biggest weapon buried below. Kills dragons."

With that, he disappeared into the cavern. Kaelyn climbed the last few feet, coughed, and peered into the shadows.

"Be careful!" she cried down to him. "It's not safe."

His head peeked out from the pit. He grinned, revealing only three teeth. "Safe? No. No, it's not safe here. It's not safe anywhere from the cruel dragons. But Bantis will kill them. Yes. Yes, Bantis will dig. Dig!"

He raised his shovel-hand and spun back into the cavern.

With a sigh, Kaelyn followed into the darkness.

"Who are you?" she called after him. "Where are you from?"

She had never heard such an accent before. Could this man be... a foreigner? Not Vir Requis like her, but a survivor of the great wars?

Kaelyn sucked in her breath.

He has to be, she thought.

She had been only a child when Emperor Frey Cadigus, her cruel father, had begun his conquests of "purification". His Legions had swept across the known world in those years, burning all foreign lands. The griffins, the true dragons of the west, the wyverns, and all other flying beasts fell. They burned in dragonfire, her father's vengeance for ancient wars a thousand years gone-by.

And he burned men too, Kaelyn remembered. Two great kingdoms of men had bordered Requiem in those years: Osanna in the east, an ancient land of forests and plains, and Tiranor in the south, a desert realm. No magic had blessed their people. They could not become dragons like the Vir Requis, but rode horses, built great cities, and lived in peace with Requiem.

Until my father burned them all, Kaelyn thought. *Until he deemed them impure, slaughtered them, and annexed the wastelands.*

Could this frail old man be a human survivor--a true human with no dragon form?

"Bantis, where are you from?" she said in the darkness.

When she crawled deeper into the cavern, she found him at the bottom. He was staring at a wall of earth and stone, scratching his head.

"Have to dig *deeper*," he said. "Deeper! Buried here, it is. Bantis feels it. Big weapon."

He knelt and began digging with his prosthetic shovel, tossing dirt and rocks over his shoulder. Kaelyn coughed and spat out dirt.

"Stop that!" she said. "Talk to me. Do you need help?" Her voice softened. "How long have you been here?"

He looked over his shoulder and flashed his snaggletoothed grin.

"They sent me here. They banished Bantis! Poor poor Bantis. The others want to fight. They don't think Bantis can help." He snorted, spitting out dirt. "All because Bantis blew up their camp. And their ship." He tapped his cheek. "And the palm grove. And maybe their last sheep." He raised his shovel in indignation. "Sheep, palm, ships, camp... Who cares? Bantis deals with explosives. Bantis deals with weapons! Bantis will find big weapon here on Genesis Isle. Big weapon to fight the dragons."

Kaelyn's breath left her.

"The others," she whispered. "Are there others like you? Others who live on these islands?"

He was digging again.

"You talk too much." He frowned over his shoulder at her. "Bantis busy digging. Bantis dig for weapon to kill you. You burned us. You burned our lands. You will die! Let Bantis dig so he can kill you."

"I'm not your enemy," Kaelyn said. "Are you... from the south? From across the sea? Do you fight Frey Ca--"

Bantis screamed.

His face twisted. He fell and cowered and covered his head with his arms.

"Do not say his name!" the old man wailed. He shivered. "Do not say the name of the demon! He will fly here. He will burn us. He burned my brothers, he is a demon, he must die, I am scared. Please, please, don't burn me, dragons. Don't burn..."

Kaelyn gasped and knelt by the man. She touched his shoulder, but he only cowered farther into the corner.

"We fight a common enemy," she said. "Don't be afraid. I too seek to kill the tyrant."

The old man peeked between his fingers. "You... you are..." He voice dropped to a whisper. "You are Vir Requis?"

"I am Kaelyn Cadigus of Requiem. I fight for the Resistance, a band of Vir Requis who hate the tyrant and seek to dethrone him. We're your allies, my friend. Will you come with me to meet our leader? Will you help us, and will you let us help you?"

He lowered his arms. His eyes lit with fire, and anger twisted his face. His hair stuck out, white and wild.

"The tyrant burned Bantis's land," he said. "The tyrant slew Bantis's brothers. Show me your army, dragon. And then... then Bantis will help you."

TILLA

They stood atop Tarath Imperium, a princess and a soldier, and gazed upon a dark empire.

From here upon the tower, a thousand feet above the world, Tilla could see for many leagues. The city of Nova Vita spread below like a breaking wheel, the tower rising from its center, its boulevards like spokes. Between the streets stood houses and shops, countless buildings of brick, their roofs white with snow. The great Castra Draco rose to the south, a castle with four towers, the heart of the Legions. The twisting, black Castra Academia rose in the east, the school that had broken and remolded her into a commander. The arena where prisoners died, the smithies where steel rang, and the monolithic statues of Frey Cadigus--they all seemed so small from here, toys Tilla could lift and break.

But it's Rune I will break, she thought. *The empire seems small from here, but it is mighty. And Rune will serve it.*

At her side, Princess Shari Cadigus spoke.

"Has he confessed his sins?" She snarled into the wind, eyes blazing. "You've had a full moon with him, Tilla Siren. Have you broken him yet?"

A gust of snowy wind whipped Tilla's hair, pinched her cheeks, and stung her eyes. Tilla was a child of the south, of warm Cadport with its mild winters and sea breezes to scatter any snow clouds. Here in the north, in the capital, there was snow and ice and biting winds like blades. Tilla wore steel plates over wool, not enough to warm her, but she was a soldier of Requiem; she buried cold, pain, and weakness deep within her.

The emperor's daughter does not shiver in this wind, she thought. *Nor will I.*

"I need more time, Commander." Tilla clutched her sword, seeking comfort from the well-worn leather grip. "He is still shocked, hurt, and confused. He will worship our glory. I will sway him."

Shari spun toward her, teeth bared. Tilla was a tall woman, but Shari loomed above her, a beast of black steel, wild dark hair, and eyes like forge fires. Her pauldrons flared out, and her gloved hands clutched the dagger and hammer that hung upon her belt.

"Your words are useless, Siren," the princess said. "I will make him confess his sins. I will have him beg to praise us." She drew her weapons, raising hammer and blade. "I will begin by cutting off his nails, then his fingers, then his manhood. I will proceed to hammer his bones, shattering one at a time, until all are broken. I will flay his skin and pull out his bowels as he watches. I will laugh as he begs for death. And I will drag him here to this tower, stand him above the empire, and make him scream his loyalty. I will make him praise the red spiral so the entire empire hears."

Shari's eyes flashed with bloodlust. She licked her lips and her chest rose and fell.

Rune tore off her wing, Tilla remembered. *She beat him bloody the day he arrived here, but that only whet her appetite. She could never hurt him enough.*

"Commander," Tilla said and lowered her head, knowing she must speak carefully. "I know Relesar. We grew up together. Please give me more time, and I can sway him. If the empire sees a beaten, flayed, mutilated wreck hailing the red spiral, it would instill only rage in their hearts. The Resistance would gain more power. More would rise up against us." She dared to meet Shari's eyes. "But if Relesar stands here tall and unhurt, and he proudly shouts out his allegiance, the empire will see that even the heir of

Aeternum worships our glory. The Resistance will lose all legitimacy. Their fire will disperse."

Shari snorted. "Yes, I've heard of your little plan, Lanse. My father told me. You begged him too for this pup's safety. He agreed with you then, I know it. The man is a fool." Shari reached out, grabbed Tilla's arm, and thrust her face so close their noses almost touched. "But I am not. I see what you're doing, Siren. You still care for the boy. You try to protect him. But you cannot protect him from me."

Tilla stared back, daring not look away; looking away would show weakness. Shari was stronger, older, and certainly higher-ranking than her, but if Tilla wanted to save Rune, she had to hold her ground.

"Care for him? Protect him? Commander, he slew my comrades in Castra Luna." Tilla allowed herself a snarl. "He cowered in my city, letting us destroy it. I survived nine moons of training to become an officer. I fought at Luna and in Cadport. I slew men for the red spiral, and I watched my own men die." She slammed her fist against her chest. "I hail the red spiral! I wear that spiral upon my shoulders. I worship our cause with every fiber of my being, and Relesar is an enemy of that cause. He will be our greatest champion. Protect him? No, Commander. I care not to protect him. I want him to fight for us--not cower for us, not bleed for us, not scream and weep--but *join* us. That will be our greatest triumph--not to torture him, but to turn him against Valien."

As she spoke these words, staring firmly into her commander's eyes, Tilla's insides shook. Did she speak truth or lie? Did she still love Rune, or did she only love the red spiral? Did she truly want him as a champion, or was Shari right--was Tilla just trying to save an old friend?

I don't know, she thought, her throat tight. *He was my childhood friend and then the man I loved. Who is he now?*

Tilla swallowed, looked inward at her fraying soul, and saw the answer. She knew why she had to convince Rune to join them.

Because I am torn between my past and my present. Because I am torn between Rune and the red spiral. Because if he joins us, I can have both, and I will no longer feel broken.

Shari stared at her, silent, still gripping her arm. She raised her dagger, bringing it between their faces. Tilla sucked in her breath but refused to flinch.

"When Relesar tore off my wing, you saved my life, Lanse," Shari said, eyes narrowed. "For that, I will grant you more time. You have until the new moon to sway him. And if you cannot..." Shari growled and tilted her blade. "This steel will make him scream so loudly the entire city will hear."

With that, Shari spun around, marched to the tower battlements, and shifted. She took flight as a dragon, one wing wide and blue, the other constructed of wood, rope, and leather. With a blast of fire, she flew into the distance.

Tilla remained upon the tower. She placed her hands against the battlements, blew out her breath, and found herself shivering. If she could not sway Rune soon, she suspected that blade would cut her too.

"Stars damn you, Rune," she whispered into the wind.

She shifted into a dragon. She flew.

The snowy wind roared around her. Tilla dived across Cadigus Square, a cobbled expanse larger than all of Cadport. Leaving the palace grounds behind, she flew over crowded streets and houses. Troops marched below and dragons shrieked above.

A mile south of the palace, she saw the Citadel, a crumbling edifice rising from snow.

Many years ago, this fortress had been called Castra Murus, the barracks of the city guardians. When Frey had established the Axehand Order, he drafted the old City Guard into his Legions, then turned the castle into a prison. The Citadel, they called it now--a place of pain, blood, and screams. No more noble warriors filled its halls. Today prisoners languished in its cellars, chained and beaten. Today blood stained the old bricks. Today she would find Rune here.

When first bringing Rune north, she had imprisoned him in a cell by the courtyard. When he would not cave, she had moved him to the dungeon. She had hoped the darkness, the echoing screams, and the smell of blood would sway him. Yet still Rune would not hail the red spiral. And so Tilla had moved him again. Now Rune languished in the cruelest cell this prison contained, a place where minds had broken, where prisoners had smashed their skulls against the wall to end the pain.

She flew above the prison courtyard and halls, heading toward the Red Tower.

Four towers rose from the Citadel, but the Red Tower was the most infamous. Its bricks were as gray and craggy as the rest of the keep; it was named after the blood that flowed within. Frey had imprisoned and tortured his greatest enemies here. Generals loyal to the old king, lords sworn to Aeternum, and resistors caught lurking in the city--all had languished here.

Tilla landed in a courtyard below the tower, shook her head to scatter her smoke, and returned to human form. The tower guards saluted her, and Tilla stepped between them and through the doorway. She climbed the spiraling staircase, heading up toward him.

She climbed many steps, and her breath was heavy when she reached the tower top. An oaken door stood here. Tilla wore the key on a chain around her neck. With a creak, she opened the door and stepped into the darkness.

The day was bright outside, the sun glittering across the snow, but shadows filled this room. Two arrowslits, vestiges of the Citadel's olden days, allowed narrow beams of light to fall into the chamber.

One beam, which lit the western wall, fell upon horror. A stretching rack stood here beside an iron maiden. Smaller torture instruments hung on pegs: hammers, thumbscrews, pliers, floggers, and a dozen other tools of mutilation. Dried blood covered the instruments; Shari had used them many times upon her prisoners.

The second beam, which lit the northern wall, fell upon Rune.

Tilla released her breath and her belly twisted.

"Rune," she whispered.

He sat against the wall, his wrists manacled behind his back. A chain ran from the manacles to a bracket, only a few feet long. Dirt and old bruises darkened his skin. Shari had beaten him the first day, but she had not tortured him yet.

I have until the new moon, Tilla thought. *Only eleven days to sway him. And then Shari will pull her tools off the wall, and when I visit Rune again, I will not recognize him.*

He looked up at her between strands of scraggly hair.

"Tilla," he said hoarsely, lips cracked.

Chains clanking, he struggled to stand up. He winced, still weak and haggard, then fell back down and sat panting.

"You used to be so strong," Tilla said. "We'd fight with wooden swords on the beach. We'd run and wrestle and swim and fly. Oh, Rune. It doesn't have to be this way."

He glared up at her, chest rising and falling, as if every breath was a struggle. Tilla stepped toward him. Armor clanking, she sat down and leaned against him.

"It doesn't have to be this way," Rune repeated, raspy. "You are right, Tilla. You are right. We could have fled this place the first day. We can still flee. You carry the key around your neck. You just need to unchain me. There are only two guards outside. We need only break past them and fly."

Tilla laid her head against his shoulder, placed a hand on his thigh, and sighed. "You know I can't do that."

Rune wriggled away as best he could in his chains. "And you know I can't do what you ask."

She turned to look at him, narrowed her eyes, and held his shoulder. "Why? Why, Rune? I... Oh stars, look at you." Her eyes dampened. "It hurts me to see you like this. Thin. Haggard. Your body bruised. I can't see you like this, Rune, chained here. If you just hail the red spiral, if you just join Frey, we can--"

"And it hurts me to see *you* like this," he said, and his eyes flashed. "Chains? Bruises? They are nothing compared to what I see. I see a girl from Lynport, a friend, a kind woman clad in black steel, bearing the sigil of evil. I see a roper's daughter, a woman I love, serving a beast and wielding his weapons and--"

"I serve Requiem!" she said, her turn to interrupt. "Frey is a beast? Yes, Rune. Frey is evil? Perhaps. But we cannot save the world. We cannot defeat him. So we must serve him, and we must serve Requiem. Rune, please. None of this should have happened. None of it! If you hadn't joined the Resistance, Castra Luna would still stand, and our friends would still live--Mae Baker and all the others. Cadport--and yes, I still call it Cadport--would still stand." She dug her fingers into his shoulders, hurting him but not caring. "But you fought against Requiem. You killed thousands. You lured the Legions to our city, and you watched that city burn, and now everyone from our home is dead. Everyone we grew up with. Everyone we ever knew. Dead, Rune. Dead because of you."

"Not because of me!" He shouted now. "I fought for our city. I fought for our kingdom. I fought for you, Tilla. I fought to save you from him, and now... now you imprison me here, and you ask me to praise your lord? To praise the man who burned our city?"

"I ask you to live!" she said. "I ask you to... to avoid that wall." She gestured at the western wall where the torture instruments hung. "She will torture you, Rune. You do not know what she can do. She will dislocate your bones. She will cut off your manhood and force you to watch her burn it. She will flay your skin, remove your organs, and make you scream for the red spiral. She's done this to enemies before. You've been in this chamber for long days. You've studied her instruments. Why do you still refuse to join us?"

Rune closed his eyes and his face paled. He shook his head.

"You won't let them do that," he whispered. "I have to believe, Tilla. I still believe in you. You will not let them do that."

"I cannot stop them. Only you can."

He opened his eyes and looked at her.

"Tilla," he said, "do you remember our last night in Lynport? Not the battle. The night before you joined the Legions."

Her throat constricted. Her eyes dampened, and she blinked and clenched her fists.

"I remember," she whispered.

"We can find another beach," he said. "We can flee to distant lands together, to unexplored countries, or to the deserts across the sea. We can be together again. Not in this place. Not here in this cruel city. We can be like we were."

Tilla tasted a tear on her lips, and she hated herself for it, and she hated Rune for making her cry. She had not shed tears for moons in Castra Academia as her tormentors burned her, but she cried here.

"Those days are gone." She held his shoulders, knelt above him, and stared into his eyes. "They are gone, Rune. They are over. You cannot flee Frey; his arm is too long. You cannot fight him; he is too strong. But we can be together here. We can serve him together, two soldiers for his cause."

He shook his head. "Never. I will never serve him, and I will not watch you serve him."

She pulled his hair back from his brow and found herself caressing it. She leaned forward, kissed his cheek, and whispered into his ear.

"Please. Please, if you have any love for me, if our memories together mean anything to you... do as I say. Worship him. Save yourself."

She rose to leave. She walked toward the door, tears in her eyes.

His voice rose behind her. "I surrendered myself to save the last people of Lynport... but also to save you, Tilla. Also to save you."

She could not bear to turn and look at him. Her tears streamed down her cheeks. She left the chamber, closed the door behind her, and bit her lip until she tasted blood.

VALIEN

He stood upon the beach, watching the old man caw, run in circles, and plead for his life.

"Calm yourself, friend!" Valien said. "We won't harm you."

The old man wore but a loincloth and a belt strung with his prosthetic hands. His eyes bulged with fear. He tugged at his long white hair, and his chest, frail enough to reveal his ribs, rose and fell as he panted.

"You... you are Vir Requis!" he said, voice high and quavering like a bird's call. "You burn us. You burn my home! You burn Tiranor. But Bantis will fight you. Bantis invents. Bantis booms things. Big weapon. Bantis dig for it. Bantis kill you all!"

With that, he resumed running in circles. He raced toward his beached raft, an old thing of rotten wood and rope. When he saw the two resistors who stood nearby, he turned the other way and ran, nearly slamming himself against two more. He fell into the sand, leaped up, and began to wave his arms like a man trying to shoo away squirrels.

Standing at Valien's side, Kaelyn sighed.

"He was like this when I found him," she said. "He was living on a rock he called Genesis Isle. I think he was alone there for a very long time. But he spoke of other survivors. I thought my father killed all Tirans, but... Oh stars, I hope he's not the last."

Valien looked at her, and as always--no matter how many times he gazed upon her--he felt his fear melt under sadness. Kaelyn had always been pale, but the southern sun had bronzed her skin. Her hair, once dark as honey, had lightened under this sunlight into a bright gold. Instead of her forest garb, she stood barefoot in the sand, clad in a white tunic, a wild thing swept from the sea onto the shore, a mythical creature of sand and sun and secrets. But her eyes were the same--hazel, soft, and kind, the eyes that had warmed Valien through the years of war.

"He's a Tiran," he said. "I visited Tiranor years ago. I was little older than you are now, and I still served the old king." He looked across the sea and inhaled deeply, remembering the scent of the southern desert, a perfume of sand and spices. "The Tirans were a proud people, tall and golden-skinned and blue-eyed, their hair a platinum so pale it seemed almost white. They lived in oases where palm trees soared, cranes sang, and limestone palaces rose into blue skies. They spread across dunes and mountains, bringing life to the desert. I spent a year there, an ambassador of Requiem. I still miss the sweetness of Tiranor's wine, figs, and dates; her music of lutes and drums; the song of her trees and birds; and mostly her people, an old enemy of Requiem grown into a close friend." Valien returned his eyes to Kaelyn and his voice soured. "Frey Cadigus burned that land and slaughtered those people, his revenge for a war seven hundred years ago. He burned the oases. He butchered mothers and babes. He toppled temples and slew every Tiran he found. I thought they had all died. And here we have this one... a survivor."

Bantis was crouched in the sand, hopping like a frog. Hearing Valien's last sentence, he looked up and tilted his head like an inquisitive owl.

"Survivor?" he said, hopping around on his hands. "Yes, yes, Bantis survived! Others too. Army! Army like this one, yes." He gestured at the resistors who covered the beach and hills of the island.

Valien looked around him and sighed.

Army? he thought. No, this was no army. These were but ragged survivors too.

The island was small, no larger than the city of Lynport back in Requiem. Valien had named it Horsehead Island due to its shape. Perhaps it had no true name; it did not appear in the maps of Requiem. Located a three-day flight from the empire's southeastern shore, it housed the remains of his Resistance. Three thousand men and women lived here in huts, caves, or simply upon the beach. Their clothes were ragged and their weapons dulled, but their eyes still shone. Some of these resistors had been following Valien for years--they had hidden with him in the ruins of Confutatis, fought with him at Castra Luna, and crawled with him through tunnels in Lynport. Others had just recently joined his command--some were men of Cain's Canyon, outcast from Requiem after fighting Frey, and others had once followed the outlaw Leresy Cadigus. They walked across the beach, moved between the huts, and climbed the hills, haggard and long of hair and tanned of skin. An army? Valien did not know.

Maybe we're little better than old Bantis, he thought.

A voice rose behind him, twisted with contempt.

"I say we put the old bugger out of his misery."

He turned to see Leresy walking across the beach, a smirk on his face.

Valien growled. "And since when did anyone care what you say, boy?"

The young, outcast prince ignored him. Strutting as if he still wore finery rather than sandy rags, Leresy approached the old Tiran. He sniffed and wrinkled his nose.

"Stars above, the old man stinks," he said. He lifted a stick and jabbed Bantis with it. "All scrawny too, ribs showing and all. I say we put him down. He's no use to us."

Bantis seemed to find his courage. He snapped his teeth at Leresy, shoved the stick aside, and barked like an enraged dog.

"Scrawny?" the old man demanded. "No use? Bantis has many uses. Bantis is an inventor. Bantis invented hand cannons. Bantis invented glass eyes that can see far. Bantis is digging--digging for big weapon. Genesis Isle is little, but *big* weapon is there. Weapon to slay dragons." He puffed out his chest. "Bantis smells like gunpowder; he no *stinks*."

With a grumble, Valien trudged forward, shoved Leresy aside, and stared at the wild-haired old man.

"Bantis, you said there are others," Valien said. "Where are they? Did other Tirans survive?"

"Oh yes, oh yes!" Bantis said and resumed hopping, spinning around, and kicking sand. "Many others survived. They live on Maiden Island. Big island, it is, big like this one. But they banished poor Bantis. All because Bantis loves explosives. Poor poor Bantis. He built them hand cannons and fireballs and lots of things that go *boom*! And poor Bantis now lives alone."

Valien looked up and met Kaelyn's gaze. She nodded and he returned his eyes to the old man.

"Bantis, will you show us there? Will you lead us to the others?"

The old man's eyes widened. He tugged at his long, white hair and bounced about in circles like a monkey on a leash, slapping the sand.

"Take you there? Yes, yes. Bantis take you to the others. Bantis trusts you. Follow! Follow. We go to their island. But not as dragons, no! Shoot you they will. Kill you with my inventions." He hopped toward his raft, which lay upon the shore. "We oar our way there, yes."

He detached his shovel prosthetic, slung it from his belt, and lifted an oar from the raft. He attached the oar to his stub, grinned, and looked at Valien eagerly like a dog begging for a walk.

"Follow, follow! Bantis take you." He began to paddle the raft through the sand, seemingly unaware that it wasn't moving. "Follow!"

Valien sighed and looked at Kaelyn. She gave him a grin, her teeth bright white against her tanned face. She hefted her bow across her shoulder and gripped her sword.

"Ready for another adventure?" she asked.

Valien's heart twisted again. Her golden hair, her blue eyes, her smile that spoke of all the fire, blood, and rain they'd flown through--every time they hurt him.

"Never and always," he answered.

He gave a few orders to his men, then began pushing the raft toward the sea. Kaelyn pushed at his side. Scrawny Bantis stood upon the raft, rowing as if he himself were moving the vessel. He whooped as it splashed into the waves.

Valien and Kaelyn waded through the water, pushing the raft deeper. Waves rose and fell. Bantis kept oaring upon the raft, but the waves grew larger, splashing and shoving the raft back toward the shore.

With a grumble, Valien shifted into a dragon.

He flattened himself so his belly grazed the sea floor, and his nostrils rose above the water. He beat his tail, driving forward and pushing the raft.

"Bantis oars fast!" Bantis said upon the raft, his oar barely even skimming the water. "No waves can stop old Bantis."

Valien rolled his eyes, snorted smoke, and kept shoving the raft. The waves crashed against them. The raft rose and fell violently, almost flipping over. Still in human form, Kaelyn climbed onto the vessel and crouched low. She pulled Bantis down beside her.

"Hold on tight while you oar, friend," she said. She looked back at Valien and winked.

The waves grew larger and larger, crashing against them. The last one would have overturned the raft had Valien, swimming behind, not held tight with his claws. Past the last breaker, he shifted back into human form, climbed onto the raft, and shook water from his hair.

"Poor poor Valien," said Bantis, looking at him in concern. "Waves were too strong for you. You fell overboard. It's okay, Bantis steered us through."

Valien grunted, spat overboard, and watched Horsehead Island dwindle behind them. A single, orphaned archway rose upon its peak, green with ivy. Three columns, the vestiges of an ancient temple, still stood upon its shore; twenty other columns lay fallen around them. Resistors moved across the beach, between the trees, and upon the hilltops.

It was not a bad life. Valien could stay there, lead his men, and find a new life with Kaelyn. A life of sunlight. Of peace. Of trees and whispering waves and no more war, no more fire or blood.

He gritted his teeth. But no. They'd been living here for a moon now. The time would come for them to fly again. To fight. To bleed.

Valien lowered his head and thought of Rune.

I will not forget you, Rune. I will not leave you to a life of torture and darkness.

He had known Rune since the boy's birth. He had fought at his side, bled with him, killed with him. Rune had become more than just the hope of Requiem.

He is like my son, Valien thought. *He is like the son Marilion and I never had.*

"And I will save you," he rasped, voice too low for the others to hear.

The island grew smaller and smaller behind them, and Bantis began to sing and dance as he rowed, surefooted even upon the swaying raft.

He oared for a long time.

They traveled south until Horsehead Island dwindled to but a green smudge upon the horizon. The sun dipped into afternoon, casting silver light upon the sea. The water spread across all horizons, deep green and blue. Fish leaped every few moments, and a pod of dolphins swam in the distance.

Kaelyn leaned against Valien. "The sea seems endless," she whispered. "There is no pain here. No people to lead. No wars to fight. I can imagine that the whole world is like this. Blue and quiet and... simple." She looked up at him. "I wish he were with us. I wish he could see this water too."

Valien placed an arm around her. "They will not kill him. He's worth more to them alive."

A tear streamed down her cheek, and she closed her eyes. "That's what I fear. Those are the nightmares that fill me, even here, surrounded by this peace. Because I know, Valien... I know that death would be a kindness to him now. I can't even imagine what--"

Valien growled. He pulled Kaelyn's face up toward his. She opened her eyes and he glared at her.

"Do not think such thoughts," he said. "Do not, Kaelyn. They will haunt you. They will hurt you. We don't know that Rune is tortured. The dragon who captured him--the white one--was his friend. She is protecting him."

Kaelyn nodded and leaned back against him. "Maybe you're right. I pray that you are. I just wish we could be with him. Fighting for him. Saving him and everyone else."

"So long as I breathe," Valien said, "so long as I can stand and fly, I will fight. We hide now, but we will seek allies, and we will regroup, and we will not abandon Rune. We will not abandon Requiem. I swear this to you."

The sun was nearing the horizon, casting a golden path across the water, when they saw Maiden Island.

Valien now understood how the island got its name. It rose from the water like a woman lounging on her side, a forested hill forming her hip. A waterfall cascaded from a smaller hill like hair from a head.

"Welcome, welcome!" Bantis said, hopping around the raft. "Bantis led you to Maiden Island. To hope. To his army. Together we will fight, yes."

As they oared closer, Valien looked for signs of life but saw only seagulls and trees. The waves whispered across virgin sands. No huts, no smoke from cooking fire, no men or women to be seen.

"Bantis," Kaelyn said, "how many survivors did you say live here?"

He pirouetted upon the raft, nearly falling into the water. "Thousands! Thousands of survivors live here, yes. Bantis's friends. Bantis's son leads them, yes. Bantis lived here too. Bantis loves explosives. Bantis lives alone now."

They oared closer. Valien guessed the island stretched two miles long, maybe three. He still could see nobody. The shores were smooth. No trees had been hewn. No huts or tents rose. Valien let out his breath.

Crazy old loon, he thought. *He's been alone too long. He invented himself an army of friends.*

They let the waves carry them to shore, then walked along the sand. Cliffs rose above them, topped with palm trees. Pelicans and gulls flew overhead. Kaelyn chewed her lip as she walked, staring up at the trees, while Valien grumbled. No footprints marred the sand; Valien wondered if they were the first to ever walk here.

Yet Bantis ran ahead, eager as a dog released from a house, kicking sand and spinning in circles every few feet.

"Come, come! Follow old Bantis. He will lead you to them. Hurry, Vir Requis!"

Valien sighed. He looked at Kaelyn and saw her sigh too.

"Let's humor him," he said in a low rumble; Bantis was running too far ahead to hear. "We'll see what he wants to show us."

Kaelyn hefted her bow across her shoulder. Her cheeks were reddening in the sun, and sand clung to her clothes.

"Might be we'll find only thousands of skeletons."

"Or thousands of ghosts," Valien said.

Bantis scampered ahead, leading them toward a rocky hill. He raced up the slope, turned toward them, and gestured for them to follow. They climbed the Maiden's waist, moving between boulders, mint bushes, and rustling pines. Frogs trilled and herons flew overhead. The waterfall sang in the distance.

When they reached the hilltop and saw the southern sea, Bantis stopped walking and stretched out his arms. "Here! Here is my army. Meet them! Meet them!"

Valien looked around and saw only the trees, the frogs, and the birds. He grumbled and heaved the longest sigh of his life.

"Not skeletons," he muttered to Kaelyn, who stood by his side, chewing her lip and searching the trees. "Not ghosts either. He led us to an army of frogs."

She grinned and leaned against him. "I suppose we could unleash them in the capital. We'll teach them to swarm the emperor and give him warts."

Valien grunted, wiped sweat from his brow, and hefted his pack across his shoulders. "Come on. Let's go back."

He had taken two steps downhill when the forest leaped at him.

A hundred people or more sprang from the trees. They wore clothes of grass, leaves filled their hair, and mud smeared their faces. They bore what looked like miniature cannons mounted upon wooden shafts.

"Capture them!" spoke one, a tall man with blue eyes peering from a painted face. "Take them alive."

Valien growled, shifted into a dragon, and soared.

He shot through the trees. Kaelyn flew beside him, a green dragon, her wings bending the trees below.

A boom tore through the air.

Smoke blasted from one of the men's sticks. Fire blazed out. A projectile whizzed by Valien's head.

"I said alive!" shouted the tall man below.

Valien beat his wings, rising higher, and growled. At his side, Kaelyn sucked in her breath, and flames crackled between her teeth. She rose, then turned and assumed a swooping position, prepared to blast her fire downward.

"Kaelyn, no!" Valien shouted, flew toward her, and knocked her aside. Her flames cascaded down the hillside, missing the men. "They're refugees. They're frightened. They're--"

Metal creaked below upon the hill.

Men covered in leaves and mud raised metallic tubes and pulled levers. Grapples shot skyward, dragging chains behind them. Valien banked, but two grapples swung across him, then tugged down. Chains wrapped around him, and one grapple dug into his leg. He howled and dipped in the sky.

At his side, chains swung around Kaelyn too. She howled and drew more fire into her maw. When she blasted the flames downward, the men scattered and vanished between the trees. The fire crashed down against boulders. From the canopy, more grapples flew.

Chains encased the two dragons. They beat their wings, struggling to rise, but the chains tugged downward, and Valien glimpsed men turning winches.

Valien and Kaelyn, dragons of Requiem, crashed against the hillside. A dozen chains swung from the trees and crashed down atop them. Men cheered.

"Cursed be Requiem!" cried one man.

"For the glory of Tiranor!" cried another.

Men leaped onto their backs, and Valien howled and tried to shake them off, but the chains held him down. Arms reached across his head, fastening a muzzle over his mouth. He growled and blasted fire from his nostrils, but he couldn't free himself--not without killing the men, which he wasn't prepared to do. From the corner of his eye, he saw a dozen men muzzling Kaelyn too as she flailed.

"Death to Requiem!" they cried. "The dragons are ours!"

LERESY

He pulled her along the beach.

"Come on," he said and rolled his eyes. "Will you stop leaning down to collect seashells?"

Crouched in the sand, Erry glared up at him. Leresy held her hand, trying to tug her along. With her other hand, she lifted a large pink shell.

"This is a *conch*, you fool," she said. "This isn't an ordinary seashell. It's rare and-- Ow! Stop pulling me."

He kept walking, squeezing her hand, forcing her to trail behind. She glared and spat and kicked sand.

"It looks like a damn seashell to me," he said. "Do you want to collect shells like a little girl, or do you want to find this big weapon the crazy old man talked about?"

"Collect shells."

He paused, turned toward her, and held out his hand. "Let me see."

She shook her head.

He grabbed the conch, wrenched it from her fingers, and tossed it into the sea.

"You bloody piece of pig shite!" she shouted and tried to kick him, but he held her shoulders at arm's length, and her short legs only kicked the air.

"Call me what you like, soon I'll be pig shite with a weapon to take the throne." He spat. "You'll be thankful I let you trail behind me then. Now come along. This is where the old loon landed with his raft. Shift with me and let's find this damn Genesis Isle he came from."

She raised her hands to the heavens. "Damn it, Leresy, how are you going to find his island? Kaelyn said it's barely bigger than a rock, and there are about a million islands around here. The man was crazy! Cawing like a bird and dancing around. What weapon could he possibly have been seeking?"

"I don't know. We'll find out."

With that, he shifted into a dragon and took flight.

Damn, flying feels good, he thought.

That grizzled fool Valien had insisted nobody shift upon the island. The man was paranoid, sure that imperial dragons were scouting the sea and would see their fire. But Leresy knew his father. The old man had his prize; the boy Relesar was his.

Give the dog a bone to chew, and he'll keep himself busy, he thought.

He rose higher on the wind, inhaling the salty air. The southern sun, warm even in winter, heated his red scales. He sucked fire into his maw and blasted it skyward.

"Erry!" he cried down to her. The urchin still stood upon the beach in human form, scowling up at him, hands on her hips. "Are you coming, or are you going to stay and sulk like a baby?

She spat and shifted too. She soared as a copper dragon, eyes narrowed and fire trickling from her nostrils. They flew east, the direction Bantis's raft had come from. The sea sprawled below them, blue and green under a clear sky, and Horsehead Island--their home since fleeing Requiem--dwindled behind.

Erry shot up to fly beside him, snorted a blast of fire, and glared. "I can't believe you're still obsessed with your damn throne. I thought you gave that up when we moved here. What about all that sweet talk? Living on an island paradise. Forgetting about the war. Making love every day, eating wild grapes, and wearing grass like beautiful savages."

"Well, that was before I heard about this big weapon."

"And now I suppose if you do find some weapon, you'll want to fly back to Requiem." She growled. "Well, I'm not going with you, Leresy Cadigus. Not for any throne or palace or gold."

He hissed. "You'd rather stay alone on this island, a dirty and miserable outcast? You'll turn into another Bantis." He shook his head. "I'm not letting that happen to me. I'm not turning into some crazy-haired, wild-eyed old man. I'll find that old bugger's weapon and slay my father once and for all."

"Leresy!" She slapped him with her tail. "There is no damn weapon. The man is crazy. His weapon is probably just an angry sea sponge he thinks he can slay monsters with."

"A sea sponge with teeth can work," Leresy said. "I'll give it to my father and tell him to wipe his arse with it."

She sighed. "Always poetry with you."

He flashed a toothy grin and flew on.

Their island dwindled behind them, a patch of gray and green shaped like a horse's head. The sea stretched on. The world became nothing but blue--the sky above, the sea below, and two dragons in the middle. As they flew, Leresy found himself antsy. Back at the island, there were many distractions--swords to sharpen, huts to build, boars to catch, trees to fell, and Erry to bed. But here, trapped between blue and blue, nothing stopped his memories from resurfacing.

An image flashed before him, and Leresy winced.

Suddenly he wasn't flying over the sea but was back in Lynport. The barrels of gunpowder rolled. Blasts tore the door open, and outside, he saw them. Men torn apart. Limbs and heads severed. Men screaming, clutching at spilling entrails and stubs. Beras the Brute swinging his axe at Erry, and so much blood, and--

No. Leresy growled and blasted flames down into the water. *No more memories. No more pain.*

His heart thrashed, and he wondered if Erry was right. Why did he need to return? Why not leave Requiem--all that fire and pain--behind?

Or course, he knew the answer.

I've left Requiem. But she did not leave me. She will not until I can return and slay those ghosts.

He looked over at Erry who flew beside him, grumbling and muttering to herself. He didn't want to leave her. He didn't want to lose her. She was the only good thing he had left, but the ghosts of his pain tainted her too. When he looked at her, he still saw Beras with his axe.

So I will slay those ghosts, he swore, flames crackling inside him. *For us.*

They flew until they saw a group of islets ahead, a dozen or more rising like a spine ridge, leafy with palms. The two dragons made their way forward, and Leresy lowered his altitude.

"I told you," Erry said, "damn too many islands here. How are you going to find the right one?"

He glided toward the first island. "Well, Bantis said he was digging, so we find the island with the big hole."

The first island he flew over seemed a poor candidate--nothing but palm trees upon a cliff. The second was barren, a mere pile of mossy rocks. He had flown over ten islands, and his wings were aching with weariness, when he saw the distant patch of green.

"There's another one there, farther off," he said. "Erry, come on."

She panted. "Can't we land on one of these? My wings hurt more than a mare in heat locked up with stallions."

"We'll rest once we find what we seek."

His own wings ached, and every breath felt like a saw in his lungs, but he forced himself onward. The sea streamed below. The distant islet lay miles away from the others, an isolated rock no larger a humble house. When he flew above, he twisted his jaw into a grin.

"Here we are. Genesis Isle."

A rocky hill rose upon the island. A hole had been blasted into the hillside, forming a cave. Rocks and dust littered the slope. Leresy glided down and landed upon the shore.

Erry landed beside him, shifted back into a human, and plopped herself down onto the sand. She lay back, closed her eyes, and let the waves wet her toes.

"Bloody stars, I'm tired. I'm going to lie here while you go searching for your toy."

He shifted back too, reached down, and grabbed her hands. "You're searching with me. We'll lie on the sand later. *Both* of us."

She gave him a sidelong look. "Oh you'd like that, wouldn't you? Bet you're after another treasure here. An island all to ourselves..." She reached down to his breeches, teased him with a caress, then slapped his face. "But since you tossed away my conch, no treasure for you today."

He sighed, grabbed her wrist, and pulled her after him. "Help me dig."

She growled and cussed but followed. They climbed the hillside between boulders and fallen trees. Items lay strewn across the slope, gray with dust. Leresy saw a wheeled cannon, a few shovels, and barrels of gunpowder.

"Hello, what are you then?" he said and leaned down by a fallen tree.

He lifted a shaft of sanded wood the length of a sword. A metal pipe was mounted upon it. A trigger, like that of a crossbow, fit his finger.

"Is this your secret weapon?" Erry said. She leaned down and lifted another one of the contraptions. "What is it? It looks like a crossbow, just without the bow."

Leresy hefted the device, sniffed at it, smelled gunpowder, and smiled.

"Very nice," he said and caressed the wood. "Very good work that Bantis did."

Erry glowered, holding her own shaft. "Leresy, are you going to tell me what this is?"

He pointed the muzzle at her. "Can't you see? It's a hand cannon."

She glowered and shoved the barrel aside. "Well, don't point that thing at me then, you dolt! Who the Abyss heard of a hand cannon? Cannons are, well... they're bloody huge."

"Not this one." Leresy pointed it skyward and pulled the trigger, but nothing happened. "Not loaded. I reckon you place miniature cannonballs into it, then go shooting down dragons."

"Leresy!" Erry stamped her feet and tossed down her own hand cannon. "The muzzles on these things are tiny. I can barely fit my finger in. How will a cannonball this small kill anyone?"

"The same way a crossbow bolt does. With a lot of speed and power." He grinned. "But this weapon here, my darling... I wager it has more power than any crossbow. Why use a string when you can use gunpowder? Let's see if we can find some rounds."

He kept climbing, moving between the rocks and fallen trees, searching for the miniature cannonballs. He wanted to try this weapon. Instead he found another strange object, one whose purpose he could not determine.

"Hello," he said, placed down his hand cannon, and lifted the new contraption. "And who are you?"

It looked like a scroll formed of tough, hardened leather bolted together. A round, wooden lid sealed each end of the tube. When he unscrewed the lids, he revealed glass circles like the bottoms of jars. Leresy had never seen anything like this.

"What is it?" Erry demanded and reached out for it. "Give it here."

He stepped back. "No touching." He brought the contraption close to his eye. "Let's see then. A cylinder of boiled leather, glass at each end. A container? Maybe the ammunition is in here."

He peeked through one glass circle, trying to see inside, and sucked in his breath. A grin spread across his face.

"Bantis, you bloody old genius," he said.

He aimed the cylinder at the sea, still holding it to his eye. Through the glass, the distant batch of islands, which should have appeared as mere specks, loomed large enough for him to count their trees. He lowered the cylinder, raised it again, and laughed.

"Give it here!" Erry demanded, leaped up, and snatched the cylinder. She stared through it and gasped. "Bloody piss pots! It's magic."

She spun in a circle, staring through the cylinder at the sea and the hill behind her.

Leresy shook his head. "Not magic. I don't think so. Bantis said he's an inventor, not a magician."

She lowered the cylinder and narrowed her eyes. "Well, how the bloody Abyss do you invent *glass* that makes things *bigger*?"

"I don't know." He shrugged. "How do you invent clocks? Or gunpowder? Or steel? Damned if I know. So long as it works. But it's not magic. Magic feels... different. You know how you feel when we shift into dragons? How it sort of... tickles, like soft light, but you can't really feel it? At least, not how you feel a feather or a blanket or heat. You sort of feel it inside you, whispering. That's how magic feels. This?" He took the cylinder from her and stared through it again. "This is clever and I don't understand it, but it feels... mechanical. It's an invention like the great clock back at Castra Luna."

Erry tapped her thigh. "So is this the big weapon? Portable cannons and a magnifying machine?" She scrunched her lips. "Good weapons for Tirans, perhaps. They need the help. But we're Vir Requis. We can turn into dragons. I'd take dragonfire any day over these hand cannons."

Leresy shook his head again. "No. Bantis said he was digging for something. Digging for a *big* weapon." He gestured at the hole that loomed above. "That's where he was digging. Let's take a look."

He shoved the cylinder under his armpit and lifted one of the discarded shovels. They continued climbing the hillside. They reached the hole--it loomed about the size of a doorway--and peered inside.

"Nothing but dust and rubble," Erry said. "Damn old man was crazy, I told you."

"Crazy enough to invent a magnifying machine and portable cannons. If he says there's a weapon here, I'm digging deeper." He climbed into the hole, thrust his shovel down, and scooped pebbles and dirt. "Now go grab another shovel and help me, damn it. I'm not digging alone."

She grumbled but she grabbed a shovel.

They dug.

They dug for a long time.

After digging through several feet of soil and rock, sweat soaked Leresy. He wiped it off his brow and stripped off his shirt.

"Feel free to do the same," he told Erry, but she only slammed the shovel against his legs.

They dug some more, and the sun began to dip into afternoon, casting golden beams into the cave. Still they dug, tossing shovel after shovel of dirt outside.

"Leresy, damn it!" Erry said. "There's nothing buried here."

"We haven't dug deep enough." He mopped his brow and dug some more.

Erry tossed her shovel down and placed her hands on her hips. Dirt covered her.

"It's an island!" she said. "A damn, stinkin' island in the middle of nowhere. Burn me, it's barely even that. More of a forsaken rock than an island. Why why *why* would there be a weapon buried here?"

He gritted his teeth and kept shoveling. "Because there has to be one."

"What do you mean?" she demanded and grabbed his arm. "Ler, what--"

He reeled toward her, teeth bared, and tossed his shovel down. It thumped against the dirt.

"I mean," he hissed, "that I'm not going to believe this is it. All right? I'm not going to believe that... that things just end like this. That my father wins. That Shari wins. That there's blood and fire and pain in Requiem, and we're just going to hide here and remember it and..." Tears budded in his eyes, and he hated himself for it. He spun away lest she saw. "There has to be some way to fight him, Erry. To kill that bastard and to kill the memories."

He stood, chest heaving and legs shaking, staring at the dirt. He felt her small hands on his shoulders.

"Ler," she said quietly. She walked around to face him, and her eyes were soft. "And if there isn't a way to fight? If this is all that's left, isn't that enough? You and me?"

He lowered his head and pulled her into an embrace. He held her tightly, crushing her against him. He smoothed her hair and closed his burning eyes.

"I thought it would be," he said, voice choked. "I wanted to forget. I wanted to just live here with you. To start a new life. Not a prince of Requiem and an orphan from Lynport, but just...

just two people on an island. But I can't forget. I can't." His voice cracked. "I still see it, Erry. All of it. The dragons burning Castra Luna and killing so many, killing Nairi and the others. And the war and blood at Lynport. And my father... my father grabbing me and Kaelyn, beating us, laughing as we bled and screamed. I can't forget it. You can't know what that's like."

She held his head with both hands and growled up at him. "Can't I? I was there with you. At Castra Luna. At Lynport. I fought through the mud and fire with you. And no, your father never beat me when I was a girl. But enough men did. I grew up a dock rat, filthy and skinny and afraid. I know what pain is. And I can't forget either, and I never will. But that doesn't mean we have to go back. We don't have to go chase that world again. That life of ours... that life is over. We have a new life here."

"I don't," he said. "I don't think I ever will. Not until I go back and face him. Not until I close that door. The door is distant, all the way across the sea, but I can feel the cold wind still blowing through it. So I have to find this weapon. And I have to kill my father." He lifted the shovel again. "So please, Erry, please. Help me dig."

Night was falling, and the cave was almost pitch black, when Leresy's shovel *crunched* and red light glowed.

His heart burst into a gallop. At his side, Erry gasped. The soft red light gleamed under the soil. Leresy drove his shovel deeper, loosening the dirt. The red glow intensified.

"Burn me," he said, knelt, and began to clear away soil with his hands. "Erry, look at this."

She knelt and helped clear away the dirt. Hundreds of red shards glowed below, each one no larger than a pea.

"They look like pomegranate seeds," Erry said, lifting one in wonder. It glowed in her hand.

"Or like droplets of blood," said Leresy.

He grabbed a few and held them in his palm. They felt unnaturally cold. He raised them to his eye, scrutinizing them. Each stone seemed made of glass, and red liquid swirled within. Their surface was angular as cut gems, though each pebble had a different shape.

"What are they?" Erry asked. "Some kind of crystal?"

Leresy smiled and closed his palm around them.

"Magic," he said. "Our big weapon."

SILA

He stood upon the deck of his ship, stared at the cove that surrounded him, and clutched the railing until his knuckles turned white.

Sila didn't know why he still came here. His ship, a three-masted carrack named the *Golden Crane*, had not raised its anchor in eighteen years. Its planks had begun to rot, and barnacles covered its hull. Its hold still whispered with ghosts. Dragonfire had blackened its starboard, and though the sails were now folded, Sila knew that burnt holes still peppered them. Only the ship's figurehead, a flying crane of giltwood, still bore some former glory.

And what of myself? he wondered. Did he too bear any lingering glory, a golden figurehead for his people? Or was he but a rotting hull, as captive on Maiden Island as his ship?

Once Sila had captained this vessel through storms and battles. Once he had led refugees out of fire and into new life. Once he had been a leader, a savior, a man who made his father proud.

"And now I linger, a relic like the rest of this wreck," he said to his ship.

And now his people needed him again. Now two of their ghosts had washed ashore with the old man. Now two demons of the past, mere nightmares for so long, breathed upon Maiden Island, this sanctuary Sila had protected for so long. Now he needed to decide. And yet he only stood here upon his deck, far from his people and their tormentors--a place of solitude, of memory, of thoughts that whispered like the sea.

Cliffs rose above the surrounding shores, topped with palms. Nestled into the small of the maiden's back, the cove faced south, hidden from the northern enemy. Five other ships rose around him, each as barren as the *Golden Crane*. Often Sila thought of burning these ships. Should the dragons scout these seas from the south, the masts would reveal their sanctuary. Yet for eighteen years, Sila had hidden his people among the trees and kept his ships alive. He had watched his daughter born and raised into a woman on this island. He had watched his people, once ragged refugees, build a new life. And he had kept these ships. He had kept his vengeance burning.

"Because I have to believe," he whispered to the cove. "I have to believe that we can go back. That we can still fight the enemy. That we can still rebuild our desert home."

Tiranor, his land of dunes and oases, had burned in the fire of the red spiral. But those dunes still whispered inside him. He kept that memory as alive as his fleet.

"Father! Father, why do you do this?"

The voice came from behind him, and Sila turned to see his daughter emerge from the hull. She joined him on the deck.

"Miya!" he said and a frown twisted his face. "How long have you been here? What are you doing on the *Golden Crane*?"

Miya glared at him, fists on her hips. "And why shouldn't I stand here? I'm your only daughter, and this ship is my birthright. She's as much mine as yours."

Eighteen years old, Miya had been only a whisper in her mother's womb when Frey Cadigus had burned their kingdom. She had been born in the shallow waters of this very cove, shaded by cliffs and palms, and grown wild along the beaches and among the trees. Today she stood before him as a golden-skinned, scabby-kneed island girl with fiery blue eyes, long platinum hair, and a shark-tooth necklace. While the older folk Sila led still wore the traditional robes of the desert, Miya was a wild thing, dressed in leaves and caked in sand, a primordial child who'd never known civilization. In her left hand, she held a spear with a stone head, and across her shoulders she wore the bow she had carved herself and stringed with vine.

"This ship will be yours when I'm dead," Sila said to her. "And I plan on living as long as your grandfather."

She stomped up closer. "Father, how long do you plan to keep this up?"

He turned away from her, leaned across the railing, and stared at the cliffs that ringed the cove. Gulls and herons flew among the trees above. Somewhere between those trees the two sat chained.

Sun God bless us, he thought with a chill. *Two living Vir Requis. Two demons from the past--here, chained on my island.*

"Father, don't ignore me." Miya came to stand beside him and glared. "You cannot simply keep them chained up like that, like... beasts."

He raised his eyebrow. "I seem to have been doing a good job of it."

She groaned. "They're not here to hurt us. They could have burned us all from the air. They didn't blow fire. They let themselves be caught rather than kill us. And now you will keep them chained and--"

"Miya!" He spun toward her. "For years, I've let you nurse baby birds that fell from nests, toss back fish you pitied, and collect your baskets of caterpillars. But these are no poor animals for you to tend to. These are dragons. These are--"

"They are not dragons," she said, eyes flashing. "Not anymore. They are humans now--a man and a woman--and you chained them to a tree."

"Shapeshifters," he said and spat overboard. "Demons. You weren't there, Miya. You weren't in Tiranor when they burned us."

She looked up into his eyes. "Did they burn us--those two? Valien and Kaelyn?"

"Oh, so they have names now?"

"Yes! They do. I've talked to them, and they have names, and they have stories of their own. They are good Vir Requis, Father. They're... different from the ones you fought."

He snorted.

The ones I fought.

No, Sila had not fought the dragons eighteen years ago. His brothers had. His friends had. They had all burned. But Sila... he was either wiser or he was a coward. Sila had fled. He had loaded his ships with survivors and sailed away. And he left the others behind. He left the millions to burn.

He looked down at the hull of his ship. He could still see those fingernails clawing at the wood, still hear the people begging to be saved.

"The ships are full!" he had shouted that day. "I will return for you. I will return!"

They had wept. They had tried to swim after him. He had loaded his fleet with men, women, and children, cramming them like cargo, a weight nearly too great to bear. He brought them to these islands. And when he sailed back to Tiranor for the others... they were all gone. He found only bones and ash and lingering screams over the water.

"They are all demons," he said, voice barely more than a whisper. "And you should not have talked to them, daughter. I forbid you to speak with them again."

It was her turn to snort. "I speak to whoever I like. Remember what you used to call me when I was a child?"

"You are still a child."

She shook her head. "I am eighteen."

He nodded. "A child."

She growled and stamped her feet. "What did you always call me?"

He groaned and felt his pain melt. "An insufferable, pigheaded, scrawny-legged pest?"

"Father!" She gave a sound like an enraged hippo. "No! You know what you called me. Princess of the Islands. That was your name for me. I was born here, the daughter of our leader. Not born in Tiranor like the rest, but born wild and free, an islander. A princess." She swept her arm through the air, gesturing at the cove. "This is my kingdom, and I go where I like, and I speak to whom I please. So I spoke to your prisoners. And they told me stories. And they want to speak to you too. Will you listen to them?"

He sighed.

He had led merchant fleets through storms. He had battled pirates and kraken. He had led thousands of refugees from inferno into safety. His arms were thick and tattooed with serpents, his shoulders were wide, and his stare, he knew, caused even the strongest sailors to mutter and look away. Yet Miya, it seemed, never saw him as a hero. To her, he was not the burly captain with the withering stare, only her lumbering, old-fashioned father.

Perhaps no man is a hero to his eighteen-year-old daughter, he thought and grumbled.

"I will speak with them once, Miya," he said. "I will let them tell their story. And if I am not satisfied... they will suffer my justice."

Miya sucked in her breath and narrowed her eyes. She began to object, but he hushed her with a glare. Sila had not condemned a man to death in ten years, not since one sailor had slain another after losing a game of dice. He had turned Maiden Island into a land of order, of harsh discipline, and of harsh justice.

If more of those beasts follow, he thought, *all this will end. The new life I built for my people will burn too.* He closed his eyes and saw the dying again, thousands in the water, screaming for him, thrashing like flies in blood, scratching at his hull as he sailed away. *If Requiem flies against us again, Maiden Island too will burn.*

They took a rowboat to the beach, then walked the hidden paths up the maiden's waist. Mint bushes rose around them, bustling with mice. Cedars grew like dark columns. Carob, olive, and pear trees rustled, heavy with fruit. Vines crawled over boulders and the branches of oaks. Frogs and crickets trilled in the grass, herons and jays flew overhead, and turtles sunbathed upon rocks.

I gave Miya a good home here, he thought, looking at her walking beside him, her face tanned deep gold, her blue eyes bright. *I will not let this place burn too.*

A mile from the cove, they reached the maiden's neck, a declivity between the hills of her head and shoulder. The waterfall crashed down ahead, the maiden's hair, and between the trees, their village sprawled.

Sila wasn't sure when he'd stopped calling this place a "camp" and started calling it a "village." They had landed here eighteen years ago as refugees, shivering and afraid and famished. Today were they still refugees or simply islanders?

Four thousand souls lived upon Maiden Island, survivors of the slaughter and those born upon the island. Their huts spread between the trees. Some elders still bore the white, woolen tunics of Tiranor, sturdy garments that had lasted the years. Most now wore clothes of *maidenspun*, a fabric they wove from local leaves and wild cotton. Some, especially the children, simply wore clothes of grass, leaves, and fur.

Looking at the children who ran around, near naked and laughing and wild, Sila sighed.

"We came from a land of golden obelisks, temples that kissed the sky, libraries with a million books, and statues of such beauty that grown men wept to behold them. We fled a beautiful, wise civilization that had ruled the desert for thousands of years." He shook his head ruefully. "And eighteen years later, we're running around half-naked in the mud."

His daughter, her own legs muddy up to the knees, flashed him a grin. "And we thank you for it."

Walking across a grassy plateau dotted with gopher holes, he saw a squad of arquebusers drilling a volley. They stood in five lines, ten men in each, holding their guns to their chests. Across the plateau rose a dragon effigy, life-sized and built of wood, grass, and wicker. Sila paused from walking and placed a hand on his daughter's shoulder.

"Watch," he told her.

The first five men stepped forward, standing in profile to Sila. They raised their arquebuses, masterworks of oak and iron, and pointed the muzzles toward the wicker effigy. They pulled the triggers, and booms *crashed* over the island, so loud that even Miya, who had seen these drills before, jumped and winced. Smoke blasted. The smell of gunpowder flared. Rounds crashed into the wicker dragon, tearing holes through it.

"Good," Sila said. He raised his voice to a shout. "Next line--faster!"

The five shooters, their arquebuses still smoking, marched behind the formation and formed a new line. There they began to reload their guns. As they worked, the next line of men stepped forward. They pulled their triggers. Five more arquebuses fired, roaring across the island, loud as cannons. More holes tore through the wicker dragon.

Sila nodded in approval. For a long time, he had insisted his men drill with empty guns. Iron and gunpowder were rare upon these islands. But yesterday two dragons had flown here, speaking of three thousand more.

"Today we drill with live fire," he said softly.

After each line of gunmen fired, they stepped behind the formation to reload. It was a slow, tedious process. Damn too slow. Sila watched, grumbling.

First the men pulled gunpowder from pouches and refilled their barrels. New rounds--balls of iron the size of marbles--followed, pushed down with ramrods. Some rounds were the wrong size; they had to be wrapped in leaves to snugly fit. Once the barrels were loaded, the men filled the guns' flashpans with more gunpowder. These small, iron receptacles stuck out from the guns like ears; when ignited, they would deliver a spark into the barrel, lighting the main charge. Once barrel and flashpan were ready, the men strung fuses through their matchlocks like tailors stringing thread through a needle. When finally ready to fire, they'd light their fuses, pulling the triggers to bring matchlocks to flashpans.

"It's still too damn slow to reload," Sila said and spat. The whole process took a full minute, even for the fastest fingers.

By the time the first five arquebusers had reloaded, their comrades had all fired their guns. This formation--ten lines of gunners, the front line firing while the others reloaded--meant Sila could maintain gunfire throughout a battle without pause. But it also meant that, at any given moment, most of his men were reloading rather than fighting.

"Grandpapa will find a way to make the guns faster," Miya said.

Sila grumbled. "Your grandfather is a dangerous man. He nearly blew himself up--and half this island--with his inventions."

"And he invented these guns you now use!" she said. "And he invented the scope, which you're always looking through. And he invented the canals to bring water from the spring to our camp. And--"

"Yes, yes, I know all about his inventions," Sila said. "Half the time they work. Half the time they nearly sink the island. We should send him back to his rock."

Miya stamped her feet. "No! You cannot send him back. He's your father. When you're that old, would you like me to banish you to deserted rock?"

"I don't blast huts apart when trying to invent an ice-making machine."

He sighed. He didn't know how he--a burly, laconic captain--had been born to a scrawny, wild-eyed inventor like Bantis. Sometimes Sila wondered if the man had simply swapped his true babe with another, too consumed with a new invention to notice.

"Keep drilling!" he called out to his men. "I want you to double your speed. When the dragons fly here, it will save your life."

They nodded and Sila kept walking, crossing the grassy plateau toward a hill thick with mint bushes, brambles, and trees. These men drilled to slay dragons, but today Sila had two dragons he needed very much alive.

When he reached the hill, he turned to Miya.

"Stay here," he said. "I'll speak to them alone."

Her eyes flashed and she raised her fists. "I will go with--"

"You will do as I say," Sila said. He sighed and softened his voice. "Miya, you are young and fiery and proud. You grew up in peace, in sunlight, wild among the trees and upon the beach. I gave you a good life here. Or at least, I tried to."

She lowered her head, then looked up again, stood on tiptoes, and kissed his cheek. "You did."

"I gave you a life most of our people never knew. They burned, Miya. I watched them burn. I watched the Vir Requis burn them and laugh. I saw flesh peeling from bones, and I saw the proud palaces and temples of Tiranor fall. I saw women and children swimming after my ships, begging for room I did not have. I will speak to these shapeshifters now. I will ask them why they did this to us. I won't hurt them, but I will demand answers. Stay here, Miya. Stay in this valley in sunlight, grass and trees and water around you. I will step back into the fire."

Tears gleamed in her eyes, and she nodded. He left her there and turned toward the hill.

He began to climb. A natural path led up the hillside, carved by eighteen years of footsteps. Alongside the pebbly trail, mint bushes, olive trees, and brambles bustled with birds and mice. Ant hives and groundhog holes rose from wild grass. Boulders of chalk and granite speckled the hillside like white clouds upon a green sky.

A twisting carob tree crowned the hill, the tallest tree upon Maiden Island. Its branches spread out like a crown, thick with dark leaves. Its roots rose from a carpet of fallen fruit. Wooden strands wove together into its bole, forming a grandfatherly face, complete with two burrows for eyes. Sila often thought of the tree as the island's grandfather, an ancient sentinel watching over him. Sila was not a religious man--back in Tiranor, he had spent little time worshiping the Sun God, the lord of the desert--yet he often thought this tree holy.

You've watched over us for eighteen years, Old Carob, he thought, climbing the trail toward the tree. *Today you watch our greatest enemy.*

Climbing the hill, he could see the island spread all around. The hills rolled down, thick with brush, to golden shores. The sea spread into every horizon, azure under the clear sky.

Maiden Island, he thought and clenched his jaw. *A new haven. I will not let it burn too.*

He took the last few steps toward the hilltop, approached Old Carob, and stared at the two prisoners tied to the trunk.

"Vir Requis," he said, hand on the pommel on his saber.

They stood in human forms now. The ropes binding them to the tree would keep them humans. It had taken a hundred men to cudgel the dragons, knocking their magic out of them. Bruised and bound, the two hardly looked threatening now, but Sila had seen their dragon forms: one dragon large and silver, missing a horn, the other slim and green.

Demons.

The silver dragon now stood as a man, his dark hair streaked with white, his leathery face thick with stubble. He stood tall and wide; his shoulders bulged under his tattered tunic. Sila was among the tallest, strongest men on this island, and this man seemed his match. He seemed on the wrong side of forty--about the same age as Sila--but his eyes seemed older, haunted with ghosts. Those eyes glared now, steaming with rage, but Sila had stared into the eyes of enough enemies to recognize old pain.

Two men of an age, Sila thought. *Two warriors with dark eyes. What secrets do your eyes keep?*

He turned to look at the second Vir Requis. This one was as different from the man as fire from ice. She was a young woman, perhaps twenty years old. Her hair cascaded in waves the color of dark honey, and her hazel eyes blazed with fury. She hadn't the skin for the southern sun, and her nose and cheeks had begun to peel, and her lips were dry and cracked, but she still exuded a northern beauty. Her sharp features and golden mane gave her feline look, a tied lioness who couldn't wait to rip out his throat.

"Two Vir Requis sweep onto our shore," Sila said, flexing his fingers around his hilt. "Two dragons are captured. What should we do with them?" He turned back toward the beefy, haggard man. "You. You have the bearings of a soldier. How did you find us?"

The man's eyes simmered like smelters. When he spoke, his voice was raspy like a man being strangled, a mere death gasp.

"I thought all Tirans were dead. How did *you* get here?"

Sila raised his eyebrows and thrust out his bottom lip. "Asking questions, are we? My friend, where I come from, the man with the sword asks the questions. The man beaten and tied answers. So tell me. We have hidden here for years. How did you find us, and how many will follow you?"

The man spat, nearly hitting Sila's boot. "You hide here from Frey Cadigus. So do we."

Sila blew out his breath and shook his head. "Of course you would claim that. Yet how can I believe you? You perhaps convinced my daughter, but she is young and naive. I've seen too many of your kind. I know your evil, weredragon."

For the first time, the young woman spoke up, straining against her ropes.

"You will not call him that word!" she said and bared her teeth. "You will not use that... slur. He is *Vir Requis*. He is the son of a noble, proud race fallen into darkness, and he fights to restore its light. You speak to Lord Valien Eleison, leader of the Resistance. For twenty years, he's been fighting Frey Cadigus, the man you fled. Show him respect."

Sila turned back toward her. "So quick to change flags, are we? I know you lie. I know you scout these islands for Frey Cadigus, your lord. Are Frey's soldiers so cowardly that a few bruises and a rope make them turncoats?"

She fixed him with a steady, haunted stare. "Yes, I am a turncoat. I turned against Frey Cadigus. But not because of your bruises or your ropes. I rebelled against him three years ago, and I've been fighting him since. I hid from him in mud and ruin. I flew through fire and rain to charge against his lines. I crawled through darkness, and I killed, and I watched my comrades die. And I still fight him. Until my last breath." Her eyes bored into him. "Frey destroyed Tiranor and he destroyed Requiem too. He burned your land; he cloaked ours in darkness. I hate him more than fire hates the rain."

For a moment Sila could say nothing, only stare into the woman's eyes. He had commanded merchant ships through storms. He had commanded ships in battle. He had led men from fire into light. He could read eyes like other men read books, and he could spot a lie like a hound spotting a hare. There was no deception in this woman's eyes. She either spoke truth, or Vir Requis could tell lies like the greatest actors.

He turned back toward the haggard man, this Valien Eleison. "How many do you lead? My father spoke of seeing hundreds of you upon your island. Why are you there? Do you plan an attack against us?"

"We plan an attack against Requiem," Valien growled, and again Sila was taken aback by the sound. The man's voice was little more than a hiss like leather dragged over stone. "We lost a battle upon Requiem's southern coast. We fled to these isles to regroup. We will fight again. You are not our enemy, Tiran. We share an enemy. I lead three thousand fighters, all sworn to slay the emperor. Free me... and join us."

Sila barked a laugh. "Even if I did believe you were a rebel Vir Requis, now you truly speak madness. We are no army here, Valien Eleison. We fled war. We built a new life here. We are people of peace now."

"Is that why I hear gunfire?" Valien grumbled. "Is that why your men carry hand cannons and grapples? Those are tools for slaying dragons."

"Aye." Sila nodded. "For slaying dragons who would attack our shores."

"And yet you did not slay me and Kaelyn. You hear me speak and doubt seeps through you. Deep inside, you believe me, Sila of Tiranor. Because I am like you, and you see it."

It was Sila's turn to growl. His fist clenched around his hilt, and he drew a foot of steel.

"We are nothing alike, weredragon," he said, and his voice shook. "I know your kind. I saw thousands of you swoop and burn my home. I saw--"

"You saw the soldiers of Frey Cadigus," Valien interrupted. "You saw dragons in armor, their helms displaying the red spiral. You saw men march in black steel, the sigil of Frey upon their breasts. You did not see me. You did not see the Resistance. And yes, Sila of Tiranor, we are alike. We both lead men. We both carry the scars of war; I see them in your eyes." His mouth twisted into a mockery of a grin. "And we both hate Frey Cadigus. The question is, Sila... will you hate him in hiding, or will you fight with me?"

Sila found that his fist trembled. Sweat trickled down his back. *Damn it. Damn it!*

He took a step closer, muscles tense and heart pounding. He stood only a foot apart from Valien and stared into his eyes, seeking deceit and finding none.

"Frey cannot be defeated," he said. "All of Tiranor fought him. Three million of my people perished in his flame. You lead a few thousand warriors. Among my people, only two thousand are strong enough to fight. We cannot defeat him."

Valien's twisted grin--a wolf's grin--only widened.

"A few thousand dragons... bearing two thousand gunmen on their backs. The world has never seen such an army. We cannot fight him? Oh... I think we can."

Sila stared at him a moment longer, silent and still.

Then he drew his sword, thrust it forward, and sliced Valien's ropes.

"Come with me to my camp," he said.

As they walked down the hillside, Sila's throat tightened and he could not stop his heart from thrashing. When he looked toward the sea, he saw the waters turn red again, and he saw the refugees begging and scratching at his hull.

I fled war, he thought, fists clenched. *Curse the Sun God. Now it returns to me not with fire, but with a whisper and a hope.*

When they reached his daughter, and she stared at him with earnest eyes, Sila decided that he believed Valien's story... and that frightened him more than a hundred enemy dragons.

LERESY

He spent all night in the hole, digging with his shovel, collecting soil thick with gems, and sifting with a canteen he'd punched full of holes. Erry had given up only an hour after sundown, then gone to sleep upon the beach, but Leresy would not sleep. This was too important.

"Here is my salvation," he whispered as dawn crept through the cave entrance. "Here is my father's death."

He had fashioned his shirt into a sack. Inside glowed thousands of red crystal shards. Each one was no larger than his smallest fingernail, and inside them glowed swirling red liquid like lava.

He straightened, and his back creaked after so many hours hunched over. He lifted the sack of shards, tossed it across his shoulder, and climbed outside the hole into daylight.

Genesis Isle sloped down around him, littered with the barrels, tools, and weapons Bantis had built. Below upon the sand, Erry lay sleeping, her cheek on her hands.

"Wake you, you lazy dog's bottom!" Leresy called out and began walking downhill. "I damn well broke my back while you were dreaming of unicorns."

She sat up, moaned, and rubbed her eyes. "Bloody bollocks, Ler. I wasn't dreaming of no damn unicorns. I was dreaming that you actually had some muscles on you." She stared at his bare torso and grinned. "A good night of shoveling didn't help that dream come true."

He stomped down to the beach, kicked sand onto her, and placed down the shards as she cursed.

"I dug them all up," he said. "What do you reckon they are?"

She spat out sand. "Ladybug shite."

"Be serious." He growled and lifted a shard; it was the size of an apple seed. "These aren't natural gems. They're polished. It looks like... like pieces from a smashed stained-glass window, but there's some liquid inside. They almost look like drops of blood." He blew out his breath. "Bantis said they're a great weapon. How do you kill with them?"

Erry chewed her lip. "Well, we can tell Frey they're candies and maybe he'll choke. Or we can call him over, then spill the shards onto the floor, so he trips and breaks his neck. Or wait--I know! We can wait until he's very frail and old, and then pelt him to death with them--death by a thousand tiny jabs." She nodded thoughtfully, lower lip thrust out. "Quite a weapon. Definitely more powerful than dragonfire."

Leresy waited and sighed. "Are you done?"

"Or maybe we can--"

"You're done!" he said. "Be quiet. Burn me, I preferred you sleeping. Let's take these shards and find Bantis. He'll know what to make of this."

He cracked his neck and summoned his magic, preparing to shift.

He cleared his throat.

He twisted his toes.

"Or maybe we can make him a necklace so pretty, he'll abandon his wars and become a bar singer named Freyina," Erry said brightly, ignoring him.

Leresy grumbled.

What the Abyss is wrong?

He strained again, tugging at his magic, but no wings sprouted from his back. No scales grew across his body. He remained standing in the sand, a human.

I'm just tired, he thought. He had been digging all night, and was just too weary to fly.

"Or maybe we can--"

"Shut up, Erry!" he said. "I'm trying to focus here."

He gritted his teeth, closed his eyes, and searched deep inside him for the old magic of Requiem, the magic that flowed from the old gods, that let his people become dragons. He felt the flickers inside him, mere whispers. He tried to grab them, but it was like trying to catch the memory of a fading dream; it slipped from his consciousness like smoke between fingers.

He opened his eyes, kicked sand, and shouted.

"Stars damn it! What the Abyss?" He looked at Erry. "I can't do it. It won't work."

She snickered, reached over, and patted his privates. "So it's finally happened."

He grabbed his wrist, tugged her hand away, and snarled. "Don't you worry about that. *That* is fine. I can't... oh bloody stars, I can't shift into a dragon."

She frowned and tilted her head. "What are you on about?"

"You heard me." He spat into the sand. "I can't shift."

"Why not?"

"I don't know. Maybe it's the damn shards."

He looked at the sack of them. They were glowing behind the cloth. And Leresy understood. He clutched his head, leaned over, and laughed.

"Oh maggoty dog vomit," he said, borrowing one of Erry's cusses, and laughed again. He looked up at Erry and grinned. "Erry! He's a genius. Bloody stars, the man is a genius."

"What are you talking about?" she demanded again, glaring. "Stop laughing like an idiot. If you can't fly home, I'm flying without you."

She raised her chin and stretched out.

Nothing happened.

She growled, strained, and hopped about.

She remained a human.

"Having trouble?" Leresy asked.

She roared and glared at him, barely five feet tall but looking fierce as a demon.

"What did you do, you gutter stain?" she said. "Damn you, you sheep-shagger, what the Abyss did you do?"

He grinned. "I didn't do anything." He gestured at the sack of glowing shards. "They did. The red shards. Don't you see?" He whooped, joy brimming in him. "They cancel out magic! They're like... like anecdote to poison. Like light to shadow. Like song to silence."

"Like booze to your brain," she said. "Pretty much wipes it out."

"Pretty much," he admitted. "By the stars, Err! The old man got it. Bantis figured it out." He gave a little Bantis-style jig himself. "No wonder the bugger was dancing about. He knew the way to kill my father all along. Imagine it! The Legions flying toward you, hundreds of thousands of dragons roaring for blood. You wave these shards around, and they fall from the sky as humans. If any survive the fall, you blast them to death with hand cannons." He punched the air. "This is what I'm talking about. This is how you take Nova Vita."

Erry rolled her eyes. "Yes, yes, that's all fine and dandy, except for one little problem. Nova Vita is far in the north across the sea. And we're, well... stuck on this damn rock!" She shoved him. "How the Abyss do we get back now? We can't fly, you idiot, and Bantis has the raft."

Leresy tapped his cheek. "We were able to fly here, back when the shards were underground." He stared at his makeshift sack of cotton. "See how they glow through the cloth? We need a thicker barrier against whatever magic they're spitting out. It's the light that does it, I reckon."

He looked around the beach, considering. If he had a wooden chest, cast iron pots, or even a sack made of thicker cloth than his old tunic, perhaps he could contain the shards' magic and fly. Would he have to rebury them after all that work?

"How about this?" Erry said. She scampered across the beach, lifted one of the magnifying cylinders, and waved it about. "The ladybug shite can go in here."

"Will you please stop calling them that?" Leresy said.

He grabbed the cylinder from her. It was made of hard, boiled leather like the armor his recruits used to wear. It could work, he had to confess. He popped off the lid, revealing the glass lens, and drew his dagger.

"Don't scratch it," Erry said.

"Be quiet. I'm working."

With a few twists and pokes of his dagger, he pried the lens off the cylinder. He revealed a hollow receptacle about a foot deep. He filled it with red shards, popped the lens back in, and screwed the lid back on. Erry, meanwhile, scurried around the beach and returned with three more magnifying cylinders in her arms. She dumped them at his feet, and Leresy filled those too. It took four cylinders to seal all the red shards.

"Now try to shift," Leresy said, holding the cylinders. "The shards are sealed. No more light. Go on, fly!"

Erry gave a few stretches, touched her toes, and shook her legs. With a clearing of her throat, she shifted.

Wings burst out from her back. Copper scales rose across her. She took flight, her beating wings tossing sand onto Leresy.

"Moldy troll toes, it works!" she said and flew over the water, heading back west. "Now come on, fly after me. We're getting out here."

Leresy unscrewed the lid off a cylinder and pointed it at her. Red light shone out the lens.

Erry's magic vanished.

She tumbled in human form and crashed into the water.

"Leresy, you dung-sucking puddle of codpiece-juice!" She floundered in the water. "I'm going to shove these shards down your throat!"

She swam back to shore, stepped onto the beach, and marched toward him. With a glower that could wilt flowers, she grabbed the cylinders from him and shoved him back.

"Give me those, you piss-drinking maggot worm breath."

"What does that even mean?"

"It means you're a damn child."

He shrugged. "I had to test them. And they work beautifully. Thank you for your dedication to our cause."

She kicked his shin, and when he cursed and leaped with pain, she sealed the open cylinder. She held all four cylinders to her chest and shifted back into a dragon, taking the vessels into her larger form. She beat her wings and flew again.

Leresy summoned his magic. It crackled through him, as familiar as a warm, old cloak. He rose as a dragon, blasted fire against the sand below, and flew after Erry.

As they dived across the sea, heading back to Horsehead Island, Leresy imagined the Legions flying toward him, a storm of scale and fire covering the sky.

And he imagined them falling.

"I'm coming home, Father," he said into the wind.

As he flew onward, a grin stretched across his face, wide enough to hurt his cheeks. He had to keep grinning. He had to keep drowning that fear under rage, or he would see the blood again, the fire and death and guns blazing.

"I will face you again, Requiem," he swore. "And this time I will not run. This time I will win."

He flew. He kept grinning--forced himself to keep grinning--even as his tears fell and his belly twisted.

RUNE

He sat in his cell, chained and bruised, and stared at the wall that awaited him.

He had stared at these instruments for so many days, they had become like people to him, staring back at him, waiting, thirsty for his blood. The thumbscrew hung from the wall, its two bolts like eyes watching him, its vise like a mouth waiting to bite his fingers.

I will crush your fingers and toes! it cried to him, staring, waiting. *Your bones will snap between my jaws.*

Rune turned his eyes toward the stretching rack. Knots in the wood reminded him of a face, sagging and cruel.

I will tear your bones from your sockets, Rune, the face hissed at him. *Come lie with me.*

The pliers laughed from the wall, tiny iron crocodiles hungry for his fingernails. The rusted hooks sang for his entrails. The floggers screamed for his flesh.

We await you, Rune! The instruments sang and danced upon the wall. *We will make you sing with us. We will dance with blood.*

Chained to the wall, Rune only smiled at them.

"I won't fear you," he said. "You're my friends. I can't fear friends."

That confused them. They fell silent. Good. Good. If they had faces, friendly faces that were funny, he would not fear them. He would only laugh at their taunts.

Friends.

Tilla had been his friend once. Once. Years ago. Eras ago. In a different world, one that had burned. A world of sand and water and dreams now buried under ash.

"Are you still my friend?" he whispered into the shadows as the sun fell outside.

He did not know. Tilla served the red spiral now. She served those who hurt him. Tilla tried to protect him, but... she wasn't always here. She wasn't here when the guards kicked him, when they spat in his food, when they spilled his water across the floor, leaving him to lick moisture from dust and encrusted blood. But she had been there when Lynport burned. She had flown above, watched their city fall, and fought for *him*.

"For the demon," Rune whispered through cracked lips.

For the golden beast. For the creature with many heads. For Frey Cadigus.

Rune could see it again in the darkness. His home burning. The golden dragon above, his minions behind him, a hundred thousand strong. Kaelyn cried for him from the tower, and everywhere below the corpses lay, all those he'd grown up with, all those he'd loved, burnt and torn apart. So many screams. So much fire. Evil itself, a blanket of scale and smoke and fang, swirling above in a storm.

And her.

"And you."

The white dragon. A single beam of light breaking through the storm, warm and kind, caressing him, taking him under her wing. His dearest friend. His love. His Tilla.

"I have to save you from him," he whispered, his throat dry, his lips cracked and bleeding. "Even if they break me. Even if all those tools on the wall hurt me. I have to save you from him."

He tried to imagine it--Tilla leading him outside the tower, holding his frail body in her claws, and flying south. Flying away from the capital. Flying to the sea, across the waters, and into distant lands where Frey could not find them. They would find another home. Another beach to walk along, sand to caress their feet, water to wash away their pain. He would hold her in the night, kiss her lips again, and they would be as they were.

"And you will be good again," he spoke into the darkness, voice choked. "You will be Tilla Roper again, not Lanse Tilla Siren, not this creature they molded you into. And I will just be Rune. Not Relesar Aeternum, not any king. Just Rune and Tilla on the beach. That's all I want."

For a year, fighting in the Resistance, Rune had prayed to see her again. And now he saw Tilla here every night. She came to him in her armor, a machine of the enemy, and she spoke to him. Sat with him in the dark. Held him in her arms, and whispered to him, and kissed his cheek, and begged him to join her.

"But I will not let this happen to us. I cannot forget who you were."

The sun fell outside, casting orange light through the arrowslits. On cue, keys rattled in the lock. The door creaked open. And there she stood.

"Hello, Tilla," he said, sitting in the corner, his arms and legs chained.

Her sword hung from one hip, her punisher from the other. She had never used the instrument on him, but when the moon fell to darkness, when her time to sway him ended, would she burn his flesh?

As always, she sat by his side. As always, she wore her armor, the fine black plates of an officer. She stared at the wall with him, saying nothing.

"A fine pair we make," he said. "Me wearing my prisoner rags, you wearing your steel. Me with my face all dirty and thin, you with your face so pale, your eyes sad."

"It doesn't have to be this way," she whispered, her voice choked. She looked at him. "You can wear armor too, not rags. You can fight with us. For Requiem."

He looked away from her, leaned back as far as he could in his chains, and smiled softly. "Do you remember the mancala board I carved that winter, the one with the seashell pieces? It was such a cold winter, too cold for the south. Rain and thunder and wind every day. We sat in the Old Wheel most nights by the fire. You'd wrap a blanket around your shoulders. And we'd play mancala and drink ale, and Scraggles would lie at your feet. Do you remember? We--"

"Stop it," she said.

He let his smile widen and closed his eyes. "And the apple pies my father would bake! Stars, the whole place would smell of apples, and--"

"Stop it!" she said, more vehemently this time, and grabbed his arm. "Rune, those days are gone. The Old Wheel burned. You know this." Her fingers tightened and she stared at him. "Our home is gone. Everything we've ever known is gone."

He looked into her dark eyes and shook his head. "You're still here."

"I am not the woman I was."

"You are Tilla Rop--"

"I am Lanse Tilla Siren!" she said and bared her teeth. "I serve the red spiral. I follow Frey Cadigus. And so will you, Rune. So will you." She rose to her feet. "I placed you in the dungeon so you could hear the prisoners scream, see their blood, and languish in the dark. And still you did not worship him. So I placed you here, in this tower, so you could stare at the instruments of torture and imagine their pain. And still you do not join me."

"And still you, Tilla, do not join me," he said. He struggled to his feet, the chains so heavy, and stood before her. "You can end this. You have the key. You can flee with me."

She stared at him coldly, face blank as always, but something filled her eyes this time, something cold and afraid. She touched his cheek and whispered.

"So I will take you to a third place. And in this place, Rune... you will join us. I promise you. This place will break you."

She reached behind him and unchained him from the wall. She left his wrists manacled, but for the first time in days, no shackles bound him to the wall.

She held his shoulder and guided him toward the door. He walked with small steps. For nearly a moon now, he'd languished in irons. His chain had been long enough to let him stand and lie down, but not to walk. Walking now, every step ached, shooting pain from his toes, up his legs, and down his spine to the tailbone. He winced and almost fell, but Tilla held his arm, a gentle jailor, helping him onward.

The climb downstairs seemed an eternity. Rune did not count the steps, but there were hundreds, maybe a thousand. Each one shot more pain through him, and his head spun. He was too weak, too hungry, too hurt. The guards had kicked him too strongly. When they finally reached the bottom, Rune panted and swayed.

They stepped through the doorway, past the two guards with the mocking eyes, and into a snowy courtyard. The walls of the Citadel rose all around them. More guards stood upon the battlements, faces hidden behind helms. From within those walls, screams rose, a chorus of a thousand prisoners mad and beaten and dying. Rune had spent his first week here with them, and just hearing their screams, he could imagine their anguished faces.

"We fly from here," Tilla said. "I'll carry you."

"Unchain me and I'll fly with you."

He had tried to shift many times in his chains, only to find he could not. Whenever he'd summon his magic, the ancient starlight of Requiem, his body would start to grow, and wings would start to sprout from his back... and then the chains would slam him back into human form, leaving him panting and dizzy. Rune could shift with clothes, with weapons, even with armor; those were parts of him like his skin. The chains were foreign objects; they shackled his human form, and they shackled his dragon magic.

Tilla shook her head. "I cannot unchain you. Not yet. Not until you join us. I'll carry you."

She stepped away from him, leaving deep prints in the snow, and shifted. Her scales were white as the snow, but her eyes were black, two pools of night against a starry field. When she flapped her wings, she scattered snow across the courtyard, revealing its cobblestones. Smoke plumed from her nostrils, and fire glowed between her teeth, a single patch of color in a white and black world. Rune stood before her, chained and shivering, and she reached out her claws. She lifted him, an owl lifting a mouse, and flew.

Wind whistled. Snow swirled around them. The Citadel dwindled below. Rune watched it shrink until it looked like a toy, just a pile of blocks white with snow. The city streets snaked around it, bustling with people, thousands of men and women and children all going about their lives. Thousands of souls who cared not for his war. Thousands of souls who knew him as an outlaw, a killer, a beast to be tortured.

They flew over the streets, the city arena, and a dozen towering statues of Frey. They flew toward a fortress with black towers, a place Rune had only seen once in darkness.

"Castra Draco," he whispered. "Bastion of the Legions."

The Legions had many forts across the empire. Some trained recruits. Most housed garrisons of troops. Some, like the Citadel, housed prisoners, and one--Castra Academia--trained nobles for leadership. Draco was the heart of them all. If the Legions were an empire of their own, this would be its imperial palace. From this place did the generals command.

Will she take me there for torture? Rune thought, watching the fortress grow nearer. *Will she place me in another dungeon and in more chains, and will the whips of her comrades tear my skin?*

Yet when they almost reached the castle, Tilla banked and descended toward a street lined with tall, narrow houses. Rune remembered this street. Last year, he had rummaged here with Kaelyn through a barrel for posters. His heart twisted at the memory.

"Kaelyn," he whispered, and his eyes stung.

Last year, running and hiding with Kaelyn through the wilderness, Rune had often found comfort in thinking about Tilla--remembering her dark eyes, her smooth black hair, her soft lips, and his childhood spent with her upon the boardwalk. Hiding with Kaelyn, a wild rebel with flashing eyes, Rune had sought his comfort with the ghost of an old love.

Today, clutched in that same old love's claws, Rune thought of Kaelyn.

For so long, Kaelyn, I wanted to escape you, he thought. *I wanted to go back home, back to Tilla, to never see you and Valien and war again. But now I miss you.*

He missed her eyes rolling at him. He missed her finger jabbing his chest. He missed the sound of her groaning at his jokes. And he missed her smile. He missed her courage, her light that shone in the dark, and her love of life and home.

He wondered if she even still lived. Last time he'd seen the young woman, she had stood upon the tower of Castellum Acta, dragon wings billowing her golden hair, and she had cried his name. Had she fled with Valien through the tunnel? Did she live now in exile, and was she thinking of him too?

Wings puffed out, Tilla descended into a side street in the shadow of Castra Draco. Narrow, three-story houses lined the street, their tiled roofs white with snow, their gray bricks frosted. She placed Rune down outside one house, shifted back into human form, and stood beside him.

Rune stood on shaky feet, shivering in the snow. He wanted to hug himself, but manacles still bound his wrists behind his back. Orange light glowed from windows, and oil lamps flickered along the street, but Rune saw no other people. Tilla walked toward the house, unlocked the door, and led him inside.

"Welcome," she said, "to my home."

A cozy room greeted them. An armchair stood by a fireplace. Leather-bound books stood upon shelves. Plates of bread, cheese, ham, and fruits stood upon a wooden table. Tilla stepped toward the fireplace and soon flames crackled, filling the room with warmth and light.

"You are a legionary," Rune said, looking around the chamber. "I thought you would live in a fortress, surrounded by blades and shields."

Tilla locked the door behind her, then began unbuckling her armor and hanging the pieces on pegs.

"The common soldiers do. I'm an officer. I'm the officer who saved Shari's life." She gave a rare, crooked smile. "Some comforts are allowed for me here in the capital. The house is mine. When I asked to be stationed in Nova Vita, the Cadigus family bought it for me, a place of my own outside my barracks."

Rune wondered who had lived here before Tilla, and if Cadigus had truly "bought" the place, or if he'd made the previous occupant conveniently vanish.

"Why did you bring me here?" he asked, hearing the bitterness in his voice. "To gloat? To show off your comfort while I languish in a cell?"

Her eyes flashed with rage, then softened, and she sighed. She unbuckled her last plate of armor and stood before him in a woolen tunic. Suddenly she looked so much like the old Tilla--Tilla Roper from Lynport--that Rune could almost smell the sea.

"Not to gloat," she said. She began to load a plate with bread slices, slabs of ham, cheese, and grapes. "To share this with you. Come, sit with me and eat."

The armchair was wide enough for two. Tilla sat in one corner, the plate on her lap, and patted the space beside her.

"Will you unchain me before our meal?" he asked, standing before her.

"You know I can't. Not yet. Sit by the fire with me. Eat and drink with me. Please."

He wanted to refuse. He wanted to barge against the door, break it open, and run into the street. Yet he doubted he was strong enough. He was barely strong enough to stand. He was too famished, too thirsty, too tired. He sat by her in the armchair, his wrists still bound behind him, and let the flames warm him. It was a tight squeeze. Pressed against him, Tilla's body warmed him as much as the fire.

"It's a bit hard to eat with my wrists chained," he said.

She held a grape up for him. "Pretend I'm not your jailor, but your beautiful serving girl, feeding you grapes in luxury."

"Is that a joke, Tilla? You can joke at a time like this?"

"Eat."

He could not refuse it. He needed this food. He took the grape into his mouth, chewed, and swallowed. The juices flowed down his throat, sweet and healing. He had never known food to taste this good.

They ate, the fireplace warming them. Tilla held out pieces of cheese, ham, and bread for him, and he ate those too. He drank wine from her mug.

"It feels almost like the old days," she said. "Sitting by the fire at the Old Wheel."

He swallowed another grape and looked at her. She stared at the fire, her face golden in the light, as if lost in memory.

"I thought you didn't like to remember," he said.

She looked at him, her eyes soft. "I always remember, Rune. Always. I never forget. We can have a life again. Together. Here in this home." She held his knee and leaned closer, bringing her face but an inch from his. "I spoke to the emperor about it already. He will let you live here with me." A tear trailed down to her lips. "You and me together again. Always."

He looked away from her at the crackling fire. "And at what cost? I would have to serve him."

"You would. You would join the Legions. You would train. The training is difficult, but you will survive it, and I will be there, watching over you. You will fight for Cadigus, a soldier like me. You will raise his banners and bear his sigil. You will hail him in the days like I do. But at night, Rune... at night you can come back here to me."

Suddenly the food tasted stale.

"I cannot serve him," he said. "How can you serve him, Tilla? How can you wear that armor? Bear the red spiral? Worship the man who killed my father, who burned our home, who crushes Requiem under his heel?"

"Because I want to live!" She grabbed his cheeks and forced his face back toward her. Her eyes flashed and her lips peeled back. "Because I'm a survivor. Damn it, you don't have to love him. Do you think I do? Do you think anyone does? Do you think I love the man who burned our home? You don't have to love him, Rune. You only have to fear him."

"Is that what you do? Fear him? Are you a warrior or a coward?"

"A survivor," she said. "I joined the Legions and I served him. I did what I had to do to live. And I'm trying to save your life too. Call it cowardice if you will. I'd rather be a live legionary than a dead resistor."

Rune thought of Kaelyn again, the woman who hid in burrows, crawled through the mud, and fought through fire and rain. He thought of Valien, his guiding star, the man who lived in ruins but sang for light. They were brave. They were noble. Did they even still live?

"I don't want to die," he said, Tilla's hand still holding his knee. "But I have to believe they're still alive somewhere. Kaelyn. Valien. The others. I have to believe there is still hope for them. For Requiem. And for you, Tilla."

She blinked tears from her eyes. She rose to her feet.

"Come with me, Rune. I want to show you something."

She helped him to his feet and headed toward a staircase. They climbed upstairs into a bedchamber. A clock stood upon a bureau. An iron spiral hung upon the wall over a bed. Outside the window, beyond a few snowy trees, loomed the towers of Castra Draco.

"What did you want to show me here?" Rune said, lips twisting bitterly. "The spiral that hangs over your bed? The fortress that shadows you even here?"

She shook her head. "No. I wanted to show you this."

She stepped toward her bed and lifted something off her pillow. When she turned back toward him, a shaky smile trembled on her face, and her eyes were moist.

A string of seashells lay in her palm.

Rune blinked and felt his own eyes dampen. The memories pounded through him. Once more he was walking along the beach under the cliffs. The waves glistened in the sun and splashed over his bare feet. A boy of fourteen, he collected seashells into a pouch, choosing only the nicest ones. He strung them along a string for her. He gave her this gift for her birthday, and she laughed and tousled his hair.

"You kept it," he whispered.

She placed it around her neck and touched his cheek. "It means more to me than all the spirals and forts in the world. It means more to me than my sword, than my shield, than my empire. It's our childhood. It's our memory. It's our love."

She kissed him. Her lips were full and soft, and her tongue sought his, and her fingers smoothed his cheeks. It tasted like salt--the salt of her tears and the sea. Rune closed his eyes and he hated her, and he hated what she fought for, and he loved her.

"I want you to come into my bed," she said. "And I want to make love to you. Because I love you, Rune Brewer. I always have, and I can't bear to lose you."

She took him into his bed. It was soft and warm and so was she. She removed their clothes, held him close, and kissed him again. Their bodies moved under the blankets, a dance more intoxicating than wine, than all their flights over the sea. He had never lain with a woman before, but this felt right. This was home.

When it was done, they lay together in bed. He lay on his back, and she leaned up on her elbows, kissed his lips, and played with his hair.

"I want us to stay here forever," she said. "Stay with me here."

He looked at her pale face, her smooth black hair, her dark eyes that spoke of so many years and lost memories. He wanted to stay here with her. He wanted to choose her kisses, not the whips and the rack.

He looked up at the iron spiral that hung above them. He looked out the window at the fortress towers. And he thought of Kaelyn--his comrade, his friend, the woman he had fought with. He thought of her still fighting in the mud.

"Flee with me," he said to Tilla. "Flee south with me, and we'll fight him together. But I cannot join him. I cannot serve him. Not for you. Not for anything. Flee with me south and fight with us... or return me to my cell."

Her tears splashed against his chest. She took him downstairs. She flew with him. And she returned him to his cell.

ERRY

She wandered along Maiden Island, tears in her eyes.

"Tirans," she whispered. "My father's people."

She reached into her pocket, found her father's medallion, and clutched it so hard it hurt.

All her twenty years, Erry had lived among Vir Requis, her mother's people, an ancient race with the magic to become dragons. She had lived with them in Lynport upon the docks. She had served with them in the Legions. And finally, she had spent moons with ragged Vir Requis refugees upon Horsehead Island. Erry had inherited Requiem's magic from her mother, and she too could become a dragon, unlike her father's people. Yet she had always felt the outcast. A half-breed. The scrawny bastard of a whore and a foreign sailor.

But here... here on this southern island shaped like a sleeping woman... here the dormant half of her, her southern desert blood, blazed with waking fire.

"They're real, Scraggles," she whispered to her dog. "Stars, they survived. They live. My people."

Thousands wandered the camp around her. Erry had imagined Tirans to be short and scrawny like her; she had always blamed her father's blood for her diminutive frame. And yet they were a tall people, maybe even taller than Vir Requis. Their hair shone a platinum so pale it was almost white. Their eyes were blue as sapphires, their skin golden. Rune had once shown her a painting of Tirans he kept hidden, and in that painting, they wore golden armor and rode horses between palisades of columns. Yet here around her, they lived as wild islanders, clad in leaves and homespun; only a few of the elders still wore old, embroidered cotton of the desert.

Erry wiped tears from her eyes.

"Damn it, Scraggles," she whispered, then knelt and hugged her dog. "We... we could have been here with them. All those years I spent on the docks. All that damn year in the Legions. All those cold, lonely, painful nights in Requiem... and they were here. In sunlight. Happy. Alive. I could have been here with them."

Scraggles licked the tears from her cheeks.

Erry kept moving through the camp. Elders sat upon logs, singing old songs about Tiranor: her golden dunes, her lush oases of fig and palm trees, her fallen temples of sandstone and platinum, and her wisdom lost. Children scampered about, laughing, the sun shining upon their pale hair. Young couples walked hand in hand, whispering and smiling secret smiles. They were refugees. Their land had fallen. And yet still they seemed to Erry happier than she herself had ever felt.

"Do you think they'd let me live with them?" she asked Scraggles. She bit her lip and her eyes still stung. "Or would I be an outcast here too?"

She was half Tiran, that was true, but she looked Vir Requis. Her hair and eyes were brown, not platinum and blue. She was scrawny and short, not tall and noble. She spoke with the rough accent of Requiem's southern coast--odd enough among northerners like Leresy, Kaelyn, and Valien--not the flowing lilt of the desert.

"But I have this," she whispered. "I have my father's medallion."

She pulled it from her pocket and slung it around her neck. She had never dared wear her father's memento in Requiem, not in that empire that had burned the desert and hunted its people. Yet here she could wear it freely, and she clutched the silver. The medallion was shaped like a sunburst, symbol of Tiranor, and it had often comforted Erry during the long, cold nights. Her father, a Tiran sailor, had paid for her mother with this medallion, hiring her for a night of pleasure before sailing back south. Some would see it as shameful--the cost of a whore--but to Erry, the medallion had always brought hope. It had always been a symbol of another world, a better place.

And now I've found that place, she thought, looking around the camp of sunlight, greenery, and noble folk of her blood.

A young woman was climbing a fig tree ahead. She was reaching for the fruit, but the figs hung just beyond her grasp. When she saw Erry, the youth waved and cried out.

"Can you help me?"

Erry stepped closer, hesitant. A life upon the docks had taught her to fear strangers; those who asked for help often wanted more than she could give.

"What do you want?" she said, approaching the fig tree. Could this girl somehow see her Tiran blood, and would she mock her for it, call her a half-breed and bastard?

"I need a push," the girl said. "Please?"

She clung to the tree trunk, several feet above the ground, straining to reach a branch heavy with fruit. Yet far as she stretched, the branch remained an inch out of reach.

Erry realized her belly was rumbling. If she helped, perhaps the girl would share the prize. She wove her fingers together, forming a little shelf with her hands, and pushed up the girl's foot. The young Tiran snagged some fruit, smiled, and hopped down to the ground.

"Thanks," she said and grinned. Her teeth were very white in her golden face. Her long hair was almost as white, a smooth flag that swayed in the breeze. Her eyes seemed like sapphires to Erry, blue and bright.

"Now give me half of those fruits," Erry said.

The girl laughed. "You deserve them, fair enough. Come, eat with me." She reached out her hand. "My name is Miya."

Erry stared at the oustretched hand, not moving. So many times upon the docks, people had offered her food, but they had always wanted something in return. So many times, Erry had accepted an outreached hand, only to have that hand beat her later. So many men had offered food and shelter for her body. Leresy too had offered a smile and meal, only for him to later use and strike her.

How can I trust anyone? Erry wondered.

As the girl's smile faded, Erry lowered her head.

I can't be the old Erry here, she thought, *afraid and angry and hiding. These are Tirans. Their blood pumps through me. Miya is only a youth, not a man who lusts for me. I'll have to be different here, or I'll forever be the dock rat.*

She reached out, grabbed Miya's hand, and shook it.

"My name is Erry. Let's eat."

They sat upon a flat boulder under the shade of a pine. Wildflowers and fallen needles spread around them. The hillside sloped down at their feet, leafy with mint bushes, mulberry trees, and swaying wild oats. Far below, a golden shore faded into the sea. For a moment, the two young women sat silently, watching the waves and eating the figs.

"Is it true?" Miya finally asked, breaking the silence. "Your leader, the man Valien... he says he can defeat Frey." She looked over at Erry, her eyes wide. "Do you believe him?"

Erry shrugged and took another bite. She chewed for a moment, considering.

"I don't know. Sometimes I think he's mad."

"And yet you fight with him."

Erry allowed herself to laugh, but her eyes stung. "Frey burned my home. And so I fight. I have nowhere else to go.

Can we win? I don't know. But fighting is better than just lying down and dying."

As she spoke those words, Erry didn't know which home she meant: Lynport... or the desert kingdom she had never seen.

Miya bit into a second fig. "He burned my home too. I've never seen Tiranor. I was born here on this island. But my father... he speaks of home often." She gazed across the sea as if she could see that distant, fallen kingdom. "He said that most of Tiranor was just desert--dunes, mountains, and endless plains of sand. But a great river flowed through it, the Pallan, a giver of life. Oases grew alongside its banks, lush with fruit trees, shade, and a thousand kinds of birds. Limestone towers rose among them, capped with platinum. Great cities sprawled between the trees, centers of learning, their libraries and universities as large as palaces." Miya's eyes gleamed. "I wish I could have seen Tiranor. But she is fallen now. We are all that remains."

Erry stared across the sea, trying to imagine it.

"It sounds a lot nicer than Requiem," she said. "I wish I could have seen it too." She reached under her collar, pulled out her silver amulet, and showed it to Miya. "Can you read the letters here? I've never known what it says."

Miya's eyes widened. "This... this is Tiran silver! This is the sunburst of our god. How did you get this?"

Erry glared. "I didn't steal it, if that's what you mean."

"I didn't mean..." Pain filled Miya's eyes. "I'm sorry. Let me see."

The young Tiran girl held the amulet, leaned closer, and examined it.

"Well, can you read it?" Erry said. She herself had never learned to read; she didn't even know whether Tiranor and Requiem used the same letters.

Miya nodded and closed her eyes, saying nothing.

"Well, what does it say, damn it?" Erry scowled. "Won't you tell me?"

Maybe she had been wrong to trust this girl. Would Miya accuse her of being a thief? All her life upon the docks, fellow girls would accuse Erry of being a prostitute, a burglar, and a bastard. Men would beat Erry; girls would taunt her, their words more painful than blows. Was Miya just one of them, a pretty young thing who thought it fun to mock the orphan?

"Well, forget it then, damn you!" Erry said. She yanked the amulet back, rose to her feet, and was about to stomp away... and froze.

Tears were flowing down Miya's cheeks.

Erry stared. "Bloody stars, what...?" She sat back down. "Miya, why are you crying?"

The young Tiran sniffed and smiled tremulously.

"The words on your amulet... My father used to speak them. I haven't heard them in many years. Your amulet bears our Old Words, the prayer of Tiranor. *We Will Never Fall.*" She blinked tears from her eyes. "For thousands of years, our people spoke those words in the desert."

Erry felt all her rage flow away, and her own eyes stung. She clutched the amulet to her chest.

"We will never fall," she repeated in a whisper. "I like that."

Miya sighed and lowered her head. "And yet we did fall. Perhaps that prayer is meaningless now."

Erry shook her head mightily. "We did *not* fall. Look around you." She swept her arm around, gesturing at the camp. "I see thousands of survivors. I see a new life for our people. This amulet is right. We *will* never fall."

The young woman looked up and tilted her head. "Our... people? Erry, aren't you--"

Before she could complete her question, a shout rose from among the trees.

"Erry Docker! Damn you, you filthy urchin. Docker, where are you?"

Erry sighed. It was Leresy.

"Oh, bloody bollocks," she said and watched the outcast prince emerge from the trees.

Leresy stomped forward, hands on his hips, his chin raised with the same old vanity of royalty. A few dried leaves topped his golden hair instead of a crown, and he wore only tattered rags rather than finery, but he still strutted around as if he owned the world.

And as if he owns me, Erry thought.

He pointed at her. "There you are. Stars damn it, woman, didn't you hear me? Come with me. The council is about to begin, and I need you there."

She glared and spat at his feet. "Go find a rotting turtle carcass to shag, Leresy. I'm eating figs. I don't need no fancy-arse council for princelings."

He groaned and rolled his eyes. "Burn me. I need you to demonstrate the damn shards. Remember? Valien will be there, and so will my sister. The leader of this rabble will be there too, some oaf named Sila."

It was Miya's turn to glare. The young woman hopped onto her feet, crossed her arms, and growled.

"Sila is a great captain," she said. "He is my father. You will show him respect."

Leresy guffawed. He looked at Miya as if noticing her for the first time. His eyes trailed up and down, taking in her golden skin, pale hair, and slim body clad in leaves.

"Well, burn me," he said. "Another damn urchin. As if one weren't enough."

Erry grabbed a pine cone and tossed it at him. "She's got more bollocks than you do, Leresy. Brains too I reckon, but so does this pine cone. And I'm not some trained monkey. You want to demonstrate the shards? Use them on yourself, preferably while flying over a campfire."

He groaned, walked forward, and grabbed her arm. "Just come on. Bloody Abyss. Eating figs! We've got more important things to do. Planning how to kill my father, say." He began pulling her down the hillside, then called back up toward Miya. "You! Little girl. You come with us too. You'll want to see this."

Miya fumed, her arms crossed and her eyes blazing. She looked ready to claw Leresy to death. But it seemed curiosity overcame her anger. Grumbling under her breath, she followed.

They made their way downhill, heading toward the southern shore. Back at Horsehead Island, where the Resistance had been camping, Erry would fly from hilltop to beach. Since arriving here at Maiden Island that morning, she had been walking everywhere.

"These people watched dragons burn down their kingdom," Valien had told her. "We don't wish to stir those memories. Do not take dragon form around Tirans."

And so they walked, though Erry's soles ached, and rocks and thistles covered the hillside. Birds and mice rustled in the bushes, wild oats swayed taller than Erry's knees, and a falcon chased starlings overhead. The stems of old walls rose from the grass, only a foot tall and smoothed to lumps. Grass, vines, and cyclamens all but covered them.

"Somebody once lived here," Erry said.

Miya nodded, walking at her side, the wind in her hair. "My father said the Ancients lived on these islands. They were a wise people who vanished thousands of years ago. Father said they were great explorers who sailed around the world, navigating by the stars."

Walking ahead of the two, Leresy snorted. "Lot of good it did them. Nothing left of the buggers but a few old bricks."

He kicked an old wall, stubbed his toe, and wailed. Erry and Miya nearly fell over laughing.

After an hour of walking, they had crossed the island's waist and beheld a cove. Erry's eyes widened and she gasped.

"Stars above," she said. "Would you look at that."

Leresy frowned. "What the Abyss are those things?"

Erry grinned, remembering the paintings Rune had kept hidden under his floorboards. "They're ships. Tirans use them to navigate the seas."

Leresy guffawed. "Those things? Primitive. I'd take flying any day."

Erry glared at him. "Is it hard work being such a horse's arse, or does it come naturally to you? Tirans can't fly, and I think their ships are beautiful."

She stood a moment, admiring them. Six ships floated in the cove, their sails folded upon their masts. From bow to stern, they looked longer than the greatest dragon from snout to tail's tip. Cannons lined their decks, and their figureheads were shaped as birds. Their hulls sported sunbursts, the paint faded to dull ocher, and beneath them appeared words Erry could now read.

"We will never fall," she whispered.

Miya nodded. "See the largest ship, the one with the crane figurehead? That's the *Golden Crane*, our flagship. My father is captain. Our council will be held there."

They walked downhill, heading to the cove. A small oared boat waited at a dock, and they climbed in. As they rowed, Erry stared up at the *Golden Crane*, clutched her medallion, and felt peace flow across her. Leresy be damned, this ship was beautiful. It was not merely a vessel, she thought, but a symbol of a better time. It was Tiranor in her golden age, navigating the seas, a proud desert kingdom of spice, song, and secrets. It was Lynport before the Regime, a thriving port town, welcoming such ships to its docks.

Long ago, these ships would sail into Lynport, Erry thought. They had brought southern silk, spice, and gems. The boardwalk had been alive then, not a ruin of rotten wood and urchins rifling through trash, but a hub of trade. Rune's father would sell his ale to these sailors, and Tilla's father would sell his ropes, and Mae's father would sell bread.

And my mother sold her body, Erry thought. *I come from these ships. They brought me too into Requiem.*

When they climbed onto the deck, she saw Valien and Kaelyn already there. They had shed their charred, torn leather and wool--the clothes they had fled Lynport with--and wore tunics of *maidenspun*, a fabric the Tirans wove from wild cotton. They still bore their swords of Requiem. A heavy, two-handed sword hung across Valien's back, an ancestral weapon of House Eleison. Kaelyn wore Lemuria upon her hip, her thin sword of dragonforged steel. They were ancient blades, weapons of honor and history and tradition.

Yet honor, history, and tradition are passing from the world, Erry thought. She looked at a rack of hand cannons that lay against the bulwark--*arquebuses*, she had heard the Tirans call them. *Our blades will rust; gunpowder will rise, a demon of greater malice.*

"Welcome to the *Golden Crane.* Welcome to my council."

Erry turned toward the voice. She saw a man emerging from the ship's hold. He was tall and wide--as large as Valien--and almost as gruff. His face was wide, leathery, and golden, his nose flat and his jaw heavy. Stubbly platinum hair covered his scalp, cut so short he was almost bald. Grooves lined his face; Erry couldn't tell if they were wrinkles or scars. He wore maidenspun, a wide belt, and baggy pants--simple garb, yet he moved with the aura of command.

Miya approached the man, kissed his cheek, and introduced him.

"This is my father, Captain Sila. Father, this is Leresy Cadigus, the outcast prince of Requiem, son of Emperor Frey. His companion is Erry Docker, once a soldier in the Legions. Both now fight for Valien."

"*With* Valien," Leresy corrected, raised his chin, and cleared his throat. "I serve no man."

Erry jabbed him with her elbow, glowered, and hissed from the corner of her mouth. "Quiet, Leresy. Nobody cares about your stupid pride."

Under the noon sun, pelicans flying overhead and the ship gently rocking, the council began.

Valien spoke the most, straining to hiss the words through his ruined throat, but never slowing his speech. He spoke of battles they'd fought: the Battle of Castra Luna, where Erry had flown in the Black Rose Phalanx, fighting against the Resistance; and the Battle for Lynport, where Erry had fought on the other side. And he spoke of older battles too, battles that had raged in the north years ago, back when Erry had still lived upon the docks. And he spoke of future battles: of his plans to storm the capital of Nova Vita, to surround Frey in his palace, and to slay the man.

Sila spoke too, gruff captain of the *Golden Crane*, and Erry learned that he not only ruled this ship, but all the island. He spoke of leading a merchant fleet years ago, of fighting the Legions when they had invaded his homeland, and of fleeing burning Tiranor with all those he could load onto his ship.

"We've trained for battle," Sila said. "My father invented the arquebus, and we've forged two thousand of the guns here on this island, melting down everything from swords to belt buckles for the metal. I've drilled an army of men and women. We know how to fight." He grumbled. "Yet we've only trained to fight off dragons should they attack our island. We've never dreamed of invading Requiem, let alone her capital. How would we? We are only a few. The Legions are half a million strong, they say."

Valien nodded. "We are few and they are many. Yet now we have new weapons. Now we have hope. Leresy!" He turned toward the former prince. "Show him the scope."

The young man nodded, rummaged through his pack, and produced one of the leather magnifying cylinders; Erry had learned the Tirans called them *scopes.* It rattled, still full of the glowing crystal shards they had found.

"Erry, go on, fly around a bit," Leresy said.

She placed her hands on her hips. "I'm not doing it again. Just tell them how it works."

"Bloody griffin vomit, Erry, they need to see it." Leresy scowled. "Just fly around, for stars' sake. It won't kill you."

Erry gave the loudest, longest groan of her life. Eyes rolling, she jumped off the ship, shifted into a dragon, and flew.

The beating of her wings blasted the hull, rocking the ship. She flew in circles, scales clattering, and blew fire upward--just to impress them a little more. She rose higher, roared to the sky, and swooped toward the ship, claws outstretched, feigning an attack.

Upon the deck, Leresy--still in human form--pointed the scope at her, then unscrewed the wooden lid.

The gems inside glowed. Their light blasted out from the lens, drenching Erry.

Like a tugged tablecloth, her magic vanished.

Erry returned to human form, fell through the air, and crashed into the water.

She sputtered, cursed, and swam back to the ship. When she stood back upon the deck, she shook herself wildly like a dog, spraying water onto the others.

"That," Leresy said, "is how we fight the Legions. I've got four scopes full of these shards. We fly to Requiem. My father's dragons will drop from the sky like dead flies." He nodded. "I've called my weapons Leresy Scopes. They will win me the throne."

The others began to growl and roll their eyes. Before they could object too much, however, a high voice rose above them.

"Big weapon! Big weapon is no Leresy Scope. Genesis Shards they are, yes. Bantis knows them!"

Erry looked up and raised her eyebrows. Crazy old Bantis, still clad in only a loincloth, perched upon a mast. His white hair billowed in the breeze and he laughed. Fast as a monkey, he scurried down the mast, landed upon the deck, and danced a jig.

"Grandpapa!" Miya said. "Have you been up there all along?"

The old man grinned. "You cannot hold councils without Old Bantis, no. Foolish boy, give me that." He reached toward Leresy, grabbed the scope full of shards, and began tugging, struggling to free it from the younger man's grip. "Mine. Mine!"

Leresy growled and held the scope firmly.

"Leresy, let him have it!" Erry said and kicked his shin.

The prince yelped, his grip loosened, and Bantis scurried back with his prize.

"These are Genesis Shards," the old man repeated. "Yes, that is their name. Bantis has been seeking them for many years, yes. They have languished underground for a thousand years. Dragons buried them! They did not want them found, no." He cackled. "Yet now Bantis has big weapon. Kills dragons!"

Leresy rubbed his shin. "Bloody Abyss. Why are they called Genesis Shards?"

Bantis hopped around on one leg, cawed like a bird, then smiled mischievously. "Created all life, they did. Ten thousand years ago, the gods created Animating Stones, *big* gems--big like chicken eggs!--that raised dust, earth, and water into men and beasts. Created us Tirans too, they did." He laughed, head tossed back. "Powerful magic, yes. Powerful enough to raise matter into life. Powerful enough to cancel out all other magic around them. Even the magic to become dragons." He winked. "The old Vir Requis found the gems a thousand years ago. They feared them. They broke them into tiny shards. They can no longer create life, no, not broken like this." He laughed and gave a quick dance. "But they can still cancel dragon magic. So they buried the shards. Buried them deep in a distant island. But Old Bantis found them! Old Bantis will take them to Requiem. And dragons will fall from the sky!"

Bantis himself fell onto his back, arms and legs splayed out, imitating a fallen dragon. He lay upon the deck, grinning.

Leresy began to pout and object, shouting that *he* had found the shards, and that they *were* called Leresy Shards. Kaelyn, Erry, and even Miya began to shout him down--and soon to kick him. Sila howled at everyone to be silent, and Bantis kept laughing. The council collapsed into chaos, and soon everyone was yelling above the others.

Only Valien stood silent, staring across the water, lost in thought. After a long moment, he nodded and spoke, but his voice drowned under the shouting.

"All of you, be quiet!" Erry howled, hopping up and down. "Valien is talking. Let him be heard!"

When finally everyone was silent, Valien stared at them one by one, then spoke again.

"We've fled here to these islands, two camps of refugees. On Horsehead Island, three thousand Vir Requis dream of reclaiming their homeland. Here upon Maiden Island, four thousand Tirans have found a new life, refugees from their fallen kingdom, and they too dream. They dream of returning to the desert, unafraid, of rebuilding their homeland without the threat of Cadigus looming. For long years, both our camps hid and fought separately, but we shared the same vision. We sang the same song. We dreamed of going home."

As they listened to the speech, Erry saw that Kaelyn and Miya had tears in their eyes. Kaelyn dreamed of returning to Nova Vita, the capital Erry herself had never seen. Miya dreamed of returning to Tiranor, land of her fathers, the desert kingdom her people still yearned for.

Yet what home do I dream of? Erry wondered. *I never had a home, unless the docks at Lynport were a home. If we truly win this war, what awaits me if not more pain?*

Valien continued speaking, voice scratchy but clear, the voice of wind over sand. "For many years, this was but a dream, a whisper of a hope. But today we found new hope--a hope that blazes bright as a pillar of fire. We no longer need hide. Together, with our magic and your machines, we can defeat the Cadigus regime. We can both reclaim our homes." He lifted a scope in one hand, an arquebus in the other. "I will lead my people into Requiem. We will fly as dragons, roaring and blowing fire. Upon our backs, we will bear you, noble people of Tiranor, and you will wield your weapons. You will point the Genesis Scopes at the Legions; they will fall from the sky. We will fly for days, felling the armies that storm toward us, until we reach the capital. We will storm the palace as men, firing our guns. The Axehand Order defends the palace, and they fight with blades; we will shoot them from a distance. We will find Relesar Aeternum, true King of Requiem, and free him from captivity. We will find Frey Cadigus, the usurper, and slay him." The grizzled man's eyes gleamed. "The war will end. Fear will fade. We will return home."

The council dispersed one by one. Leresy shifted and left first, flying off with a puff of smoke, still muttering about how *he* had found the shards. Kaelyn followed him, a slim green dragon, calling him a woolhead for all the island to hear. Miya left in her boat, while Bantis opted for leaping off the hull, crashing into the water, and swimming to shore. Valien departed with a grumble, a silver dragon with clattering scales and one horn.

Erry remained standing on the deck, watching the others leave. She placed her hand upon a cannon, remembering the battles she had fought, the friends she had seen die, and the men she'd killed. She lowered her head.

A voice spoke behind her.

"Will you not fly with your friends, Erry of Requiem?"

She turned to see Captain Sila. His golden, weathered face still seemed rough to her, a patch of leather left out in the sun, but she saw softness in his eyes.

"They're not my friends," she said. "I'm just here because..."

Because what? she wondered. Because the docks had burned? Because Tilla had turned into a killer, little better than Shari Cadigus? Because Leresy fed and sheltered her, or because she felt she had to heal him?

Sila nodded. "I understand. You are here for the same reason I am."

"And what is that?" she demanded.

He smiled wryly. "Because there's nowhere better to be."

"Valien thinks there is. And he wants to fly out and fight for it. Will you fight with him, Captain Sila? Will you leave your haven for a chance to win this war?"

He cleared his throat, came to stand beside her, and placed his hands upon the railing. They both stared at the beach.

"My people mistrust dragons," he said at length. "Some were born here upon the island, but most remember the war. They remember thousands of dragons burning their homes, killing their families, and toppling their kingdom. They might not distinguish between the Resistance and the Legions; both are beasts to them. Yet I will do my part to sway them. I believe we should fight with Valien. I believe he is an honorable man."

Erry swallowed. "Maybe I... maybe I can help sway them. Your people, that is. The Tirans here." Her throat felt so tight, and her eyes dampened. When she looked back up at Sila, her vision was blurred. "I can tell them that not all Vir Requis are bad."

He smiled. "What makes you think they'd believe you and not me?"

Now her tears did fall. She had never told anyone here of her heritage--not Valien, not Kaelyn, and certainly not Leresy. Yet now she blurted out the words, voice choked.

"I'm half Tiran." She trembled. "I'm... I'm a bastard orphan. My mother was a Vir Requis from Lynport, a town in southern Requiem. My father was a sailor from Tiranor, though I never met him. I can shift into a dragon like a Vir Requis; I got that from my mother. But... I'm Tiran too." She rubbed her eyes. "I'm one of you, or at least half of me is. I can tell the people. I can tell them that Vir Requis and Tirans can work together. I'm living proof."

Sila laughed softly, and Erry sucked in her breath, sure that he was mocking her, but his smile was kind.

"There's no shame in mixed blood," he said. "Do not cry, Erry. Did you know? After the great Griffin War, a massacre a thousand years ago that left only seven Vir Requis alive, Requiem's survivors mingled with the people of Osanna and Tiranor. Most Vir Requis today carry some mixed blood."

Erry blinked at him, tears still falling. "Really?"

He nodded. "Many years ago, there was a great queen in Requiem, Luna the Traveler of House Aeternum. She visited Tiranor and appears in our lore. They say she wed a Tiran prince, and that her children inherited the magic of Requiem and became princes of your realm. Perhaps all Vir Requis have some Tiran blood deep inside them. Be proud of it, child. You are a noble daughter of starlight and of sand."

She nodded, blinking her tears away. That didn't sound too bad. A thought struck her, and she reached under her shirt, slung her medallion off her neck, and held it out.

"This is my only memento from my father," she said. "He was a Tiran sailor. He gave this to my mother in Lynport twenty years ago. Sila, you commanded a merchant fleet. Maybe you recognize this medallion?" Her voice shook. "Maybe you knew my father?"

His eyes narrowed and he took the medallion from her palm. He examined it, turning it over and over, and exhaled slowly. Old dreams seemed to dance in his eyes.

"I know this medallion," he said.

Erry trembled like the last leaf on a tree. "Do you know who gave it to my mother?"

He nodded, placed the medallion back in her palm, and closed his hands around hers. He smiled again, a soft, secret smile full of pain and memory.

"Of course I do. I did."

TILLA

"The moon is new," said Shari. "The time for his torture has come."

They stood in the Citadel's courtyard, torchlight illuminating the falling snow. The walls rose all around them, lined with cells. From behind a hundred oaken doors, prisoners howled, wept, screamed, and begged. Below Tilla's feet, she could feel the cobblestones trembling; down in the dungeon, racks turned, whips lashed, and flesh tore. The very stones of this place shook with pain.

Now that pain would tear through the man she loved.

Tilla looked up at the Red Tower. It rose into the night, wreathed in snow, a bone rising from a grave. In that tower he waited, chained, foolish, still hoping he could sway her to his cause. In that tower he would now scream.

"I will begin with my punisher," Shari said. "I will burn every inch of him. His skin will crack and fall." She sucked in her breath. "Every day I will introduce a new instrument. Tonight the punisher. Tomorrow the rack. The third day the hammers. I wonder how many days he will last."

Tilla returned her eyes to her princess. It was the first time she had seen her commander without armor. Shari had not dressed for battle today; she had dressed for torture. She wore tall boots over black leggings, a leather apron, and thick gloves. Her mane of dark curls cascaded down her shoulders, and her eyes shone with bloodlust. Her punisher crackled in her hand, red energy racing across its tip.

Today she does not look like a warrior, Tilla thought and shivered. *Today she looks like a butcher.*

"Commander," Tilla said, "I need more time. I am beginning to sway him. I--"

"You've had long enough," Shari said and caressed the dagger that hung on her hip. "Are you softening to his cause, Lanse? Whose side are you on--ours or his?"

Tilla's heart pounded. Her voice was weak. "Commander, a flayed, beaten, broken man cannot fight for us. He cannot break the spirit of the Resistance, only embolden them. If I can sway him with words, and he joins us willingly, the Resistance--"

Shari snarled, reached out, and grabbed Tilla's throat.

"The Resistance is scattered!" she said and squeezed. "They fled into the sea with their tails between their legs. Most likely they all drowned." Shari growled like a feral dog. "I grow tired of your excuses, Lanse."

Tilla gasped for breath. The fingers were crushing her. She thought Shari would snap her neck. Stars, the woman was strong. How could anyone be so strong? She grasped at Shari's hand, trying to pry her fingers off, but could not. She was seeing stars and her legs were wobbling when Shari finally released her.

Tilla clutched at her throat, wheezing, and stared up with burning eyes.

I saved your life! she wanted to say. *Rune almost killed you, and I saved you from him!*

Yet she could not speak those words, even if she had breath for them. To speak them was death. Shari was too enraged now.

I am her groom, Tilla thought, sucking in air. *And I saved her life. And I fought at her side in battle. Yet if I cross the line, she will still kill me. And she will enjoy it.*

"Commander," she managed to say, voice raspy. "Let me do it. If I cannot sway you, let *me* hurt him."

Shari laughed, the laugh of a madwoman. "A moment ago, you were pleading for him."

Tilla took a deep breath, unable to conceal its shakiness. "I thought I could sway him with words. But if we must use pain, we must hurt him fully. We must break him." She allowed herself a small, crooked smile. "What would hurt him more than his dearest friend torturing him?"

Please let her agree, Tilla prayed silently. *Please, old and new gods, let her agree.*

If she could torture Rune herself, she could perhaps hurt him less than Shari would. She could make him scream, but not cause permanent damage. If Shari tortured him, she would drive all her malice into her work; she would break his mind. Tilla could still save him... save him by burning him herself.

Shari reached over and touched Tilla's punisher, which hung at her hip. Her gloved fingers caressed its leather grip.

"You will torture him," she said and sucked in her breath. "Yes. That will hurt him, and it will harden you. We begin. Now. We enter the tower."

They crossed the courtyard, a chorus of screams rising from the cells alongside. They entered the Red Tower, climbed its stairs, and emerged into his cell.

Oh, Rune, Tilla thought, and her eyes stung.

He stood bound, arms chained to the ceiling. He met her gaze and did not break it. He knew what was coming. He had been waiting. He was ready.

"Begin," Shari said.

Tilla wanted to flee. Yet if she fled, Shari would give him a worse fate. She wanted to plead with Shari again, but if she did, she too would suffer this pain.

I'm sorry, Rune, she thought.

She drew her punisher.

She did as she was trained.

At first he withstood it. Then his screams joined the rest of them.

"You don't have to do this!" he cried, voice torn, as her punisher burned his flesh. "Tilla, you don't have to--"

But his voice drowned in his agony.

And she kept working.

It seemed an hour, maybe more, before Shari nodded and placed a hand on Tilla's shoulder.

"Good, Lanse," she said. "Good." She admired the welts that rose across him. "You did well for tonight. Tomorrow you will continue. You've made me proud."

Tilla stood shaking. Sweat and tears burned in her eyes. She looked at her commander.

"Will you not ask him to join us?" she whispered. "Will you not ask him to hail the red spiral?"

"In time," Shari said and smiled. "When he's suffered enough. Not this night. Not until my vengeance is sated. Your work here only begins."

With that, Shari turned and left the chamber. Tilla remained in the tower. A moment later, she heard a roar and, through an arrowslit, saw a blue dragon fly into the distance.

"Tilla..." Rune spoke in a choked whisper.

Now she could not curb her tears. They stung her eyes and streamed down her face, and she took two great steps toward him. She wanted to embrace him but froze; embracing him would only double the pain in his wounds. Instead she stood trembling and touched his cheek, the only part of him not scarred.

"I will heal you," she whispered. She rummaged through her pack for bandages. "I will bring you laceleaf milk for the pain. I--"

"I don't want you to heal me," he said, hanging from his chains. "Will you heal me only to hurt me again? Tilla... flee with me."

She shook her head, tears streaming down her cheeks.

"I cannot," she whispered. "He would hunt us. He would kill us. I have to make you serve him. I have to save you."

His eyes softened, and alongside the pain, she saw pity in them. Despite what she had done, he pitied her.

"And I must save you," he whispered. "I must save you from what you've become, what they turned you into. My body is burned. But worse is the pain of seeing your soul broken."

Tilla closed her eyes and trembled. She remembered Nairi burning her a year ago; that pain had only lasted for several minutes, and it had left Tilla in an infirmary for days. Now she had burned Rune for an hour, maybe longer, and still he only thought about her. Still he cared for her soul more than his pain.

She opened her eyes and kissed him, a kiss deeper than any they had yet shared, and she loved him more than any love she had felt.

"You are noble," she said through her tears, "and you are brave, and you love me. But you are wrong. My soul was never broken. I do what I must to survive. Please, Rune. Tomorrow when Shari returns, hail the red spiral. Worship Frey Cadigus. And this pain will end."

"It would only begin," he replied.

She looked at his manacles. She had the keys on her belt. How easy it would be to unlock him, to fly with him again! They could fly like in the old days, find some distant beach, heal together, kiss in the sand, and--

No, she told herself and tightened her lips. Those were the dreams of youth. She had to follow this path--for Requiem, for herself, and for his life.

She left him in the tower.

She returned to her home.

She sat upon her bed, pulled out her string of seashells, and held them all night.

ERRY

She sat on the islet, eyes burning, and stared out across the sea.

"Pissy pig-shagging maggots," she said, eyes burning, and clenched her fists--small fists no larger than a child's. "Damn bloody gutter shite." She snarled and shouted to the waters. "Damn you, you latrine-licking dog's son, and damn all of you beef-witted cockroaches, you... damn..."

Her throat tightened. Her eyes watered. She pulled her knees to her chest, lowered her head, and let her body shake.

"My father," she whispered. "He is my father. Damn him. Oh stars, damn them all."

She looked at the sea. The waves shimmered through her tears. It was easy to remember like this. It was easy to pretend that she still sat at home, on the beaches of Lynport.

Her belly rumbled with the old hunger, and she remembered rifling through trash for scraps, eating live fish when she could catch them, dead ones that washed ashore when she couldn't. She remembered all those men who had taken her in the sand, all those times she had spread her legs for a meal, a roof in a storm, or a broken promise. And most of all, she remembered the demon inside her, the icy tendrils that clutched her belly and heart and mind, pulling her into shadows of loneliness and gloom worse than any blow. So many times she had lain in the sand, stared up at the stars, and prayed to die. So many times she had walked into the sea, sunk under the water, and tried to drown but never found the courage to swallow the water.

"I spent eighteen years on the docks," she whispered. "I lived with cats and I became a feral beast, and I fought and I hurt. And you weren't there. You left me to that nightmare."

She still clutched his medallion in her palm. She looked at it, her face twisted, and she emitted something halfway between growl and sob. She had thought this amulet a symbol of hope, of home, of a better world. Yet now it disgusted her.

She whispered through tight lips, "You abandoned me."

She rose to her feet. She tossed the amulet into the sea.

The sun began to set, and Erry stood watching it, frozen as a statue, just standing, just staring, alone. So many nights she had stood like this, watching the waters, dreaming of what lay beyond. But now she knew.

"They were there. My father. My sister. Living in peace. They left me."

Darkness fell and the stars emerged. It was her seventh night alone on this islet. The others had been searching for her; she had seen the dragons flying overhead, calling her name. She had hidden among the trees until they passed.

"They can all leave," she said. "They can all fly to their war, and I will stay here, and they can all go die. Especially him. Especially Sila." She clenched her fists. "I hope he dies first."

She howled at the moon, fingers raised like claws.

But no. She could not let him die like this. Not yet.

She shifted into a dragon, rose into the air, and roared fire across the sea.

"You will answer to me first."

She howled in the darkness. She beat her wings. She flew through the night.

The sea spread below her. The sky spread above. Erry flew between black and black, her fire lighting the way. Her blaze reflected against the water, and her roars pealed. The night was clear but she was a storm.

"I've been hiding and running all my life," she spoke into the wind. "But now I will learn the truth. Now I will learn why I suffered."

She flew for hours before she saw Horsehead Island ahead, a dark patch upon the inky sea. They would be mustering for war now. Tomorrow they intended to fly out, to invade Requiem, to kill and to die. That was their war; Erry fought her own, a battle that had been raging inside her since her birth upon the boardwalk.

She crashed down onto the beach in a cloud of smoke and flame. Valien had forbidden them to light fires, worried the Legions were patrolling the seas, but Erry didn't care. She howled and sprayed her flames, lighting the island.

"Sila!" she cried upon the beach. "Come see me. I'm here. Come face me!"

She tossed her head, scattering fire, not caring that others saw. She beat her wings, raising the sand into a storm. They stood upon the beach, Vir Requis and Tirans, gaping at her.

Let them gawk, she thought, eyes burning. *Let them see the orphan, the dock rat, the creature. He made me this thing.*

Through the smoke and flying sand, he emerged, walking grimly and staring ahead. Captain Sila of Tiranor. Her father.

"Erry," he said.

She growled and snapped her teeth at him, still in dragon form. He stood before her, wide-shouldered, leathery-faced, gruff and strong and weathered, but still only a man. She was a dragon. She was fire and claw and fang, and she could kill him. She could make him hurt like she hurt.

But her eyes only dampened again.

She lowered her head, blasting the sand with smoke, and growled and clawed the beach.

"Why?" she said, spitting the words out with spurts of fire. "Why did you do this?"

He stood before her, not cowering back even as her smoke and fire flickered. Sparks from her flame burned upon his tunic, but still he stood firmly, staring at her steadily. His eyes were still hard, his face inscrutable.

"Will you face me as a woman?" he said.

She growled. "Will you face me as a man? I don't see a man. I see only a coward. I see only a whoring sailor. I see a dog who... who abandoned my mother." Her tears streamed now, steaming in her fire. "A dog who abandoned me."

He met her gaze steadily. "Return to human form, Erry, and we will talk."

She howled. She wanted to blast him with fire. She wanted to dig her claws into his flesh. But he only kept staring, eyes hard, lips tight, silent. He stared her down. With a yowl, she blasted a pillar of fire skyward, and she released her magic. She returned to human form and stood in the sand, panting. Her flames rained around her as sparks.

"Speak to me!" she said. "Tell me why you did it. You abandoned me!"

"Is that what your mother told you?" he asked.

She could barely see through her tears. "She never told me anything! She died when I was only five. You didn't even know, did you? You didn't care. Frey killed her, and you only lived here on the island. You never cared about her. You only fled here, a coward."

People were gathering around them, but Erry didn't care. She panted and rubbed her eyes and stared at this man she hated.

"Erry, where is the medallion I gave her? The medallion you carried all these years?"

"I threw it into the sea. It's a piece of garbage. Meaningless. It's a trifle you paid for a whore." She snorted through her tears. "I hope you enjoyed bedding her that night. I hope it was your best damn time. I hope your silver bought you an hour of joy. It bought me a lifetime of pain."

He remained calm and cold. If any pain filled him, his eyes did not betray it. He had a captain's eyes, eyes for staring down mutinous sailors and enemy ships, for staring down death and life.

"You have lived for years upon the docks. You have served in the Legions. You have seen the underbelly of the world. Have you ever, Erry, in all those years, seen a man hire a whore with a silver medallion?"

She gritted her teeth. "You probably spent your last few coins on booze."

He shook his head. "I never did drink booze, not then and not now. No, Erry. I did not hire your mother for a night of cheap passion. I loved her. I courted her. I wanted her to marry me, to return with me to Tiranor. When she refused, I gave her my amulet, a parting gift. I never knew she was with child. You must believe that. Had I known, I would have returned for you."

"I don't believe you!" Her body trembled, and she could barely breathe. "If this were true, my mother would have told me."

"Would she have? Would she have told a toddler of these things even adults struggle to grasp? Yes, Erry, I loved her. She was a flower blooming in the sand. I found her living in boardwalk squalor, and I wanted to save her, to show her a better life. I would have brought her to the desert and built a palace for her. But she would not leave her home. Her heart was in Requiem, land of her fathers, not my desert. She stayed--with my medallion, with my heart... and with my daughter."

Erry shook her head, staring at her feet. "I am not your daughter. By blood? Maybe. I don't care." She looked up at him, and her voice cracked. "Do you have any idea how I suffered? I was an orphan. I slept on the docks. I always wanted to know who you are, but now... now I hate you."

Finally something changed in his eyes. Finally some of that hardness shattered, and for a moment, his soul shone through, and it was hurt. It was as hurt as hers.

He took a step toward her. "Erry," he said softly. "Erry, I am sorry. I am so sorry."

Her tears fell. "I hate you."

"I know." Now his voice too cracked with pain. "You are my daughter. And you suffered. And I hate myself for this too. Erry, my child. I cannot change the past. I cannot make you forgive me. I cannot undo any of this or make any of it right."

She sobbed. "So what can you do?"

"Be with you now," he answered, reaching out to her. "I cannot heal you, and I cannot make you forget those years, but I can be with you now and always. You are my daughter. Let me learn how to love you. Let me learn how to be your father."

A shadow appeared behind him. A platinum-haired girl stepped around the captain. Slim, golden-skinned Miya walked across the sand, and her eyes shone with tears. She reached out to Erry.

"I have a sister," the girl whispered. "I have an older sister."

Erry wept. She looked away. She wanted to fly. She wanted to flee this, to return to her island, to roar her fire, to drown in the sea, or to be a wild beast, but not face this. Not feel her heart shatter. Not feel love fill her; love hurt too much. She had known too much pain to feel love now. It frightened her more than all the dragons and horrors in the world.

Yet she could not move, and when Miya embraced her, she could not resist. She wept against her sister's shoulder. Miya was only eighteen, two years younger than Erry, but taller and stronger. Erry had grown up with a tight belly, and she was so small, a runt of a thing, but her sister held her nonetheless, and she felt warm.

"I have a sister," Miya whispered and cried. "Erry, you are my sister. I see it in your eyes."

Erry looked up. Sila stood there, a foot away, looking upon them, still gruff, still the captain. But then his throat bobbed, and he sucked in air, and he took a great step forward and joined their embrace. Erry wanted to scratch and kick him, to break free and burn him, but she found herself holding him tight. She pressed her cheek against his chest and wept.

I have a sister, she thought. *I have a father.*

She spoke through her sob, voice shaking. "I'm so scared."

They held her close, keeping the night at bay, strong and warm and enveloping her.

"I know," Sila said. "But we'll be here with you. We'll help you face it. We'll help you heal. You'll never more be alone."

Held in their arms, Erry raised her head. She looked at the sky. The Draco constellation shone there, stars of Requiem.

"And... you don't care that I'm half Vir Requis? That half my blood is that of your enemy?"

Sila laughed and squeezed her tight. "The only thing I care about," he said, "is that you curse more than most sailors in my fleet."

She closed her eyes. "You're talking bloody pig shite," she whispered.

She stood in the sand, letting them hold her, and she thought of home. Mae had died, Tilla had betrayed her, and Leresy could go lick codpieces. Erry sniffed and rubbed her eyes.

I have a family.

VALIEN

They flew above Horsehead Island in the sunset, one dragon scarred and silver and brawny, the other green and slim and fast. They glided silently. They surveyed their army that mustered below.

"Three thousand Vir Requis," Valien said, voice nearly lost in the wind. "Two thousand Tirans strong enough to fight, each armed with an arquebus. A handful... against the might of half a million legionaries."

Here was his new Resistance, a patchwork. Only a seed of his original fighters remained. The rest Valien had woven in from other forces. A few hundred had served as Leresy's Lechers. A thousand had been men of Cain's Canyon. Now two thousand Tirans joined his cause, foreign warriors who could not shift into dragons. A patchwork, that was all. A few thousand souls who hated Frey enough to join here upon these beaches.

It wasn't enough.

Flying at his side, Kaelyn grinned, showing all her teeth. "Since when did we care about being outnumbered?"

Valien snorted a puff of smoke. "Since we lost most of our men in Lynport."

Since I lost my wife, he thought. *Since I fled the capital with Rune in my arms and Marilion's blood in my nightmares.* Yet he did not speak those words. He would not speak of Marilion to Kaelyn, this new woman in his life.

She lives! She lives in my dungeon, you fool!

Emperor Frey's words still echoed. They filled his mind now as they did every waking moment. Valien had seen his wife die. He had held her lifeless body. Her blood had coated his hands.

She lives!

He knew the emperor was lying. He knew that Frey only wanted to hurt him. Yet still Valien dreamed--even as he flew here above the island. Still her eyes haunted him, and still he saw her in the lighthouse, smiling at him, waiting for him always.

When I fly to free Rune, will I find you in that dungeon too? Have you been waiting for twenty years, Marilion?

He growled. *No. Frey lied.* Valien blasted fire. *All he does is lie.*

Kaelyn flew around him in a circle, nudged him with her tail, and smiled. "Come, Valien, let us land and sleep. Night falls. Tomorrow our battle begins."

Below upon the island, men and women sheathed swords, slung arquebuses over their shoulders, and retreated into huts and tents. Even flying high above, Valien could sense their fear; their every movement spoke of it. These people had seen war and death, and tomorrow they would fly back into the fire. Valien growled, forcing his own fear down his throat. *The battle-hardened always fear war more than the green soldier.*

The two dragons spiraled down and landed upon the shore. When they shifted back into humans, Valien looked at Kaelyn, and his heart twisted. The sun dipped into the sea behind her, painting her orange and gold. The wind blew her hair and dress, and she seemed so sad to him, a sea nymph lost upon the shore.

"Kaelyn," he began, voice low, but could say no more.

I couldn't bear to lose you too, he wanted to say.

Stay on this island in safety, he wanted to say.

I love you more than Requiem and all that's in it, he wanted to say.

Yet he could say none of those things. And so he only stood in the sand, looking at her, at the sunset in her hair, at her soft eyes, at her tanned and feline face. And Valien realized that for the first time in three years, when he looked upon Kaelyn, he did not see the woman she looked like. He no longer saw Marilion.

"I see you, Kaelyn," he whispered.

Here upon the beach, on this last night before the fire, she was not a ghost, but a living flame.

She embraced him and whispered into his ear, "I'm afraid."

He cupped her pale cheek in his hand. "I know."

She clutched his hands and squeezed them. "I'm afraid for Rune. And for our people. But mostly I fear this night, this darkness, this silence before the storm." She smiled shakily. "The last night before battle always seems so long, doesn't it?"

He nodded. "I never know if I want these nights to end quickly or last forever."

"To last forever," she said and touched his cheek. "I wish tomorrow would never come. Valien, will you share my hut tonight? Hold me on this long, dark night, for tomorrow the fire will burn."

They walked to her island home, a shelter woven of branches and leaves. Valien had spent his nights sleeping alone upon the island's peak, perched upon the hilltop in dragon form, always half awake and ready to fly should the Legions find their haven. Yet tonight he entered her hut, a little nook with a bed of grass, womb-like and warm.

He stood at the entrance. Kaelyn sat down upon the grass, pulled her knees to her chest, and looked up at him. Suddenly she laughed shyly and lowered her eyes.

"I'm sorry!" she said. "It's not very roomy, but... it's warmer and cozier than the hilltop you sleep on."

She looked down at her knees and her cheeks flushed.

Feeling awkward and cumbersome, far too clunky and rough, Valien cleared his throat. He sat beside her, leaned back, and allowed himself a smile.

"Very warm and cozy," he said. He lay down and placed his hands behind his head.

She lay on her side, facing him, her hair brushing his shoulder, her body an inch away from his. She looked at him silently, and Valien was struck by how young she seemed. She was only twenty. He was more than twice her age--and probably twice her weight. Lying beside her, he felt too old, too grizzled and ragged, a disheveled bear sharing a den with a graceful young lioness.

"Valien," she whispered as darkness fell, "can we win this?"

"We will win."

"Do you think... do you think Rune is still alive?" Her voice trembled.

Valien closed his eyes. He hadn't stopped thinking of Rune since arriving on this island. Yet tonight, Kaelyn's soft breath against him, he did not want to remember Rune or Marilion or Requiem. He wanted this one, last night in shadowy warmth. He wanted no more ghosts, only this woman beside him.

"I don't know," he said. "All I know is that we must fly. We must keep fighting. We must fly to victory or death. We are Requiem. Our wings forever seek our sky."

She nodded. "For so long I hid in darkness. For so many years, my father beat me, burned me, broke my body, and I hid under my bed, and in the dungeons of our tower, and in the shadows of my own mind." She held his hand tight. "You taught me to fly, Valien. And I will keep flying with you. Always."

He wiped a tear from her cheek. She gazed at him with damp, huge eyes, and her lips shook. She placed a hand on his cheek, leaned forward, and kissed his forehead. He smoothed her hair, and she kissed his lips.

She had never kissed him before. Her lips were small but full, pink and very soft, and they shot warmth through him, warmth better than all the rye he would drink in his years of darkness. She was too young for him, her hair too soft in his calloused fingers, her eyes too fair for the pain he carried. Yet he held her close, her body lithe and warm under his hands, and he kissed her, and she smiled. He had never known eyes so large and bright, even here in the shadows.

She climbed atop him. She began to unlace his shirt, her fingers shy and hesitant at first, then gaining speed, and soon she tugged at the cloth with the hunger of a starving man for food. His hands moved over her body--large, rough hands that could encircle her waist. He pulled the tunic off her, and she sat atop him, naked in the last glimmers of sunset. Her body was slim, her breasts small and pale, and he kissed her neck, and she buried her hands in his hair.

He wanted to stop this. She was too pure, too young and virginal, too full of life for an old, scarred wreck. But he could not stop. He needed this; he needed her now more than he'd ever needed his rye or vengeance or starlight. They moved faster, naked in the darkness, and the last light faded. He rolled atop her, and she gasped and moaned and clutched his shoulders. He held her hands, and she shuddered and arched beneath him, legs wrapped around his back. He moved above her. In the darkness he felt like a dragon flying through a storm, fleeing a burning city, roaring in pain as the terrors of the world chased him.

I couldn't save you, Marilion.

He clutched the babe in his claws and flew, rising and falling on the wind, seeking shelter in the night. Still he flew through that storm. Still that darkness wrapped around him.

Fire blazed through him, and Kaelyn gasped below him, and her fingernails almost tore his skin. She bit his shoulder to stifle her cry, and they lay still.

He rolled onto his back, and she nestled against him, her head on his chest, her body soft and small in his arms. She mumbled and smiled and slept, her breath playing against his neck like waves over the sand. He held her close and the pain dug through him.

Valien had bedded women during his long years of exile. He had found comfort with outcasts, wanderers, and urchins, women who came and left his life during the long years on the road. During his darkest hours, when the rye would not dull his pain, he had found comfort in brothels, and those memories still throbbed inside him like old scars. But he had not loved a woman until Kaelyn. He had not slept with one in his arms since Marilion.

He kissed her head, and his throat constricted, and he was afraid.

Love weakens us, he thought. *I cannot lose you, Kaelyn. Tomorrow we fly to war. Tomorrow I will be afraid for Requiem... bust mostly for you. Mostly for you.*

Only a beam of moonlight lit their bed. Kaelyn mumbled something in her sleep, nestled closer, and smiled softly. Valien lay awake for a long time, holding her close.

The dawn rose gray and rainy. As fighters took formation on the beaches, they frowned skyward, cursed, and muttered of signs. For many days they had lived here in sunlight and warmth; on the eve of battle, the sky gods raged. Wind whipped the palms, the waves crashed like watery demons, and the sand blew.

The land itself rages today, Valien thought. He stood on the beach, staring north into the roiling waters. *Today the wrath of man and sky will descend upon you, Cadigus.*

His fighters stood around him, standing still in their formations, staring north with hard eyes. The wind whipped their hair, and the rain stung their faces, yet they did not flinch. Five thousand fighters marshaled here. Vir Requis and Tirans stood together; today they were one army.

Valien looked at them one by one. He wanted to see warriors. He wanted to see howling, bloodthirsty fighters chanting for victory. He wanted to see a hammer ready to crush the Legions.

Instead he saw friends.

He saw families.

He saw Kaelyn, the woman he loved, her hair a banner of gold under the clouds.

We are not warriors, he thought. *We are husbands, wives, brothers, sisters. We are outcasts and we are dreamers. We are a single light shining through the storm.*

He shifted. He stood upon the sand as a dragon, roared so the island could hear, and blasted fire upward, a pillar to lead his people.

"Arise!" he howled, his voice still strangled but loud enough to peal across the beach. "Arise, dragons of Requiem! Arise, warriors of Tiranor! Today our hiding ends. Today we fly--to war, to glory, to victory!"

Around him, his fellow dragons shifted too. Three thousand scaly beasts roared, blew fire, and lit the storm.

Glory? he wondered. *Victory?* What did those have to do with war? War was not glorious. War never ended with victory. They flew to men screaming in the mud, limbs torn off, bones shattered. They flew to more grieving widows. To more pain. To more death and nightmares that would forever haunt them.

Yet Valien was a leader. He was heir to great rulers who had led Requiem in battle. Roaring upon the beach, he thought of those who had come before him: the legendary King Benedictus who had fought the griffins, the noble King Elethor who had defeated the phoenixes, and the wise Queen Lyana who had slain demons and raised Requiem from ruin.

I am no noble, brave leader like they were, Valien thought, the rain peppering his scales. *I am too hurt, too haunted, too afraid.*

Yet the people needed that leader now. They needed a king, a hero, a leader of legend. And so he roared for glory, for victory, for freedom. And so he gave them the courage he himself lacked.

The Tirans, men and women without the ancient magic, mounted the dragons. Each fighter wielded an arquebus, a saber, and a spear. Miya climbed onto Kaelyn's back, grabbed the horn of her makeshift saddle, and raised her chin. Her father, the gruff Sila, climbed onto Valien's saddle.

"So," said the merchant captain, "I've gone from leading a fleet of ships to a flight of dragons."

Valien grumbled beneath him. "You could steer your ships, captain. This dragon flies where he will." He gritted his teeth. "Hold on tight. You might have sailed through storms, but you've never flown through one."

With that, he kicked off the sand, beat his wings, and soared.

Around him, the dragons of Requiem rose, roaring fire through the rain. The wind whipped them, but their wings beat powerfully, driving them forward. They soared through the storm. The waves crashed below. Fire, wind, and water churned like a primordial world before creation.

They left the island behind. They left the children, the elders, and the infirm. They flew through the storm, five thousand souls, a drop against the ocean of the Legions. The sea rolled beneath them. A haze of darkness lay ahead.

Valien looked at Kaelyn, who flew at his side. Their eyes met through the rain. Her scales glimmered with raindrops, and her eyes were sad yet hopeful and knowing. He thought of last night, and the memory warmed him.

I fight for the memory of Requiem. I fight for a legacy of light. But I also fight for you.

The storm clouds broke ahead, and a single ray of light fell into the sea, a glowing column of gold. Valien flew toward it. It would guide him home.

TILLA

Rune hung on the chains before her, welts covering his body, his eyes swollen and his lips bleeding. He moaned, head lowered. If not for the chains that held up his arms, running from his wrists to the ceiling, he'd have collapsed.

"Tilla," he whispered through cracked lips. "Please."

She had not wanted it to come to this. Why wouldn't he just speak the words? Why wouldn't he join her, worship the red spiral with her?

"Oh, Rune," she whispered, punisher in hand. "Why do you do this? You can make it end. Just say the words..."

He looked up at her, blinking, his face pale and splashed with blood. And yet he managed to fix her with a stare, a deep gaze like the one he would give her at home. In his eyes she saw Cadport again--their youth in the sand and sun and their home burning. His lips were silent; his eyes did the speaking. And he was speaking to her of home... and of the woman she used to be.

"Hurt him some more!"

Shari stood at her side, wearing her butcher's apron, her voice thick with bloodlust, her eyes alight. She seemed like a woman in rapture. Her teeth were bared in a wolf's snarl. Her chest rose and fell as she panted. Rune's blood stained her clothes.

"Drive your punisher against him!" the princess commanded, hissing through her teeth. "Make him scream. Make him worship the Regime."

And Tilla obeyed.

And he screamed.

But he did not obey.

"Just speak the words, Rune," Tilla whispered. She touched his cheek. "Just hail the red spiral. And you will join me. And this will end."

He raised his head, spat out blood, and stared at her.

Silent.

Tilla turned toward her commander. "He will not join us. I've hurt him more than anyone's hurt another. This is hopeless."

She prayed that Shari would listen. She prayed that Shari would abandon this quest of pain.

Just... just let Rune be our prisoner! she wanted to cry out. *Let him stay in this cell, but make his pain end.*

Yet Shari only smiled and licked her lips. "His pain is only beginning," she said. "The punisher is but a caress compared to what I still plan. It's time, Tilla. It's time to make him truly suffer. Draw your dagger."

Tilla's eyes burned, but she tightened her lips, refusing to show emotion. Her insides trembled.

She didn't want to do this. She didn't want to hurt him. She wanted this to end--to flee this tower, this blood, this pain. Yet if she ran, Shari would never stop hurting Rune. If she ran, they would hunt her down, and she would hang here too.

"Rune," she whispered. She held his cheeks, moved her face close, and pleaded with him. "Please, Rune. Do as I say."

Hands grabbed her shoulders. Shari tugged her back.

"Lanse!" she said. "Do you disobey me? Draw your dagger. Do it now!"

The princess growled, face red and wild, the face of a demon. If Shari lunged at her, sank her teeth into her flesh, and feasted like a wolf, Tilla would not be surprised.

"I'm sorry, Rune," she whispered. "I must do this."

She coiled her trembling fingers around her dagger's hilt. Her breath shook as she drew the blade. The dagger felt so heavy in her palm. It caught the torchlight and gleamed red as if already bloodied.

"Now..." Shari tapped her fingers against her hip. "This boy tore off my wing. He crippled me. He made me only half a dragon. I think... it's time to repay him in kind. What do you think, Lanse?"

Tilla swallowed.

Please don't make me do this, she prayed. *Please, stars, please, old gods or new.* Her heart raced. Sweat drenched her. Her chest tightened and she thought she would collapse.

"I... Commander, what do you plan?"

Shari laughed, approached Rune, and stroked the manacles binding his left arm.

"We don't need him chained by two arms. I do believe he can hang from one just as well." She licked her lips. "A hand for a wing; seems fitting, does it not?"

Tilla felt the blood leave her face. "I can't," she whispered.

"You will!" Shari said. "Do the deed. Now. Cut him. He took my wing; you will take his hand."

Rune began to pant. He looked up, bleeding and beaten, and his chest shook, and finally fear seemed to fill him.

"Tilla," he said and pulled his chains. "Tilla, please. Don't. You can end this. You can--"

"Cut him!" Shari screamed. Her voice echoed in the chamber. "Cut him, and we will force him to eat his own hand, and he will scream, and he will worship us. Hurt him!"

Tilla stood trembling. She wept. Her dagger wavered.

"Please, I cannot... I can't do this..."

"You must cut him! You were his love. You were his friend. You must do this deed." Shari laughed maniacally. "Watch, boy. Watch! The woman you loved, the woman you wanted to bed--she will cripple you. Lanse Tilla, cut him! Cut him or you will join him in chains."

Tilla shook. No. No! She couldn't do this. What could she do? She took a step closer to Rune. He tugged mightily on the chains, struggling, shouting at her.

"Please, Rune," she whispered, tears on her lips. "Please..."

She raised the dagger. He trembled. She positioned the blade, ready to cut through the joints of his bones.

"Do it!" Shari screamed.

"Rune, please," Tilla whispered.

He stared at her.

The room seemed to freeze.

All sound died, and even the torches seemed to fall silent.

He lowered his head, and his chest shook, and he nodded.

"I hail the red spiral," he whispered.

Tilla let out a sob, trembled, and gasped for breath. She pulled her dagger back. It was over. Thank the stars, it was over. She could be together with Rune now--like they used to be. They could leave this place. They could worship Frey together. It was over.

"Speak it louder, Rune," she said, smiled tremulously, and touched his cheek. "Worship the red spiral with all the strength in you."

He shook, his teeth ground together, and he let out a howl, a howl louder than any of his screams of pain.

"I hail the red spiral!"

He swung on his chains, heaving and shaking.

He raised his eyes and looked at her... and she expected to see relief in them. She expected to see resignation or pain but also relief... relief that the game was over. That he had lost and the agony would end.

But instead... instead she saw horror.

It was not only horror for himself. She could see that. His eyes were haunted for her.

She saw her reflection in them--a young woman, her face so pale, her heart withered. She looked upon herself as she was. She looked upon herself in his memory. She saw both her lives, past and present. A ropemaker's daughter and a torturer.

And she understood.

He's given up on me, she thought. *That is the horror in his eyes. He thought that by taking my pain, he could save me. And now he realized I'm lost to him forever.*

She knew then that even now, even if Shari freed him, even if he lived with her in her home, she was lost to him. They would never be together as they were.

The Tilla he loved died. I killed her.

Shari nodded.

"Good...," the princess said, savoring the word. "Good, very good. He's finally broken. Sooner than I'd have liked, but I'm pleased."

Tilla lowered her head, trembling, not knowing if she was relieved or terrified. "I'll take him to my chamber," she said softly. "I'll find him armor. Tomorrow he can join the Legions and serve the emperor."

Shari raised her eyebrow. "Oh... my dear lanse. I believe you've misunderstood. He's not yet paid his price. Raise your dagger! I will still have you sever his hand."

Tilla gasped. She could barely see, and she heard Rune gasp too. She raised her head, eyes wide, and stared at Shari.

"But... Commander! He's broken. He hailed the spiral. He--"

"He is not broken," Shari said, smiling thinly. "He's still in one piece, isn't he? My dear child, you are young and innocent. Relesar is lying. He hailed the red spiral only to save his hand. His words reek of dishonestly." Shari snickered. "But I see through his lies. You will break him. Fully. You will sever his hand. And then you will shatter his bones. And then you will cut off his manhood and burn it. You will have him crawl in the dust, no longer a man, no longer human, but a creature, a sniveling maggot that you created with your blade and hammer. But you'll leave his tongue so that he can still scream and worship the spiral. It will be all he can do. And then... then he will be fully broken. Then I will be avenged. Then, Lanse Tilla Siren, you'll have proven yourself worthy." Her voice rose to a shout. "Now obey me and bring me his hand!"

Tilla stared at her princess, barely able to breathe.

She's mad, she realized. *She's gone mad entirely.* Tilla's eyes burned. *How... how can I do this? How can I worship her? Even Frey did not want this! Even Frey sees reason, not just mad vengeance.*

"Your father--" she began.

"My father isn't here! I am your commander. It is I you must obey. Obey me! His hand!"

"Tilla!" Rune cried, voice choked. "Tilla, please, don't listen to her--"

"Cut him!"

Tilla shook. What could she do? Stars, what could she do? For so long, she had blamed Rune for this. For so long, she had thought that if Rune only worshiped the spiral, this would end. But it wasn't ending. The pain would only grow, and her soul would only darken, and Rune would only wither into a beast.

"This is not the way, Commander," she whispered. "The red spiral is about the glory of Requiem. If Rune can join us, he--"

"He will join us as a freak, as a creature for a cage! Cut him! Maim him!" Shari screamed, saliva spraying from her mouth. Sweat soaked her hair. She seemed not a human, not a dragon, but a demon. "Cut him now, or I will cut him, and I will cut you, and I will sew your twisted bodies together, forming you into conjoined, diseased twins for my court. Cut him! Cut him or you will suffer!"

Tilla turned back toward Rune.

She shook so madly she could barely grip her dagger.

She took a step toward him.

Rune stared at her, eyes wide and damp, and shook his head. His lips trembled.

"Tilla, no," he whispered, voice cracking. "Please. Tilla..."

She took a shuddering breath.

She placed her dagger against his wrist, and he closed his eyes and whispered prayers.

She saw it again--the sea at home. She wove ropes with her father. She sat in the Old Wheel, drinking ale with Rune, petting his dog, feeling warm and safe. She walked along the beach, barefoot, and he gave her a seashell necklace, and she kissed him. And he bled. And her home burned. And so much blood covered her hands.

I'm scared too, he had said to her that day two years ago, standing with her on the beach in the night, the night before the Legions had drafted her. *But it will be fine. I promise you, Tilla. Everything will be fine.*

"You promised," she whispered, tears on her lips, and she kissed him again, a last kiss like their first one, a kiss that tasted of her tears and his blood.

She nodded.

"I have to do this," she whispered... and spun around.

She thrust her dagger with a scream.

The blade crashed into Shari's chest, driving between her ribs and into her heart.

Shari's eyes widened. She stared, mouth wide, and for a moment the chamber froze. Nobody breathed.

"When we first met," Tilla whispered, "you told me that you'd keep an eye on me. You should have kept closer watch."

Snarling, Tilla twisted her blade.

Blood spread across Shari's tunic. She stared, silent, and her lips peeled back, and her eyes blazed, and her hands rose... and she crashed to her knees.

Tilla yanked her blade back. Shari Cadigus, heir to Requiem, crashed facedown onto the floor. Her blood pooled.

Tilla spun back toward Rune. He hung from his chains, frail and beaten, struggling for every breath. Tilla's fingers shook so madly she could barely grab her keys.

"We have to flee," she whispered. She touched his cheek and tears stung her eyes. "It's over now, Rune, but we must flee. Fast. We must run."

Her heart pounded. Stars, if they were caught...

She unlocked his manacles, freeing his arms from the chains. For so long, only the chains had held him standing, not his own feet. Now he wavered and nearly fell. She grabbed him. She held him up. He leaned against her, legs rubbery; she supported all his weight.

"I'll have to tie your wrists," she said. "There are guards downstairs. They'll think I'm moving you to another cell."

He nodded weakly. She took a rope from a table. She tied his wrists, making sure the knot was weak.

"Now let's go," she whispered. "Step by step. I'm with you."

She slung his arms across her shoulders. She began to walk. One step. Another. Holding him up. He moaned and his feet all but dragged across the floor. He was too hurt, too famished, near death perhaps.

"We have to keep moving," she said.

He limped along, his weight against her, and she heard the smile in his voice.

"I knew you were still there, Tilla. I knew it."

They reached the chamber door. Tilla yanked it open, revealing the staircase that spiraled down the tower. She took the first step, holding Rune tight. He wavered and Tilla nearly fell. She grabbed the wall for support.

"I know you're hurt, but we'll have to do this quickly," Tilla said.

With every step, her heart raced faster, and sweat trickled down her spine. She tried to calm herself. Shari had died silently; no guards would know Tilla had slain her. She just had to keep descending, step by step. She just had to pass the guards outside; they had seen her move Rune through the Citadel before, and they would let her pass.

And then... what then?

She kept climbing down, Rune's arms around her.

And then they would have to leave the city. To flee into the wilderness. They would be hunted. Frey would never rest from hunting them--the heir of Aeternum and the woman who slew his daughter.

"We'll find some faraway place," she said, and her voice shook. "Like you wanted, Rune. We'll fly as far as we can. We'll keep flying--to the very end of the world. We will not let them catch us."

She knew what the wilderness held. Soldiers. Forts. Perhaps starvation and thirst. It was likely they would fly to their deaths. Yet they would die together, holding each other, Tilla Roper and Rune Brewer. It would not be a bad way to die. It would be infinitely better than the death Frey would give them.

After what seemed like hours, they reached the bottom of the tower.

Tilla froze and steeled herself. She forced a deep breath. Behind those doors, two guards awaited, armored and armed with halberds.

They will know, she thought. *They will see Shari's blood on my hands. They will know and raise the alarm, and a thousand more soldiers will swoop upon me.*

"Be strong, Rune," she whispered. "You'll have to walk now on your own. I'll pretend to manhandle you. Act like my prisoner; there are guards outside."

He nodded.

With another deep breath, she opened the door.

They stepped out into the courtyard.

The two guards stood there, covered in black steel. They slammed their gauntlets against their chests.

"Hail the red spiral!"

Tilla shoved Rune forward. He stumbled and all but fell, but she grabbed his arms and manhandled him forward. She glared at the guards as she passed by.

"Stand straight, men!" she barked. "You're slouching again. Commander Shari will descend soon, and if she sees you hunched over, she will flay your hides."

They straightened like blades, chins raised.

"Yes, Commander!" they said.

Tilla inspected them, eyes narrowed. Despite the horror pounding through her, she still outranked these men. She nodded and kept walking, shoving Rune before her. He limped and stumbled, his blood dripping.

"Move, worm!" she shouted at him.

The courtyard seemed miles long. Walls and towers rose around her; screams rose with them. She kept walking, shoving Rune forward. Step by step. Past more cells. Past more towers. Past more guards who marched, armor clanking, whips in hands.

"Move!" she screamed at Rune as five guards marched by. "Move, maggot, or I swear, I will break every segment in your spine. Move, scum!"

She kept shoving him, and the guards marched by.

Oh stars, they will find Shari soon. They will shout. They will descend upon us.

She walked. Step by step. Drop by drop of blood.

It seemed hours before she reached the Citadel's gates. More guards stood here, their black helms spiked, their hands clutching swords.

"I'm taking this one to Tarath Imperium," she told them and forced herself to snicker. "The emperor wants to see his blood. I will return him tonight."

She sucked in her breath. The guards stared at her silently. Tilla nearly fainted and her heart pounded. Surely they sensed the ruse. Surely they would capture her, capture Rune again, torture them both, and--

"Yes, Lanse," the chief guard finally said. He drew a scroll from his belt--it held the names of all prisoners who came and went--and made a marking. "Hail the red spiral!"

She shakily returned the salute.

The guards opened the gates... and Tilla and Rune stepped out into the city streets.

Snow fell around them. The houses rose alongside. The city seemed strangely beautiful to her--the snowy roofs, the trees glimmering with icicles, the small sun behind the clouds... On any other day, she would marvel at this beauty.

She turned toward Rune. He stood looking at the snow too. He stood on his own now, frail and burnt, but he inhaled deeply. He smiled and tugged his bindings, freeing his bloodied wrists.

"I'll carry you in my claws now," Tilla said. "But once we're outside the city, we'll fly together. Side by side. Like we used to."

She shifted into a dragon. She beat her wings, scattering snow off the cobblestones, and rose several feet into the air. She reached down and scooped Rune up into her claws.

She flew.

The city spread beneath them, countless houses and streets, statues and forts, ponds and parks, a million souls who knew none of her pain. Tarath Imperium, palace of the emperor, rose in its center, a thousand feet tall, the heart of the empire. Once Tilla had dreamed of serving in that palace. Once she had stood below it, shouting for the spiral, worshiping the tower's might.

Today she flew away.

She flew south.

She flew across Nova Vita, over the city walls, and above a frosted forest.

She flew into the wilderness, Rune in her grip, and her heart shook and she could barely breathe.

VALIEN

Sunset gilded the land when he beheld the shores of Requiem.

He had been flying all day. His ruined throat wheezed, his lungs burned, and his wings shot agony through him with every stroke. The scars on his body blazed as if freshly cut. He was too old, too wounded, too haunted for these long flights and so many battles, and yet he flew on.

His army flew around him, a thousand dragons. Each beast bore several riders, a mix of Tiran arquebusers and Vir Requis in human forms. They had been flying for three days over the sea. Every few hours, they swapped--one Vir Requis rider would leap from the saddle, shift into a dragon, and take the load, allowing the exhausted flier to resume human form and ride. They slept in the saddle. They kept flying northwest. Three days and three nights of water.

And finally the shores of Requiem emerged.

The coast stretched ahead, a mere hint upon the horizon. All around Valien, dragons chanted for home. They sang the old songs of the forest. They cried for starlight and birch leaves and marble columns. They sang for Requiem, but Valien only lowered his head.

No. This was not Requiem ahead. This was not Aeternum's kingdom. They flew now toward the shore of another realm, a fallen land once named Osanna, an ancient kingdom Frey had burned. Valien had spent years hiding in these ruins with the Resistance. He had seen thousands of Osanna's burnt skeletons littering the ash. Frey had annexed his conquest years ago, and today his banners flew here too, but no--this was not home, no more than the ruins of Tiranor were.

"We will free Osanna too," Valien said as he flew over the water. "We will liberate this fallen land for the memory of her people." He raised his voice to a howl. "Children of Requiem! Every Vir Requis--take dragon form. Every Tiran--load your guns. Scope bearers--ready your beams."

As the coast drew nearer, his army formed ranks.

All Vir Requis in human form leaped from saddles, shifted into dragons, and howled. Jets of fire lit the twilight. Soon three thousand dragons roared, flying in four units. Upon their backs rode Tiran arquebusers. They streamed over the water, chanting for victory. Valien roared with them, hoarse but pealing his cry across the sea.

"Death to Cadigus! Dragons--fan out!"

Their four formations spread side to side. Ahead of each flew a scope bearer--a Tiran rider clutching a cylinder full of Genesis Shards.

Valien led one group, and upon his back rode Sila; the gruff captain held one of the scopes. Kaelyn and Erry each led another group, scope bearers upon their backs. Leresy held the fourth scope in his own claws; the prince had refused to let anyone ride him.

Only four scopes, Valien thought with a grumble. Even with a hundred, fear would have filled him today. They had tried dividing the shards into smaller batches, but found the magic too weak, and so with four scopes they flew, and fear filled his belly.

He looked across his army. Three thousand dragons. Two thousand riders. Four scopes. It wasn't enough. Even with the Genesis Shards and the arquebuses, superior weapons, it wasn't enough. Not against half a million legionaries, howling for blood and firing cannons.

We must fly to Nova Vita without rest, he thought and snarled. *We must engage no enemies along the way. We must storm the palace and slay Frey, fast and deadly as an arrow shot from shadow.*

He roared. The coast loomed only ten miles away. There would be a small patrol; the Legions patrolled every mile of this beach.

"Slay every legionary you see!" Valien called out. "Let none flee to bear news."

They streamed toward the shore. The sun sank below the horizon. The sea vanished into shadows.

From ahead upon the shore, thousands of flaming pillars blazed skyward.

Roars pounded across the sky.

"Hail the red spiral! Hail Frey Cadigus!"

Valien felt as if a hammer slammed against him.

By the Abyss...

The horizon blazed. Fire streamed like a storm of comets, like an erupting volcano, like the Abyss risen into the world. Shadows broke apart from the distant shore, rising like demonic crows from a rotten tree. Ten thousand dragons ascended from fire, shadow, and smoke, shrieked to the sky, and streamed across the sea.

He knew, Valien thought, for a moment unable to breathe, barely able to flap his wings. *Frey knew we were coming.*

Around him, his fellow dragons cursed and roared. They glanced around. They blasted flame in a confused array.

"Damn it, Valien, you said these coasts weren't guarded!" Leresy shouted somewhere in the distance.

Valien growled and snapped his teeth. He beat his wings mightily, rising higher in the night. The sea streamed below him. The beasts raced ahead.

"Dragons of Requiem!" he howled. "Show the enemy no mercy. Fly! Meet them head-on. For Requiem!"

Upon their backs, the Tirans blew their war horns. The cries trumpeted across the sea. The dragons of the Resistance answered the call, roaring their own battle cries, wordless howls of rage. Ahead, the Legions streamed across the miles--five miles away, then four, then three--bellowing and hailing the spiral.

"Scope bearers!" Valien shouted. "Ready your weapons!"

The armies streamed closer. Three thousand dragons of the Resistance. Ten thousand legionaries, a cloud of flame and shadow.

"Hold!" Valien howled.

They flew, howling. Three miles. Two.

"Ready your scopes! *Hold!*"

The Legions howled and laughed ahead. Their flames crackled, lighting the sea below. The dragons of the Resistance growled and snarled. Not a gun or flaming jet fired.

"Hold!"

Two miles.

One.

"Slay them all!" roared the Legions.

"Break their spines!"

"Feast upon their flesh!"

"Hail the red spiral!"

Valien gritted his teeth, sucked in his breath, and reared in the air.

"Scope bearers--fire!"

At his side, Kaelyn's rider unscrewed a scope first. The red light blazed out in the night, a beam piercing the shadows, an explosion as bright and furious as dragonfire. A heartbeat later, beams blasted out from Erry and Leresy, humming and slamming forward. Upon Valien's own back, Sila howled and his beam shone, nearly blinding Valien, stretching over his head to crash into the imperial dragons ahead.

The Genesis Beams hit the Legions with the fury of ten thousand cannonballs.

Where the red light struck, dragons vanished. Men and women tumbled, screaming, to crash into the sea below.

Valien howled. "Resistance--dragonfire!"

He blasted his flames. They rained onto the falling legionaries, burning them as they fell. The troops tumbled, blazing comets, to slam into the water. Around Valien, thousands of dragons roared their fire.

The legionaries screamed. They fell. They died. The beams ripped through them like great, glowing blades. Hundreds tumbled into the water.

"Slay them all!" Valien roared. "Show them no mercy. Leave none alive!"

The two armies crashed together.

Valien barreled through a swarm. Legionaries flew everywhere, a dark horde, their armor bladed, their fire raging.

"Sila, cut them down!" Valien said.

Upon his back, the captain spun his beam, clearing a path. All around, the legionaries fell. Any who flew near met the beam, lost his magic, and crashed down in human form.

"Break their lines!" Leresy shouted somewhere in the distance, laughing.

The battle descended into chaos. Legionaries flew at all sides, mingling with resistors. Beams shot every which way. Fire blazed. Arquebuses fired. The air exploded into a storm of gunpowder, flame, and light.

"Scope bearers, fan out!" Valien roared. "Leresy! Erry! Fly to the east. Kaelyn, take the south. Surround our forces!"

He cursed, trying to find them. Their formations were falling apart. A phalanx of legionaries flew toward him, roaring fire. The flames blasted Valien's belly and he yowled.

"Sila!"

The captain's beam fell upon the enemy. They fell. Valien bathed their tumbling human bodies with fire.

"Scope bearers, surround our forces! Hold the enemy back."

He whipped his head from side to side, seeking them. He howled curses. They had drilled for this. On order, the four scope bearers were to surround their army, forming four pillars of defense, cutting down the enemy while allowing their comrades to blow fire from within the shield. Yet now they flew in disarray.

"Leresy, damn it, take the east!" Valien roared.

The red dragon was crashing into the enemy above, laughing madly, clutching a scope in his claws. He spun it around every which way. Behind him, legionaries--still in dragon form--were crashing into resistors, tearing them down.

"Leresy, damn you!" Valien roared.

The red dragon blazed his beam upward. When humans tumbled down, he caught them in his jaws, bit their bodies apart, and spat out the pieces.

"Valien!" the young prince shouted, laughing, blood on his teeth. "We will slay him. We will slay my father!"

Valien blasted fire. "Leresy, behind you--"

Ten imperial dragons swooped from above. Their claws reached out. They crashed into the prince.

Leresy yowled, a high-pitched sound, and reared. His beam shot out wildly, whipping from side to side. A legionary bit into the prince's back. Leresy's claws opened, and the scope tumbled from his grasp.

"Damn it, Leresy!" Valien said. He shot forward and reached out, trying to grab the scope.

The cylinder spun wildly as it fell, shining light every which way. The beam blazed against Valien.

Like a sword pulled from his back, his magic vanished.

Valien tumbled through the sky, a human. Above him, Sila tumbled too, torn free from the saddle, his beam still shining.

The water raced up toward them.

Valien roared, swearing to slay the boy.

An instant before he could slam into the sea, he emerged from the beam's light. He sucked in his magic. He shifted back into dragon form.

His claws grazed the water. He beat his wings and soared. He grabbed Sila before the captain could crash into the sea.

"Back into the saddle!" he said.

He rose higher, looking around him. The battle had become a brawl. Rather than protect their comrades, the scope bearers flew aimlessly. For every legionary they cut down, ten swooped from behind. Arquebuses fired, cracking and shattering the air. Dragonfire blazed.

"This is no battle," Valien growled. "It's a bar fight."

He soared higher. Sila blazed his beam upward. They tore through the hosts, legionaries falling around them.

"Kaelyn!" he said, spotting the green dragon ahead. "Take the east. Go! Erry--go west. Shine that beam. Leresy, damn you, find your scope!"

The red dragon still flew, blood seeping down his shoulders, his scope gone from his claws. Kaelyn and Erry roared and darted out, blazing their beams, holding the enemy back. Thousands of legionaries still flew, mingling together with the resistors.

Valien cursed. "Sila, what can you do?"

Upon his back, the captain shouted, "Damn armies are too mingled! I can barely shine the light upon a legionary without hitting a resistor too. This is a damn mess."

"Do what you can. We have to separate the forces."

The battle continued for hours. Dragonfire, Genesis Beams, and gunfire lit the night. Men and women fell all around, some still alive and blazing, others charred corpses. Legionaries flew everywhere. The beams mowed down some; others crashed into the Resistance, blowing fire and lashing claws. Smoke and blood rained into the sea below.

Dawn rose before the Resistance made its way onto the empire's shore.

The sunlight rose upon a world coated in blood and ash.

Valien filled his wings with air, grunted with the pain of a dozen cuts, and landed upon the beach. His fellow resistors landed around him, wheezing and puffing smoke. Their scales were cracked and charred. Cuts and burns covered them. Their blood dripped. Upon their backs, many Tirans clutched wounds and welts. Some dragons bore only corpses upon their saddles.

All around them, the bodies of legionaries swept onto the shore. Every wave brought a new pile of their bloated, lacerated corpses. Death covered the beaches, thicker than the seashells, a blanket of flesh.

Sila dismounted and Valien took human form.

"Teramil, bring me reports!" Valien barked at one of his lieutenants, a tall and dour man with cold eyes. "Count the living. Aranor!" He turned toward another commander, a former priest turned resistor. "Organize the survivors into new phalanxes. Make sure every man is armed. We fly within an hour. They know we're here."

He moved along the beach, giving orders. With every wave, new corpses floated toward him. Blood painted the sand. Most of the dead were legionaries, clad in black armor; many were resistors, wearing only leather and wool, their flesh burnt black, their mouths open in silent anguish.

Some soldiers washed ashore still writhing and screaming. Some had lost limbs; they clutched at their bleeding stumps. Others screamed with burns, their skin peeling, their flesh twisting. Some bore gaping wounds, exposing or losing organs, crying for home. They had brought only a hundred healers--not enough, Valien knew. Not enough. With every step he took, another wounded man or woman fell silent, joining the dead.

So many more dead, Valien thought, walking among them, gritting his teeth. *We should have stayed on the islands. Stars damn it, this shouldn't have happened. Frey knew. He waited for us.* Valien's throat tightened. *And now more blood stains my hands.*

Yet as he walked among the dead and dying, his thoughts centered on only one soul.

"Kaelyn," he whispered.

He walked through the sand, seeking her. He saw her in every charred body. His fists shook. He wanted to shout out for her, but could not; the leader of the Resistance could show no emotions for one woman. He kept moving, quickening his step, his boots slogging through the blood.

I can't lose you too, Kaelyn. His breath shook behind his clenched teeth. *Where are you?*

"Valien!"

Her voice rang across the beach. He turned and saw her there, and his eyes dampened.

"Thank the stars," he whispered.

He took three great strides toward her. She ran and crashed into his arms, and he held her. Blood smeared her.

"Kaelyn, you're hurt," he said, her golden hair a tangle beneath his chin.

She shook her head. "The blood isn't mine. Not most of it. I'm scratched and a little burned, but I'm fine." She looked up at him, her eyes large and afraid. "He knew we were coming. How did he know?"

Still holding her in his arms, Valien looked over the beach. For a mile or more around him, the corpses lay. Crows and crabs were already swarming for the feast.

"He always knew we were on the island," he said, throat tight and voice a mere hiss. "I should have known islands that size, even so far away, would not go unnoticed. He patrolled from the air or from the sea, but he knew, and he waited for us."

When his lieutenants returned with the news, Valien felt his stomach sink. His head spun. He gritted his teeth and could only stand in the blood, fists clenched. He had flown here with five thousand souls; four thousand remained.

This was always a fool's quest, he thought, head lowered.

Kaelyn clutched his arm. Her hair flew in the wind, stained red. A cut ran down her cheek, but her eyes still blazed.

"We fly on," she said. "We tore through the Legions upon the beach. We will tear through them at the capital."

Valien growled and shook his head. "We've lost too many. Even with full force, we were unsure. We lost a thousand warriors before even landing on the beaches."

"And yet we did land," Kaelyn said and bared her teeth. "Valien Eleison, do not give up hope now. Keep fighting or I will smack you." She dug her fingers into his arms, her head no taller than his shoulders, her eyes shining like the red beams of ancient stones. "We fight on. You and me. As we always have. We fly to the capital and we win this."

Valien looked around. His fighters surrounded him and he gazed into their eyes, each one in turn. Sila and Miya stared back steadily; their faces were ashy and bloody, but their backs were straight. Erry stood with her chin raised, snarling, her eyes lusting for the fight. Thousands of fighters spread beyond them--cut, burnt, and weary, but their eyes all shone the same. They shone for battle. For victory.

They are brave and strong, Valien thought, *yet I am afraid. They need me to lead them, but do I only lead them to more death?*

"Move. Move it!" An arrogant, high-pitched voice rose among the crowd. Leresy came trudging forward, elbowing men and women out of his path. "Where's Valien, damn it?" When the prince emerged from the crowd and saw them, he glared. "Are you having a council without me?"

Kaelyn rolled her eyes. "Brother, do be quiet."

Her twin snorted. "Me, be quiet? My scopes won this battle for us." He raised his chin. "*I* dug up the Genesis Shards. *I* built the scopes. Thanks to me, we're in Requiem now. What are you planning next? I demand to know."

Valien growled. His rage fumed inside him like dragonfire. For many days, he had ignored this pup, letting Kaelyn and the others scold him into silence. Today, these dead around him, this blood on his boots and hands, he could not curb his fury. He marched through the sand.

When he reached Leresy, the prince smirked at him. Valien could not stop himself. He growled and backhanded the boy, putting all his rage into the blow.

Leresy yowled like a kicked dog. He cowered, raising his arms to protect his face, and scampered back. Valien would not let him flee. He grabbed the boy, twisted his collar, and glared down at him.

"You foolish child," he said, clutching the prince. "You lost a scope. You were too proud to bear a rider, and you let your scope tumble into the sea. Did you find it?"

Leresy tried to shove him off, but could not, so he only raised his chin and glared. His lips shook, and his cheek reddened where Valien had struck him.

"How the Abyss can I find it?" His voice cracked, but he swallowed and glared, struggling to reclaim some pride. "The damn thing sank. It fell by you. Why didn't you grab it?"

Valien howled and shook the prince. "Its light tore away my magic. I could have died because of your foolishness, boy. I let you carry a scope, and you proved yourself useless."

Leresy clenched his fists and glared, but his knees trembled and sweat drenched him.

"Unhand me!" he demanded. "I am Prince Leresy Cadigus. I am the son of the emperor. I order you to--"

"You are a fool," Valien said and spat.

He shoved the prince away. Leresy tumbled into the sand, hissed, and glared. Valien turned and marched away. He shouted out for his army to hear.

"Warriors of the Resistance! We will not linger here. We fly! Carry the wounded with you. We fly on."

They took flight, four thousand souls, one of their scopes lost, leaving their dead to the sea. They would need to set camp soon. They would need to rest, to eat and drink, to sleep, to nurse their wounds before the fight ahead. But not here. Not upon this beach of death.

They flew through the night, a small light in the endless darkness. As Valien flew at their lead, he could not swallow the pain that filled his throat.

RUNE

They had flown for barely a league when the city erupted behind them.

Rune had never found flying harder. He had not taken dragon form in many days, not since surrendering himself. His wings felt as creaky as the old chains. His scales clanked and slammed together, sending jolts of pain through him. When he twisted his head and looked at his body, he did not see the slim, strong black dragon he had been, but a wretched beast, haggard, his ribs pushing against cracked scales.

He looked at Tilla. She flew at his side, a white dragon clad in black armor, the red spirals still blazing upon her steel. She looked behind her and cursed.

"They found her," she said. "They found Shari and they'll scour the sky until they find us."

As Rune flew, he again glanced over his shoulder at the city. Alarm bells clanged. Pillars of fire shot skyward, thick as a forest. Dragons began to rise, tens of thousands of them, like flies rising from a disturbed carcass. Their shrieks rolled across the land. The Legions began spreading out from the city in every direction, a puddle oozing across the forest.

"Oh stars damn it!" Tilla said and panted. "They'll find us. They'll bring us back. Oh stars."

Rune shook his head. He wheezed and barely forced the words from his lips.

"They won't find us," he said. "I've hidden from the Legions for two years. Follow me."

He spotted the place ahead. Two piney hillsides dipped down, creating a fold between them. The trees were thick and white with snow, but Rune knew that a stream ran beneath them, hidden from the air. He began descending, the wind rushing against him. Fire crackled and shrieks rose behind.

"What are you doing?" Tilla said. "We have to fly far. We have to fly south. They're chasing!"

"Trust me," he said. He slapped her with his tail, gesturing her on. "Follow. I know a hiding place. Don't blow fire. Glide dark and silent as a ghost."

He glanced behind him. The Legions were swarming closer. Firelight glinted against armor. Tens of thousands of dragons were flying out, shrieking, blowing fire and lighting the night. Rune was a fast flier, but he was too weak now, too slow and hurt. They would have to hide.

He dived down, silent in the night. Tilla dived beside him. They crashed through the forest canopy, stretched out their claws, and landed on the forest floor. Rune allowed only a glint of fire to fill his maw. The orange light fell upon a frozen stream, boulders, and snow. Hillsides flanked them, thick with birches and pines, forming two walls.

"We're too close to the city," Tilla said. The white dragon glanced up nervously. Their pursuers shrieked above; they would fly overhead in moments. "They'll uproot every tree here."

Rune grunted and wheezed. "Uprooting trees takes a while. And they won't burn the forest. They want us alive or dead. Burning us gives them only ash. Follow me. We're close. It's somewhere around here."

"What is?" she said. "Rune, we must head south. We must get as far from the capital as possible. I can carry you if you can't fly. But we--"

"We cannot flee," he said. "They're too many and too fast. Tilla, trust me. I've spent two years fighting with the Resistance. I know how to hide. We walk in human forms from here; walking as dragons disturbs the trees."

He shifted back into a human. His head spun and he nearly fell. Tilla had burned him with her punisher; every inch of his skin ached. But she didn't know of his deeper wounds, those kicks and punches the guards had given him at nights while she slept. He could barely walk. Every step blazed. Yet he forced himself to move, one step after another.

Tilla walked at his side. Perhaps sensing his weariness, she held his hand.

"Are you all right?" she whispered.

He could barely see her; she was but a shadow in the night. He squeezed her hand.

"Keep walking. Let's be silent. We're almost there."

His throat burned. More than he worried about the dragons hearing him, he worried about his voice cracking. They walked atop the stream, the ice coarse with fallen pine needles. The dark trees creaked, a wolf howled, and the dragons screamed above.

"Find them!"

The cry rang out. Wings beat. Wind howled and trees bent.

"Find the heir! He's in these trees. Find him!"

Rune cursed and began to move faster, limping. Wings thudded above. Claws tore at trees. Firelight blazed overhead.

"Rune..." Tilla said. She clutched the hilt of her sword. "I won't let them take us alive. I..." She shook. "It doesn't have to hurt. One thrust into the heart. I--"

He growled and grabbed her wrist. "What are you talking about? Stars! Come, quickly. We're close."

They ran along the stream. Ice creaked and the fire blazed above. A thousand shrieks rose.

"Find the prisoner!"

A dragon swooped ahead. A lashing tail shattered a pine. Branches snapped and icicles fell. To their left, claws uprooted an oak. Dirt and snow rained.

Tilla froze, whispered a prayer, and lifted her sword.

Rune grabbed her and tugged. "Here!"

As trees snapped behind them, they scurried up a hillside. Brambles tore at their legs. Rune knew this place. Boulders should rise in a henge nearby, their surfaces carved with ancient runes. He ran among the trees, seeking them.

"Come on, where are you?" he whispered, and fear pounded through him. Had he flown to the wrong riverbed? Had he already passed the boulders?

"Uproot every tree!"

Fire cracked. Branches tore. Red light blazed against scales, and Rune cursed and ran at a stoop.

There!

In the firelight, he saw the boulders. He ran, ignoring his pain, pulling Tilla behind him. He raced around the henge and behind an oak. He knelt, fished through snow and fallen leaves, and cursed again.

"Where are you...?"

A tree ahead crashed down. Claws glinted. Rune's hand closed around the rope.

With a tug, he opened the trapdoor, revealing an earthen tunnel. He leaped in and pulled Tilla with him. He tugged the rope again, and the trapdoor closed above.

They slid down in the darkness, mud and moss smearing against them, and landed in a cold chamber. They lay silent for a long moment. Rune barely dared breathe. He couldn't see in the darkness, but he felt Tilla grab his hand.

"Did they see us?" she whispered.

He squeezed her hand. Her body pressed against him.

"No," he whispered back. "But wait. Listen."

They lay in the burrow. Above them, he heard the shrieks of the dragons, claws lashing at wood and soil, and wings beating. The Legions howled. Fire crackled. With every heartbeat, Rune squeezed Tilla's hand tighter, praying the dragons didn't find the trapdoor.

After what seemed an eternity, the shrieks grew distant. The dragons flew on.

Rune let out a shaky breath.

"We're safe for now," he said. He leaned his head back against the soil. Every part of him throbbed with pain. Every last shred of his skin burned. His bones themselves felt ready to shatter, his muscles to tear. He could do nothing but breathe.

In the dark, Tilla reached her arms around him. She held him and kissed his lips, and her tears splashed his face.

"I'm so sorry," she whispered, voice trembling. "I'm so sorry that we hurt you. I love you."

He held her for a moment, too pained to move or speak. Finally he raised his head.

"Let's crawl deeper in. There's food and supplies here."

They wriggled through the darkness. Rune felt around, arms outstretched, tracing the walls. He soon felt the wooden chest, opened it, and rummaged. It took long moments to find what he sought: a tinderbox and an oil lamp.

He rubbed flint against steel. When the lamp flickered to life, it illuminated a chamber the size of his old prison cell. Shelves lined the walls, laden with jars of preserves, dried meats, jugs of wine, and wheels of cheese. Swords and crossbows hung upon another wall. In a second chest lay blankets, bandages, cloaks, and leather boots.

"What is this place?" Tilla asked. She stood hugging herself and shivering in the cold.

"A gopher hole," Rune said. "The Resistance uses them. Hundreds exist across Requiem. They're safe places for us to hide and recover from injuries." He smiled wanly. "I suppose I no longer have to worry about sharing our secrets with you."

He took a step toward a shelf of food, but his legs swayed. His knees buckled, and he found himself on the ground.

"Rune!"

Tilla knelt above him. She placed her hands on his cheeks, her eyes soft with concern. He looked up at her. Her face was so pale, her eyes so large, her hair so smooth.

"There you are," he whispered. "My Tilla. Tilla Roper."

The coldness, the cruelty, the red spiral--they were gone from her eyes. In them he saw his old friend, his *best* friend, the woman he loved. The woman he had saved. In her eyes, he saw the waves and sand of their home.

"I'm going to heal you," she said. "I'm going to nurse you back to health. When you're strong enough, we'll find a place for us. A safe place to live."

Rune's eyes fluttered. He tried to hold her, but he had reached the end of his strength. She bustled around the room, fetching supplies. She bandaged his wounds. She laid fur blankets atop him. She held a mug of cider to his lips, and she fed him preserves and cheese and wafers.

"What else can I do?" she asked. "Tell me. Would you like more food? More drink? Another blanket?"

He laughed softly. "You've gone from soldier to a fussy old aunt. I want to sleep. Sleep beside me, Till. Remember how we used to sleep on the beach at home, wrapped in a blanket, watching the stars?"

Eyes damp, she nodded. "Of course."

She removed her boots, tunic, and leggings, remaining in her underclothes. Gently she crawled under the blanket and huddled close to him, embracing him.

"Does it hurt when I hold you?" she whispered, her lips touching his ear.

He shook his head. "Never."

She held him tighter, her body warm. "Good. I don't want to ever let you go." She blinked away tears. "You should never forgive me, Rune. I don't deserve your forgiveness. But know that I'm sorry. Know that I love you. I'll never let you go, and I'll never let you forget that." She kissed his lips. "Goodnight, Rune Brewer of Lynport."

"Goodnight, Tilla Roper."

The lamplight guttered away. They slept in each other's arms.

LERESY

As the high command convened, moving pieces across maps and discussing battle plans, Leresy crossed his arms, stood in the shadows, and fumed.

How dare he slap me? he thought, grinding his teeth. *How dare he? I am prince of Requiem!*

Fists clenched, Leresy stared at this Valien Eleison, this ragged, outcast knight--no better than a common outlaw--who styled himself the leader of the Resistance. The vagabond stood at the table, moving his finger across a parchment map. His hair was long, scraggly, and streaked with white. Salt-and-pepper stubble covered his cheeks, while the rest of his face looked like beaten leather. Even his dress was coarse; the man wore leathers, furs, and wools, the raiment of a beggar.

And my sister follows him? Leresy scoffed.

"At dawn, we fly northwest," Valien said, tracing his finger along plains and forests. "We head straight to the capital. We cannot win a slow war; we are too few. We must seize Nova Vita before the Legions learn to fight our Genesis Shards. Speed is our ally."

His lieutenants stood at his sides: Kaelyn with her ever-present bow and quiver, that southern creature Sila, and a dozen resistors with gaunt cheeks and somber eyes. The rest of their forces camped below the hill, a few thousand men and women nursing wounds, eating and drinking, and polishing swords.

They are a rabble, Leresy thought, disgust rising in his throat. *They are nothing but outlaws. They only won a battle because I found the*

Genesis Shards. He looked back at Valien and hissed under his breath. *And Valien takes credit for this victory.*

"Let us fly out at once," said Kaelyn, chin raised. "We've lingered here long enough."

Valien shook his head. Leresy was surprised the decrepit thing didn't shed dust with every movement.

"We'll fly at dawn," the outlaw said. "We've been flying with no rest for days now, and too many are wounded. Our fighters need one night upon solid ground, not in the saddle. They need a night to nurse their wounds, to eat, to ready their weapons and their souls. At dawn we fly. We will fly for seven days and nights, and we will fall upon the capital." He pointed at the map. "And we take the throne."

Leresy hissed again from the shadows. They had invited him to their council, but he would not speak here. He would not dignify this mob rabble with his wisdom.

You want the crown for that pup, Rune, he thought, glaring at the man. *You want to pull his strings even as he sits upon the Ivory Throne. I know your mind, Valien Eleison, traitor of Requiem.*

Leresy couldn't help it. He had vowed to remain silent, but words fled his lips.

"I demand another Genesis Scope," he said, taking a step closer to the table.

All eyes turned to stare at him. Some glared with open disdain while Kaelyn sighed and gazed with pity. No emotion, however, filled Valien's eyes; his stare was cold and dead.

"You lost your scope, Leresy Cadigus," the outlaw said. "You insisted on clutching your scope in your claws, for you were too proud to bear a rider. You will have no new scope. Kaelyn, Erry, and I will bear the remaining three."

Leresy bared his teeth and hissed. "It's I who found the Genesis Shards. They are my weapons! It's my ingenuity that won us the battle upon the coast. I will have a new scope!"

Valien himself bore one scope upon his belt. Leresy marched up toward the man, prepared to wrestle the scope free, but froze a few paces away. His heart raced and sweat trickled down his back. Leresy was a strong warrior--he had proven himself in battle--yet Valien was still taller and wider.

"Hand me your scope!" Leresy barked. When Valien said nothing, Leresy spun toward his sister. "Kaelyn--you bear a scope too. The one I gave you. Return it to me! Or give me half the shards within so I can build a new one."

His sister shook her head. "Stars damn it, Ler, you're drunk. There aren't enough shards to go around, and you know it. Go to bed. Sleep it off."

Leresy cackled. "Oh, I'm very sober. I see things very clearly." He pointed a shaky finger at them. "You want the throne for yourselves! You want to use my weapon--mine!--to seize my prize."

"Leresy!" Kaelyn shouted, her voice ringing across the hill. She stomped forward, eyes blazing, and grabbed his arm. She leaned close, sniffed, and wrinkled her nose. "Damn it, you reek of booze." She looked back at the council. "I'll take him to his bed."

When she began dragging him downhill, Leresy struggled, but she was damn strong for her size. He couldn't pry her fingers off his arm, so he only stumbled after her.

"I had only a few sips," he said, tugging his arm but failing to free himself. "Kaelyn, damn it! Release me. Give me my scope back. You want the throne too! You want all the glory, and you don't care about anything I do." Tears of rage stung his eyes. "I found the weapon. I should lead this rabble, not you and that outlaw. Did you bed him, Kaelyn?" He spat. "The camp says you did. Are you a princess or a whore?"

She gave his arm a twist. Her eyes blazed. "Leresy, damn you!" They reached his tent, which stood in a valley by an oak.

"Sleep it off. I'll forget what you said here, but promise me--sleep it off, and no more booze tonight."

With that, she shoved him into his tent. He stumbled backward, his heels hit a chair, and he fell down hard. The tent flap closed, and he could hear Kaelyn march away, returning to her council.

Leresy wanted to run after her. He wanted to shout, to fly as a dragon, to torch the council and burn them all. How dared they steal his weapons? How dared they send him to bed--as if he were some temperamental child, not a prince? He grabbed a bottle of rye from his pack, uncorked it with his teeth, and drank deeply.

"I am prince of Requiem!" he said, speaking to his bottle. "I'm the one who found the Genesis Shards. And now they plot to take my throne. Valien wants what is mine!"

His head spun and the spirits burned down his throat. He barely felt the hand touch his shoulder. He spun around, spilling half his drink, and saw Erry there.

The little urchin was staring up at him, her eyes solemn, that ridiculous short hair of hers falling across her brow. Leresy had forgotten he'd let her stay in his tent, warming his bed at night.

"Ler," she said softly and tried to take the bottle from him. "You've had enough."

He scoffed. "I can hold my liquor. I'm larger than a shrimp like you. I'm a man! I'm a prince. And Valien..." He hissed and took another swig. "He's a pig who plots to steal what is mine."

The solemnity left Erry's eyes; they flashed with rage. She pulled the bottle from his grip and tossed it aside.

"You fool!" she said, teeth bared, no taller than his shoulders but snarling like some wild beast. "Valien doesn't want the throne. He's fighting to restore the throne to Rune. You know that. You're drunk, Leresy. Go to bed."

He stared at the fallen bottle; its precious liquids had seeped into the earth. He spoke through a tight jaw.

"Oh, but Rune is only a puppet. Valien is the one pulling the strings. Even should he place Rune upon the throne, Valien would still be the master, controlling the boy-king's every move." He looked back at her, shaking with rage. "It's not right, Erry. The man is a cunning devil, a slimy worm. Why should I follow at his heel like a dog? I cannot bear him!"

Something cold and afraid filled Erry's eyes. She froze for just an instant, a deer staring at a hunter. Then the moment was gone. She tightened her lips, stepped toward him, and pressed her body against his.

"Forget about them for tonight, my prince," she whispered and reached down to his pants. "Come to bed. I'll help you forget them."

He shook his head, but let her stroke him. "I will not forget their insolence. I'm their prince. I do not forget. I do not forgive."

She reached into his breeches, her fingers deft. "Let them play their games, then, my lord. The important thing is that they'll kill Frey. That's why you're here, isn't it? To help kill Frey?"

He snorted, wanting to push her away, but letting her do her work; it was why he kept her.

"Killing Frey is no longer enough for me," he said. "I now have a second enemy. Valien must die."

Erry's fingers froze. She inhaled sharply. She pulled away and stared silently.

"You are a fool," she whispered. With one fluid movement, she pulled her tunic over her head. She stood naked before him. "Come to bed, Ler, and forget this foolishness."

He stared at her naked flesh and licked his lips. He stepped forward, grabbed her arms, and shoved her onto the bed. He mounted her at once, making her gasp.

"I can't kill him in the open," he said as he moved atop her. "No... the men would see me as a murderer, a usurper. I could kill him in the capital... yes, in the chaos of battle, I could kill him."

Erry closed her eyes and placed her hands in his hair. "Be silent, my prince. Be silent and take me harder."

He took her harder, but he would not be silent. "No, if I kill him in the capital, it would be too late. The capital must see me as a savior, *leading* the Resistance to slay the tyrant, a hero liberating his homeland." He hissed down at Erry. "Valien will have to die soon, and I will take over this ragtag army of his."

Erry moaned, moved her body beneath him, and placed a finger against his mouth.

"Please," she said, eyes closed. "Please stop talking. Harder."

He snarled, fists clenched, moving faster atop her. "I'll have to slay him in the shadows. No one must know it was me. And then, Erry... then I can take over his Resistance, use my Genesis Shards to claim the throne, and be hailed a hero." He grinned, breathing heavily. "Valien will be dead, I will be a beloved emperor, and you will be my concubine."

He closed his eyes and gritted his teeth, then lay atop her, drained and weary. She held him close, silent, her eyes still afraid.

TILLA

She lay in his arms, the burrow cold and his embrace warm, and she had never felt so lost, and she had never felt so much in just the right place.

"I never want to leave," she whispered, nestled against him under the blankets.

Lying on his back, he laughed. "So we'll spend the rest of our lives here, in a gopher hole a league outside the capital?"

She shrugged. "It works for gophers. Why not for us?"

They had been here, in this underground hideaway, for three days now. They had been the worst three days of Tilla's life: three days of nursing Rune's wounds, shivering in the cold, and mostly worrying. She worried about the Legions finding them. She worried about her father and whether he'd survived the slaughter at Lynport. She worried about where they'd go next, whether they'd spend their lives in hiding or seek distant lands. Yet they were also the best three days of Tilla's life: three days of holding Rune close, kissing his lips, making love to him in the dark, and whispering of memories.

"Last I checked, we were Vir Requis," Rune said, "meant to fly as dragons, not huddle underground as gophers."

Tilla propped herself up on her elbows, leaned over him, and kissed his lips. "But I like huddling here. It's safe and it's warm and it's better than any of that damn world above us, a world of fire and blood and cruelty. Here there are none of those things. Here I'm happy."

She kissed him again and he touched her hair.

"I have to check your wounds," she whispered and began to unlace his shirt.

"Again?" he asked.

She nodded, pulled off his shirt, and began to work at his trousers. "You were very wounded. I have to make sure you're all right."

He raised an eyebrow. "So why are you removing your clothes too?"

"I have a little scratch. Can you check it for me?"

He nodded. "Show me. Where--"

She did not let him finish his sentence. She kissed him again, a deep kiss, their hands clutching. She needed this. She had needed it for so long--during her cold days in the Legions, during those bloodred nights of seeing him chained, perhaps for years upon the beaches. She had him now. She had him here underground, hers alone, her Rune. All her world had burned above. All her dreams, her hopes, her life itself had collapsed, and yet she had him. He was all she had left. She would not let him go. And so she made love to him again; she had lost count of how many times she'd loved him here underground. Countless times was not enough.

She lay in his arms for a long while. She looked around the burrow, seeing shelves of food and drink, enough to last for moons. A soft laugh fled her lips.

"I was an officer in the greatest military the world has known," she said. "I lived in a large home all my own. I commanded men in battle. I was groomed by the princess of Requiem herself. But I'm happier here. I would be happy staying in this burrow forever with you."

"And yet we can't stay forever," Rune said, one hand against the small of her back, the other on her thigh. "My wounds are healing. We'll have to move soon."

Tilla closed her eyes. She had known this day would come, though she feared it.

"Let's run far away, as far as we can," she said. "We'll travel across Requiem, through the ruins of Osanna, and to the eastern sea. We'll fly from there. We'll head south to Terra Incognita, the unexplored country." She squeezed Rune tight. "We'll find a new life there, far from the Regime, far from everything we've ever known. Just you and me."

She tried to imagine that southern land of myth. The empire of Requiem stretched across forests, seas, mountains, and deserts. Yet there were lands beyond the empire too, lands no dragon had ever flown to. What lay beyond the edges of maps? Would they find lush forests full of fruit and game? Would they find foreign civilizations or strange animals? Were there forests there or deserts, mountains or plains? Would they find a new life, Tilla and Rune in unknown landscapes of adventure? She nodded, tightened her lips, and drew comfort from the warmth of his body.

Yet he remained silent, and when Tilla looked at him, his face was somber.

"Rune?" she said and touched his cheek. "What's wrong?"

He sighed, staring at the ceiling of wooden slats. "Can we really abandon home?"

Tilla leaned her head against his shoulder. She spoke softly. "Our home burned. Lynport is gone."

I burned it, she wanted to add, but her throat tightened, and she could say no more. The memories and guilt clutched her. She saw herself a dragon again, flying over Lynport, burning its roofs, shattering its columns, slaying its defenders. Her eyes stung.

"I don't just mean Lynport," Rune said. "All of Requiem is our home. This is the land of our forebears. The land my father governed. Can we truly abandon it, flee to distant lands and forget all who suffer here?"

She gripped his shoulders. "I will not have you imprisoned again. I will not lose you again, Rune Brewer. Do you understand?" She squeezed his shoulders painfully. "You might be thinking you can find the Resistance, that you can fight on, but I won't let you. I won't. I..."

Her eyes dampened, her throat constricted, and she could only lie against him and hold him close.

"I must find them," he said, embracing her. "Valien and Kaelyn still live. Hundreds of resistors still live, and they will fight on. *I* must fight on." He smoothed her hair. "I won't ask you to join me. If you want to flee, you can--" He bit down on his words and scrunched his lips. "Oh, bloody Abyss. I *will* ask you to join me. I *am* asking you. Find the Resistance with me. Fight with us."

She squeezed him so tight he grunted. Her rage exploded inside her like dragonfire, and she almost shouted. Her heart thrashed and she forced herself to take slow breaths between her clenched teeth.

He wants me to fight for Valien! she thought, reeling. He truly thought she'd fight for the man who had murdered her brother? She dug her fingernails into him. He wanted her to fight with Kaelyn, that... that little harlot he lusted for? Tilla ground her teeth, her tears drying under her anger. She had heard tales of Kaelyn Cadigus's beauty. Rune's eyes had always wandered to beauties in Lynport; he would have noticed Kaelyn too. *Did he bed her too, kiss her like he kisses me?*

Rune grunted and Tilla forced herself to loosen her grip on him. She would not sway him with anger. She knew Rune; whenever confronted with anger, he became stubborn like a mule. She'd have to sway him with calm words, not shouts.

"You can't keep fighting," she said. "Damn it, Rune, look at you. You're still wounded. You're still too thin. I've had enough of fighting." Her eyes watered and her chest shook. "I slew too many. I want to run away from all this. Maybe that is weakness, but I don't care. This whole empire is rotten. I want to run. I never want to kill again. There is enough blood on my hands."

He nodded and whispered, "That is why you must stay."

"To kill more? For more blood and death?"

He shook his head. "For redemption."

She rolled away from him. "I redeemed myself when I slew Shari Cadigus. I redeemed myself when I saved you, the heir of Aeternum."

He placed a hand on her waist. "Yet in Terra Incognita, would I be an heir? You saved Relesar Aeternum. That is who I am; I cannot run from it. Not while Frey still lives and still subjugates our people."

"The Resistance is smashed," Tilla said. "It burned in the fires of Lynport. It is gone."

Rune shook his head. "Not so long as I live. Not so long as Valien and Kaelyn live." He touched her cheek, turning her head back toward him. "Tilla, you saved me from the Red Tower. And now I must do what I can to save my friends. I must keep fighting."

Finally Tilla could not hold back the pain. She let the words slip from her mouth; they tasted like poison. "Fighting with the man who killed my brother."

Rune became quiet. For a few breaths, he said nothing. When he spoke, his voice was low and careful.

"Valien slew many, it's true. Did he himself kill your brother? Maybe. So many died in battle on both sides. War makes victims of us all."

She snorted, trying to feign some strength as her tears fell. "Is that some poetic way of saying I should forget Valien's sins?"

"He himself does not forget his sins. I've seen Valien drink, brood, and howl in the night, lamenting those he killed and those he let die. He bears much blood on his hands. So do we. Our hands will never be cleansed; perhaps there is no true redemption for us, killers in war. I don't believe there is running from this. I don't believe that even distant, unknown lands could purify our souls, could wipe the memories and grief away. So I will stay. I will keep fighting. You cannot run from a demon, only charge him head-on and slay him. Our demon is Frey Cadigus. I will not rest until he's dead. Tilla, fight him with me."

She sat up and regarded him. She ran her fingers along his face, tracing the old familiar features, and she wondered if she even still knew him. Was this truly still Rune her friend? Or was he now fully Relesar, a stranger? He needed to fight, but she needed different things. She needed him far from war. She needed him away from Valien, who led him into blood, and she needed vengeance for her brother. She knew what she must do, and it chilled her.

I must kill Valien.

She nodded. "All right, Rune. I'll help you find the Resistance. We'll find them together."

And then I will slay him, the man who took my brother from me, the man who's taking you away too.

Rune didn't seem to suspect her deeper motives. He pulled her into an embrace.

"Thank you. I promise you--once you meet them, you'll see the Resistance in a different light. We'll fight this together, you and me."

She rose to her feet, leaving the warmth of the blankets. The cold air raised goose bumps across her naked skin, and she grabbed her clothes and began to dress.

No, Rune, she thought. *I will not fight with you. We will be together, yes... but not like this.* She tugged up her leggings and slipped her tunic over her head. *I will kill anyone who comes between us. When your friends are dead, I will be avenged.*

She buckled her sword to her waist, but she left her armor behind; it would slow her down in the wilderness, and her days of donning imperial steel were over. They left the gopher hole, carrying what supplies they could, and emerged into the forest.

Dawn fell between the branches and the snow glittered. Icicles hung from birches, oaks, and pines. No dragons flew above, and the scents of the forest filled the air. It was a beautiful morning, but darkness filled Tilla. She walked silently, staring ahead, not speaking to Rune and not squeezing his hand when he held hers.

She gripped the hilt of her sword and took a deep breath.

I will do as I promised, Rune, she thought. *I will help you find your friends... and then I will drive this sword into them.*

VALIEN

"The boy is a burden." He sneered, facing the tent wall. "He's been a burden since he joined us."

He heard Kaelyn sigh behind him.

"He is an oaf," she said. "He is a whiny brat. Yet he fought with us at Lynport. He slew legionaries. And he did find the Genesis Shards."

Valien spun toward her, enraged, but his snarl died on his lips. He found it impossible to rage against Kaelyn. She stood before him, looking up with those large eyes, and his anger melted. He too sighed, a creaky sound.

"You have sad kitten eyes," he said. "You always get what you want with those eyes, don't you?"

"I don't want any of this," she said. "I don't want Leresy here, but... what can we do? I can't just banish him now. He's my twin. And he means well."

Valien snorted. "He still hopes to seize the throne for himself."

"Leresy doesn't know what he wants. He only knows that he hates our father. He has no cunning, no wit, only hatred. He's foolish and rash, but I know him. I can control him."

Valien grumbled. "One more mistake or outburst from him, and I banish him. Simple as that, sad kitten eyes or not."

She touched his cheek. "Do not weary your mind with him. We have greater things to worry about."

"And I worry about them all. Tomorrow we will fly again, and we will not rest for days, not until we reach the capital. It all ends now. This is our last battle, for victory or for death.

Perhaps worrying about Leresy is easier than thinking about the battle ahead."

"Think of neither tonight," Kaelyn said. "My brother is in his tent, Erry is soothing him, and the fight continues tomorrow. Tonight let *me* soothe *you*."

She unclasped her cloak and let it fall. With a single movement, she pulled her tunic over her head. She stood nude before him, her body slim and pale, and gave him that look of hers, her kitten eyes. She pressed herself against him, stood on tiptoes, and kissed his lips.

"Think only of me tonight," she whispered. "Let me love you. This is what you need. This is what *I* need."

She tried to kiss him again, but he turned his head away. She held him, but he took a step back.

"I can no longer do this," he said. "The last time was a mistake."

He saw the hurt in her eyes; this time it was real hurt, deep and cutting.

"Why?" she whispered.

"Because we are warriors. Because we cannot love. Love weakens us."

She laughed mirthlessly. "Must warriors feel only bloodlust? That is my father speaking, not you."

He looked away from her. He stared at his cot, remembering a night long ago when he had found her, Marilion, in his old bed in the capital.

"For years I refused to love you, Kaelyn," he said in a rasp. "Do not make me love you now."

She came to stand beside him. She held his arm.

"Is it because of her?" Her voice was soft; there was no jealousy there, only compassion and understanding.

He turned back toward her. He held her hands in his, two white flowers in his calloused paws.

"The gods, fate, or chance have been cruel," he said. "You look like her. For years, I refused to love you, for you were as a ghost. But now I don't see you as an echo. Kaelyn, you have flown by my side through fire, blood, and rain. You have been my torch in these cold, dark years. I love you, Kaelyn Cadigus, for the woman you are. And that is one emotion we cannot feel. If one of us should fall, the other must keep fighting, heart whole, fire bright. I cannot bear the fear of losing another love."

Tears filled her eyes. "And I love you, Valien Eleison. I came to you as a muddy, bruised youth, a frightened girl fleeing her father's rod. For a long time, you were as a father to me, wiser and nobler than my true father ever was. But I now love you not as a daughter, but as a woman. And I cannot quell that feeling. I will not. And I will not believe it weakens me. Tomorrow we might fall, so let us love today all the brighter." She began to undo the lacing on his tunic. "Save your troubles for tomorrow. Tonight you are mine."

He closed his eyes. He let her undress him, and their naked bodies pressed together, hers slim and soft, his scarred and rough. The candles flickered around them and he loved her. And he forgot about all else.

LERESY

He slunk through the camp, clad in cloak and hood, the clouds hiding the moon above. The booze still coursed through his blood, but he walked silently, the yellow grass muffling his boots. Inside the shadows of his hood, he grinned, licked his lips, and hissed.

"Backhand me, will you?" he whispered, still feeling the sting on his cheek; it had left an ugly bruise. "You do not strike the prince of Requiem and live, old man."

His hiss rose into a chuckle. He reached into his cloak and gripped his dagger. The cold hilt felt heavenly. Thrusting this blade into Valien would feel better than thrusting into a woman.

"You all abandoned me," he whispered, slinking between the shadowy tents. "You all stole my Genesis Shards. Now you will pay. Now you will bow down to me, and I will be your emperor."

His chuckle rose into a laugh, and Leresy bit down, cursing. No. He could not laugh now. He would save his laughter for later. For now he must move silently as a shadow. No one must know it was him who struck this night. He wanted to be remembered as a savior, not a murderer.

The camp slept around him, thousands of soldiers exhausted from the long flight and battle, many of them wounded. They lay as lumps in the night, wrapped in blankets, sleeping upon bare grass. As Leresy moved among them, they breathed and snored in a chorus. A few guards patrolled the perimeter of the camp, but they were gazing outward and upward, scanning for the Legions. Here among the sleeping troops, cloaked in darkness, Leresy walked alone, no eyes upon him.

Fools! he thought, adjusting the scarf that hid his face. *They should be watching the enemy within, not shadows beyond.*

A hill rose ahead, a slumbering giant in the night. Tents stood atop it like warts. Leresy growled. The high command slept upon that hilltop, Valien leading the Vir Requis and that glorified fisherman Sila leading the Tirans. Both men were filthy, common outlaws. Leresy sneered. He would have lunged uphill now and slain them, but guards surrounded the hill, a ring of sentinels armed with swords and shields. Leresy could not attack those tents now, not unless he shifted into a dragon. As a dragon, he was a great warrior, a champion, a beast of red scales and flame who had slain many... but tonight he was a shadow. Tonight he would strike as a viper.

"If I cannot sneak past your guards, I will draw you to me," he whispered.

He kept creeping among the sleeping men and women, common soldiers who lay upon grass, no tents above them. He only had to find a suitable one, a frightened one, one who would scream. Yes, she would have to be a screamer.

As he passed soldier by soldier, Leresy frowned. Most were men. Among the women, most were ugly freaks, their faces scarred with war, their lips chafed and their hair in disarray. Truly, this was a rabble of filthy commoners.

Finally, by a clump of maple trees, he found a match. He grin widened and his mouth watered.

The girl slept below him, her face upon her palms. Even in the darkness, her beauty shone.

"Miya," Leresy whispered.

Erry's half sister.

He had been eying the girl for a while, a wild thing with golden skin, bright blue eyes, and platinum hair. She was young and blooming into womanhood, a forbidden fruit, and Leresy was famished. He had known no woman but Erry for too long.

Foolish girl, he thought, standing above her. *You should have stayed with your father upon the hill, safe behind guards, not here among the commoners.* He licked his lips. *Tonight you are mine, Miya. You sister is mine and you will be too. And then... then my dagger will strike.*

He glanced around him. The other resistors all slept. Leresy sucked in his breath and knelt above Miya.

"Hello, my sweetness," he whispered, kissed her cheek, and caressed her hair.

She mumbled in her sleep. Leresy reached down to undo her clothes.

"Hush and sleep," he whispered and kissed her.

Her eyes opened. She gasped and he clutched her throat, constricting her, and smiled. She sputtered, staring with wide eyes, and kicked.

"Are you ready to scream?" he said. She kicked madly. She punched him, but he only hissed and ignored the pain. He kept tearing at her clothes.

"Now scream, little one," Leresy said, grinned, and released her throat.

She sucked in breath... and she screamed.

He stepped back from her. She leaped up. All around, soldiers rose from their slumber, drew swords, and came running forward.

"Father!" Miya cried, tears in her eyes, and began racing uphill. She clutched the tatters of her clothes to her body. "Father, help!"

As the camp erupted into chaos, Leresy crept behind the maple trees, disappearing into shadow.

Resistors ran through the night. A dragon took flight and blazed fire overhead, lighting the camp. Miya was still running uphill, crying for her father. Atop the hill, Sila emerged from his tent, ran downhill toward her, and embraced her. Men burst out from the other tents too, the officers of their force.

Leresy grinned in the shadows.

The camp had fallen into chaos.

"What is the meaning of this?" rose a raspy voice. Valien emerged from his tent and marched downhill, scowling and drawing his sword. He wore but a tunic, no armor. "Miya, what happened?"

Men were gathering around the haggard old knight. Miya wept and began blubbering about a masked man attacking her. Resistors began sweeping through the camp, holding torches.

In the madness, Leresy crept uphill, moving through the crowd.

"A man... a masked man," Miya said, tears on her cheeks. "He choked me. He tore my clothes. Father..."

Sila held his daughter in his wide, tattooed arms, and his eyes burned. Kaelyn stood nearby, whispering soothing words to the girl, while dozens of others gathered around.

Leresy crept closer, step by step, the people crowding around him.

Valien stepped toward Miya, his lips tight. Unlike the others, the gruff outcast had no embraces or soothing words. He was gritting his teeth, and his eyes burned with rage rather than pain.

"Miya," he rasped in his gravelly hiss of a voice. "Can you describe him? Do you know who did this?"

Leresy crept around the group, placing himself behind Valien, and inched closer. He reached into his cloak and clutched his dagger.

Miya shook her head. "I... I don't know, I... he wore black, and..."

Leresy stepped around a few resistors. Valien stood only two feet away.

Sweat soaked Leresy's back.

Do it now! a voice screamed inside him. *Now, while they're all distracted! Stab him! Kill him!*

Sweat covered his palm. Inside his cloak, he almost dropped the dagger. People were still shouting and moving about. Chaos covered the hill like a kicked ant hive. It was the time to strike, yet Leresy could barely breathe. The sweat now soaked his tunic, and his pulse thudded in his ears.

"We must find him," Valien said. "Sila, take Miya into your tent. I'll search the camp."

Stab him! Kill him before it's too late!

Leresy shook and his throat constricted.

Valien took a step away.

I can't do it, Leresy thought and tears filled his eyes.

He closed his eyes, and he saw his father again. He saw Frey beating him. He saw the emperor spitting upon him, casting him from his court, banishing him into the wilderness, turning him from a prince into this wretch.

Leresy had to kill the emperor. He had to. He had to seize Frey's throne for his own. And only one man stood between him and the crown.

Valien took another step away.

With a hiss, Leresy leaped forward. His dagger gleamed. He slammed the weapon against Valien's back.

His blade slashed through the man's tunic... and clanged.

Pain shot up Leresy's arm.

He yowled, dropping the dagger like a man dropping a viper.

So fast Leresy could not react, Valien spun around and grabbed him. Leresy yelped and Valien twisted his arm behind his back.

"You..." Leresy sputtered, clutched in the man's grip. "You... you should be dead! What kind of man wears armor under his tunic?"

Valien growled and tightened his grip. Leresy struggled, but the man was too large, too strong; Leresy would have better luck breaking iron shackles.

"Unhand me!" he screamed, tears budding in his eyes. "Leave me alone, savage!"

Resistors were gathering around, shouting. Some eyes widened with shock; others blazed with hatred. All the faces swam around Leresy. He could barely see them. He thought he saw Kaelyn there, her eyes sad. Sila was shouting something. Miya was gasping and pointing at him. A thousand others swirled around him like some mad puppet show.

"I did nothing!" Leresy screamed. "Let me go."

Valien gripped him only tighter; Leresy thought the man would break his bones.

"I think," Valien rasped, "we have found our villain. Is this the man, Miya?"

She nodded tearfully, and Leresy screamed louder.

"She's lying! I never touched her. Let me go!"

Valien began manhandling him forward. "Make way."

Leresy screamed and howled, but the men pushed and dragged him. A path cleared through the crowd. He kicked and pressed his feet into the dirt, but too many hands now gripped him, moving him forward. When Leresy saw the fallen log ahead, he began to weep.

"Please," he said, mucus and tears running down his face. "Please, don't... don't kill me. I didn't do anything."

Valien growled. "You assaulted a woman, and you stabbed me in the back, Leresy Cadigus. If I hadn't been warned of your treachery, you'd have killed me. Now be silent, place your neck upon this log, and I will make your death painless. Struggle and I will make it hurt."

Leresy howled to the sky. He kicked wildly. He could barely see through his tears.

"Treachery!" he cried. "Who warned him? Who? I've been betrayed!"

He panted, shaking and trembling... and he knew.

He had told only one soul.

Oh stars, no...

Icy water seemed to flow through him, drowning his fear and rage, replacing it with something colder and deeper--the ghostly stab of betrayal.

"Erry..."

He looked through the crowd, seeking her. Not Erry. No... she couldn't have betrayed him. She... she was his woman. She was his love. Not Erry...

"Erry," he said, weeping. "Erry, where are you?"

He raised his head, still clutched in the grip of so many men, and saw her ahead.

His tears fell.

She stood among the crowd. Men almost hid her from view, but he could see her face. She gazed at him, her expression hesitant, almost shy. Her eyes were soft, the eyes of an abandoned child. Suddenly she seemed so young to him. She *was* only a child, only a little doll.

"I vowed to protect you, Erry," he whispered. "You were my woman. You told him?"

She looked at him and her eyes dampened, but she said nothing. And he knew the answer.

She betrayed me. Erry Docker, the love of my life, the only woman I've ever loved... betrayed me.

They shoved him toward the log. Hands gripped his neck, pushing it down. Steel hissed against leather. Cheek pressed against the wood, Leresy raised his eyes, and he saw Valien drawing his sword. The sword was massive, a hunk of steel wide enough to behead an ox.

Leresy did not want to gaze upon this. No. He did not want to see this bear of a man and his steel; that would not be his last vision.

He turned his eyes back toward Erry.

He looked at her--at her soft face, her small features, her short hair he would always mock. She was beautiful. He would die gazing upon her.

"I love you, Erry Docker," he said, waiting for the steel to fall.

The camp fell silent all around.

Leresy held his breath, waiting to die.

A single, high voice broke the silence.

"Wait."

Leresy twisted his head and saw her there, golden through the veil of his tears.

His twin.

The second half of his soul.

"Kaelyn," he whispered.

She held up her hand, a sign of redemption, of mercy, pointing upward to the heavens and stars of his forebears.

"Wait," she said. "Valien, wait. Don't kill him. He is my brother."

"Sister," Leresy whispered. "Kaelyn... he hurt you... I'm sorry. Please. He hurt you so much. He would beat you. I have to kill Father... I have to..."

His twin looked upon him, eyes soft and full of pity. She stared at him, but she spoke to Valien.

"He is miserable, he is sad, he is drunk and pathetic and a wretch. But he is my brother. Please, Valien, spare his life."

Valien growled, a deep sound like a wolf disturbed in its den. He held his sword high above Leresy's neck.

"He assaulted Miya," he said, eyes staring down, cold with fury. "He stabbed me in the back. And you would spare his life?"

Kaelyn nodded and now tears streamed down her cheeks. "He deserves death, it's true. I've tried to kill him myself in our years of battle; I gave him that scar on his cheek. But now I look down upon him and I pity him. And I see myself. His soul is bound to mine. Our father would beat us; he would beat us until we bled, wept, and blacked out. He nearly beat us to death. I fled from my father, but Leresy was not as strong. My father broke his soul. All my brother does--all his sins--are driven by his madness."

Valien refused to lower his sword. "Life is hard in this land. Many children suffer under the scourge of Frey Cadigus. Past suffering does not excuse present cruelty. Leresy is no longer a child but a man--a man capable of his own choices, a man responsible for his actions."

He raised his sword higher.

Leresy whimpered.

"He saved my life!" Kaelyn blurted out. "Please, Valien. He saved me. When we were children... one night... oh stars." She trembled. "One night Father beat me so badly, all because I picked fruit from a garden tree. He meant to kill me. He *would* have killed me. Leresy begged. Leresy pleaded with our father. 'Beat me instead!' he said. 'Kaelyn did nothing, beat me! I picked the fruit!'" Kaelyn lowered her head. "And he beat Leresy so badly he broke his arm. My brother saved my life that night. Let me save him now. Let me repay that debt. Please, Valien, I cannot watch him die. Banish him from our camp, but let him live. I love him."

Leresy lay still, face pressed to the log, watching his sister, and the pain of that night returned to him. He remembered his father's fists striking him, his punisher burning him, his boots bruising him. But as bad as that pain had been, it was better than seeing Kaelyn hurt. He had saved her that night; it was the best thing he'd ever done.

"I love you too, my sister," he whispered. "I'm sorry for what I became. I'm sorry for the man that I am. I'm sorry I could never be strong like you. I know what I am... and I'm sorry. I love you."

The silence seemed to stretch forever.

Valien stood, sword held above.

Nobody spoke. Even the wind seemed to die.

Finally, with a grunt, Valien swung and slammed his blade down. It banged against the log an inch from Leresy's face, scattering chips of wood.

Leresy gasped and flinched, for a second not sure if he was alive or dead.

"Get up," Valien said in disgust.

He grabbed Leresy's collar and yanked him to his feet. Leresy stood on shaking legs. His pants clung to him, and he realized that under his cloak, he had wet himself.

"Thank you," he whispered.

Valien shoved him away from the log.

"Leresy Cadigus," he rasped, "I will spare your life tonight, but if our paths cross again, I will slay you. Do not doubt that. Leave this camp. Leave into whatever exile you choose. Fly from here now and thank the stars for my mercy."

Leresy wobbled. The world still spun around him, and he fell to his knees. The resistors all wavered, a sea of faces, and Leresy hissed at them.

"Stand back!" he screamed. "Do not touch me!"

He leaped up and shifted.

He beat his wings. He soared as a red dragon, a legendary beast, a monster none could hurt. He blew fire, lighting the sky.

"You will regret this!" he howled. "I am your prince. I will be your emperor. The throne will be mine, and I will hang you all!"

He soared uphill. The tents rose ahead. Cackling, Leresy stretched out his claws, grabbed Valien's tent, and tossed it aside, exposing the bed and table within.

"You will all kneel before me, and I will break you!" he shouted.

Laughing madly, he reached down his claws.

"Leresy, no!" Kaelyn shouted.

He ignored her. His eyes damp with laughter, he could barely see. He grabbed Valien's Genesis Scope from the table. He soared.

"Stop him!" rose a voice behind. "Bring him back! Kill him if you must."

Leresy beat his wings and flew, racing over the hill, a field, and trees. A jet of fire blasted above him, searing the tips of his horns. He looked over his shoulder to see dragons chasing, a hundred or more. Fire blazed his way.

"Requiem will be mine, fools!" he cried. He tore the lid off the scope and pointed it at them.

Red light bathed the world.

The dragons lost their magic and tumbled.

Laughter in his throat, tears in his eyes, and fire in his heart, Leresy turned and flew. He raced into the night, blowing flames, leaving his love, his sister, and his hope behind. He wept and laughed as he flew.

"You banished me," he said into the darkness, "but I will not forget you, Requiem. I will win my throne. You will all see and you will all be sorry, but I will not forgive you. I will be Emperor Leresy Cadigus and you will worship me."

Over a dark forest, miles from the camp, he crashed down onto a bed of pine needles. He shifted back into human form.

He lay down, pulled his knees to his chest, and shivered until the dawn.

VALIEN

They crossed the border of Old Requiem at dawn.

Sunbeams broke between the clouds, shining golden over frosty forests and fields. The southern islands had been warm, but here in the north winter covered the land. A distant ruined castle caught the sun and blazed, a beacon of molten bronze. A frozen stream snaked across the land, glimmering silver in the light. Hills rose from mist, earthen children waking from slumber.

For days now, they had been flying over the ruins of Osanna, a fallen kingdom Frey had burned and annexed into his empire. Yet now... now they flew over the ancestral home of the Vir Requis, an ancient land of memory and starlight. Flying at the head of his army, Valien whispered the Old Words, the prayer of his people.

"As the leaves fall upon our marble tiles, as the breeze rustles the birches beyond our columns, as the sun gilds the mountains above our halls--know, young child of the woods, you are home, you are home. Requiem! May our wings forever find your sky."

At his side, Kaelyn spoke the prayer with him. He turned to look at her. The green dragon bore four riders on her back: a Tiran scope bearer and three Vir Requis in human forms, resting from flight. All four slept, wrapped in their cloaks. Gliding on the wind, Kaelyn met his gaze, and her eyes shone.

"We're home," she said.

Valien looked to the east. The sun was rising, but they would not see the capital this day. Even flying without rest, Nova Vita still lay days away.

"If Frey knows of our scopes, he will send no more dragons our way," he said. "He will hole up in the capital, ready his cannons, and sharpen his swords. He will fight house to house, chamber to chamber, not in the sky. We should have a clear flight to the city, but once there..."

He let his voice trail off. The thought had been rattling through his mind for days now. The boy Leresy had lost one scope in the sea, then stolen another. Valien looked over his shoulder at his army, and his heart sank deeper. Four thousand fighters, that was all. Four thousand against the might of the Legions.

"We're down to two scopes," he finally said. "We are outnumbered more than a hundred to one. We are home, Kaelyn, yet my heart is heavy. We might be flying to our deaths."

She nodded. "I am willing to die for Requiem."

"Yet I want to live to see you live." He spat flames. "Kaelyn, we can still turn back. We can return to our islands. We can find another life together, you and me, away from all this."

The idea had been taking root inside him. With every disaster--the lost scopes, the fallen men upon the beaches, the betrayal in their camp--the temptation had grown stronger. He could flee. He could find new life with the woman he loved--with Kaelyn, the light of his heart. He needn't fly here to war, to blood, to death.

"We can," Kaelyn said. "We can find a small island, and we can grow old together, and we will never know war again. But we would not know peace, Valien. Forever we'd be haunted. Rune would languish in his prison. Requiem would moan under the scourge." She shook her head, scattering smoke. "I don't want to die. I want to live too. I want to win."

"Can we still win?" he asked. "We were to fly here with four scopes, one on each side of our army. We shouldn't have lost so much so soon."

She snarled and her eyes blazed. "We lost men, it's true. And we lost scopes. But we smashed an army on the beaches, and we will smash the capital. This is the greatest flight of our lives. Poets will sing of us."

He twisted his jaw. "Aye, but will they be our poets, or those of the emperor?"

Such was youth, he thought. *Rune is like this too; he is like her. They are young. They fly with conviction. Justice lights their hearts. But I am old and I've seen that justice often fails, that the righteous often die while evil lingers.*

And yet he flew on, for he knew Kaelyn was right. He would find no peace upon a distant island. He was a soldier. He had been a soldier for most of his life. All he could do was fight on.

Even if the battle is hopeless, I will fight it, he thought. *Better to die fighting than to flee and wither in pain.*

They flew on, the valleys and hills rolling below.

They flew over sprawling Lanburg Fields where snow glimmered, the place where long ago the griffin armies had slain all but seven Vir Requis, the last of their race. They flew over the rolling farmlands of Oldnale, the great wheat basket of Requiem for thousands of years. They flew until they saw King's Forest ahead, its birches coated in ice, where the Vir Requis had first risen, where their magic had first shone.

They flew across Old Requiem, land of their ancestors, until at sundown the first roars of the enemy sounded.

They looked ahead and saw them upon the wind.

A host flew their way, and Valien hissed and felt his belly knot.

"Resistors!" he called and blasted fire skyward. "Spear formation! Cut through them."

His dragons roared behind him. Roused by the alarm, those Vir Requis who slept in human forms leaped off their saddles, shifted into dragons, and blew their flames. Tirans leaped from dragon to dragon in midair, spreading themselves out across the hosts.

Ahead, flying from the west, the Legions covered the sky. Ten thousand or more flew toward them, clad in armor, chanting their battle cries. The banners of Cadigus flew upon them, black streams emblazoned with red spirals. They were a storm, a demon of the air, a great beast of metal and fire and scale. They howled for death.

Valien growled.

If Frey sent this host our way, he thought, *he knows we're coming. He knows of our triumph on the coast. He knows of the scopes. And he knows we'll fell his dragons from the sky.* Valien bared his teeth and hissed. *He sends myriads to die under the Genesis Light... just to slow us down.*

"Kaelyn!" he shouted. "Take the right flank."

She nodded and banked north. Miya rode upon the green dragon's back, her hair streaming, a scope ready in her hands.

"Sila, ready your scope!" Valien said to the rider on his own back. "And hold tight."

He banked south, and their army flew forward, a great snake in the sky, driving toward the enemy. Valien and Kaelyn flew ahead of the force like two horns.

The Legions swarmed toward them.

Dragonfire blazed.

Red light beamed.

Screams filled the air.

The Genesis Light tore through the sky, two beams thrusting forward. By the hundreds, dragons lost their magic. Human legionaries fell from the sky, screaming.

"Kaelyn, keep your beam on those falling!" Valien roared. "I'll keep sending them down."

She nodded and dipped in the sky. Legionaries tumbled down, and Kaelyn followed, shining her light upon them, not letting them shift back into dragons. They crashed against the hills.

"Sila, sweep the beam across them!" Valien said.

They flew, swinging their beam from side to side, tearing into the dragons, scattering humans like a broom scattering a swarm of vermin. The legionaries tumbled.

"Burn them!" Valien howled.

Behind him, his fellow resistors roared. Jets of fire blasted, burning the falling legionaries. Arquebuses blasted and iron rounds tore into dragons and falling men alike. Some legionaries managed to dart around the beams, reach the Resistance, and blaze their fire, but they too fell; the arquebuses punched through scales like arrows through flesh.

Valien roared. "Slay them all!"

Only four thousand souls, the Resistance tore through the Legions like a wolf tearing through a herd of deer.

Resistors were chanting for victory, and even Valien's heart was rising, when he heard the howls behind him.

"Slay the Resistance!"

"Hail the red spiral!"

"Hail Cadigus!"

The roars shook the sky. Fire crackled in a typhoon. Heat blazed.

Valien turned his head... and felt his heart sink down to his tail.

A second army flew from the south, twenty thousand strong--two brigades chanting for death and spreading out wide, a claw ready to engulf them. For several heartbeats, Valien could not move.

"Slay every last resistor and drink their blood!" the Legions cried. "Hail the red spiral!"

The western host, cut down to half their size, roared with renewed rage. The eastern host stormed. From the north and south, more forces appeared, chanting and blasting fire.

We are trapped, Valien thought. *We are encircled. We will die.*

He growled.

Then let us die well.

"Resistance!" he said. "Do not lose heart! I, Valien Eleison, fight with you. Howl for Requiem! Blow your dragonfire! Fire your guns! We will overcome."

They gathered around him, a small host of survivors trapped in a storm, and they roared for their home, and they blasted their fire.

"Valien!" Kaelyn said. She flew up toward him, eyes damp but burning with rage, and upon her back Miya was aiming her cone from side to side. "Let us fly around our men in rings."

He nodded. "Fly clockwise! I'll fly the other way."

She nodded.

They flew.

Darkness swarmed from every side.

They fought like a sun engulfed by night. The Resistance roared their dragonfire and shot their guns. Their beams blasted out, felling legionaries, but they could not cover the entire sky, not with only two scopes. Always they left a flank exposed, and the legionaries swooped against it, blasting fire and lashing claws. Valien flew from flank to flank, cutting the Legions down, but only exposed more resistors behind him.

Blood rained.

Corpses littered the hill below.

The sun sank and still they fought. Fire lit the night.

When dawn rose, it illuminated a world red with blood and black with soot.

Lashed with claws, his scales cracked with dragonfire, Valien descended toward the hills. He grunted and puffed smoke, his blood leaked, and every flap of wings blazed. He landed upon a hilltop and wheezed. The bodies of legionaries spread around him, tens of thousands. The survivors of the Resistance landed too, lacerated and burnt, coughing smoke and all but collapsing.

Valien resumed human form and walked among the dead, clutching his wounds. Kaelyn strode toward him, her cheeks ashy, her clothes torn and bloody.

He marched toward her and she crashed into his arms. Blood smeared her hair. Crows cawed, picking at the fallen.

"We won," she whispered, holding him tight.

He nodded, looking around at the dead, the screaming wounded, and the gore covering the grass.

"We lost half our people," he said. "But yes, Kaelyn, we won. We won."

She wept against him, and he held her in his arms as ash fell from the sky.

The capital still lay leagues away. They were down to two thousand fighters, and horror clutched Valien's heart so tightly it could barely beat.

RUNE

They crouched between the trees as the sky burned.

The Legions swarmed overhead, a storm of howls, blasting fire, and swirling smoke. The trees bent as if cowering from the host. The scents of fire and oiled steel filled the air, overpowering the smells of the forest. When Rune peered between the branches, he couldn't see the sky, only scales, armor, and smoke. Ten thousand dragons or more flew above, shrieking and chanting.

"Death to the Resistance! Hail the red spiral."

Rune scrunched his lips and crouched lower. Tilla knelt at his side. Both wore garments woven of pine branches, lichen, and twigs. Even kneeling beside her, Rune could barely see Tilla; to the world, she looked like a snowy evergreen.

"They're flying to battle," he whispered. "The Resistance must be near. They're still fighting."

Hope sprang inside him, but fear too. This meant Valien, Kaelyn, and the others were still alive. It meant there was still light shining in the darkness. It also meant war was flaring again... that everyone Rune still cared for could burn.

"How far do you reckon the Resistance is?" Tilla said.

"I don't know," Rune said, "but the Legions are flying east, so we'll follow. We'll follow until we find them."

They knelt until the last formations passed overhead, leaving a sky of smoke and raining ash. With the shrieks distant, Rune and Tilla rose to their feet, two leafy figures like storybook monsters invented to frighten children away from the woods. They shivered, brushed snow off themselves, and kept walking.

The snow was deep and progress was slow. The trees rustled, their icicles gleaming. Rune could not stop shivering, and soon he began to cough. Taken from the gopher hole, his clothes were woven of thick wool, and his cloak was wrapped tight around him, but still his teeth chattered.

"I wish we could fly," he said. "I'm never cold as a dragon. We should fly tonight."

Tilla shook her head forcefully. "No flying! Not until there's a cloudy night. We would be seen in the moonlight. You know only legionaries are allowed to fly as dragons. And you know those legionaries are looking for us."

Rune grumbled. "At this point, I'd welcome a fight against the legionaries. This snow is nastier than every dragon who serves Frey."

Tilla's eyes flashed, and she seemed ready to snap at him, but she bit her lip, stared ahead, and walked silently. Her body was stiff, her shoulders squared.

Rune looked at her and sighed.

What's wrong, Tilla? he wanted to ask but dared not. For the past couple days, it seemed whenever he asked her anything, she had only an angry retort. Her eyes were always flashing, her mouth was always frowning, and fire always seemed to simmer inside her. A root snagged her boots, and Tilla swayed and cursed. When Rune reached out to hold her hand, she glared and pulled herself away. She kept walking silently, not looking at him.

Bloody stars, Rune thought, looking at her, but she ignored him. *What happened to you?*

For three days--for three wondrous, magical days in the burrow--Tilla had kissed him, whispered of her love, and... Rune's blood heated to remember what else they would do, their naked bodies moving together under the blankets, their lips locked together, their...

He forced the thought away. As lovely as those days had been, they seemed over. Since he'd insisted on seeking the Resistance, Tilla had been cold as a statue.

"Tilla," he said, making one more attempt to soothe her, "I was thinking that after this war is over, we can return to Lynport. Maybe we can rebuild the Old Wheel. I--"

She spoke harshly, not bothering to look his way. "Don't talk to me of Lynport. Please. Just walk silently, all right?"

Rune sighed again; he had lost count of how many times he'd sighed since leaving the burrow.

"I know you're angry," he said, voice softer. "I know you wanted to flee Requiem, not seek the Resistance, not march right back into war. But I promise you, I--"

"Rune!" She snapped her head toward him. Her eyes narrowed and her cheeks flushed. "I told you. I don't want to talk. I agreed to find the Resistance with you. So we will find them. But that doesn't mean I feel like talking to you, all right?"

Rune lost his breath. He had never seen Tilla so angry. He had argued with Tilla before--he had spent his childhood bickering with her about a mancala move, wrestling her on the beach, or just arguing about minutiae like the name of a star. But this was worse. Tilla had changed in the Legions, grown both colder and more fiery. She seemed like a growling wolf now, not even human.

He nodded.

"All right, we'll walk silently for a while."

"Not just for a while. For the rest of the way."

They kept walking. He spoke no more, but his mind raced.

Was Tilla simply mad because he'd insisted on rejoining the Resistance? Or could something darker be stirring in her mind? He glanced at her as they trudged through snow. She stared ahead, face pale, eyes hard, her mouth a thin line. Her hand clutched the hilt of her sword, ready to draw and fight. She moved like a warrior, a slinking beast ready to pounce.

Rune swallowed. Tilla had trained for a year in the Legions. She had fought for them in battle. She had killed for them. Could she still be loyal to the red spiral?

Stars, he thought. *Did she free me so I could lead her to the Resistance? So she could draw her sword and slay Valien, the man who killed her brother?*

Rune felt dizzy. His throat dried out. Tilla wore pine needles and twigs now, no longer armor, but her every movement still spoke of a huntress, a warrior, a woman ready to kill. Rune felt faint. Was he leading an enemy into his camp?

No, he told himself. *No!* It was impossible. Tilla had saved him. Tilla had slain Shari. Tilla had made love to him in the burrow. This was no ruse. She was simply... simply mad that he refused to flee with her. That was all.

And yet Rune decided to keep a close eye on her, and he couldn't eliminate the chill in his belly.

They walked in silence, following the trail of fire that blazed across the sky.

In the afternoon the forest thinned out, and they found themselves walking in open sunlight. The snow was deeper here, and Rune began to worry about their tracks being seen from the sky. Maples and ash trees grew upon scattered hills, and frozen streams crossed the land. Rune stuck his hands under his armpits, but he couldn't stop shaking, and his cough ripped at his throat.

As the sun dipped behind them and dusk painted the sky, clouds moved in from the east. Another mile and the clouds thickened above, hiding the sky. Fresh snow began to fall. Finally, after hours of silence, Tilla spoke.

"We will fly."

Without waiting for a reply or even glancing his way, she shifted. She rose as a white dragon, soared straight up, and vanished into the clouds. With a breath of relief, Rune shifted too and followed.

Stars, this feels good, he thought. He had not shifted in so long. Fire filled his belly and throat. The magic warmed him, flowing through his veins like wine. For the first time this winter, he felt warm.

For a moment he flew blinded, seeking Tilla but seeing only snow and clouds. He pounded his wings, trying to clear the clouds, but they were too thick.

"Tilla?" he called.

He flew on, grumbling, wondering if she'd flown off and if he'd ever see her again. Perhaps she had decided to abandon him, to find her own life away from his war. His belly sank.

"Tilla!" he called again.

A grumble rose in the darkness. Her head thrust out from clouds, and her wings blasted him with air.

"Hush!" she said. "The Legions fly here too. I spotted a battalion flying east about a mile away. We're heading the right way. Now fly quietly!"

Her words were harsh and biting as ever, but Rune breathed in relief. Angry or not, at least she was still with him.

They kept flying, the clouds streaming around them, the snow flurrying. Rune kept close to Tilla, but he could barely see her; he only caught glimpses of her white scales between the wisps. Every few moments, the two dragons rose higher, emerging above the clouds, then sinking again, like whales rising for a breath. During these breaches, Rune could see the Legions ahead beyond the storm. The armored dragons flew east, their fire bright, their howls a distant thunder.

They fly to Valien... and to Kaelyn.

At the thought of Kaelyn, his heart gave a twist, and his eyes stung. He missed her. He missed Valien too, and he missed Erry, and he missed all the others... but he mostly missed her.

With Tilla's words still stinging, Rune yearned for Kaelyn's kind eyes, soft touch, and smiling lips. He thought back to that night in the ruined, hilltop temple, the night they had kissed.

I always thought Tilla was the love of my life, but now I miss you, Kaelyn. Now I wish I were back there in those ruins, holding you.

He looked at Tilla, who flew beside him, her scales glimmering, and guilt choked his throat, and he had never felt more confused.

A roar sounded ahead, and fire pierced the clouds.

Rune started. At first he thought it was Tilla roaring fire, but she looked just as bewildered. Rune sucked in his breath and stared ahead. Tilla's eyes narrowed and she bared her fangs.

The roar sounded again, five hundred yards away or closer, and more fire blazed, painting the clouds red.

Rune snarled. The main battalion was still distant; this was probably a lost soldier or a small patrol. Rune dipped lower in the clouds, gestured at Tilla, and she followed his lead. They sank fifty yards, staying within the cloud cover.

"Keep flying," he mouthed and pointed his claws ahead. "We'll fly under them."

She nodded, moved closer to him, and they shot forward through the clouds, silent and straight.

The roars continued above and fire cascaded down.

"They betrayed me!" roared a dragon; perhaps there was only one. "They stabbed me in the back. But I will make them kneel."

Rune frowned as he flew. He knew that voice from somewhere.

"How dare they banish me?" The dragon flew directly above now. "I'm their prince. I'm their savior! I--" The voice halted, then spoke louder. "Who flies below? I see your wake through the clouds. Is it you, sister? Have you come to kneel?"

Rune cursed and kept gliding forward. He gestured with his claws for Tilla to follow. He cursed under his breath. They'd been spotted, but perhaps they could still lose this dragon in the clouds. Tilla glided beside him, silent.

A jet of fire crashed down, missing Rune by a foot. Wings beat, scattering clouds, and air whistled. The dragon above was swooping.

"You cannot escape me!" cried the beast. "I see your wake. Come and die, dragons! I will kill you. I will kill you all."

Rune growled and filled his maw with fire.

"Stars damn it, there's only one," he said to Tilla, not caring if the beast above heard. "Let's kill the bastard."

Tilla gave a battle cry, and flames crackled to life between her teeth. She and Rune reared, soared, and blasted flame upward.

The fires roared, scattering the clouds. From the smoke and flame and mist, a red dragon came barreling down, bellowing and clawing the air.

Rune's heart skipped a beat and his anger flared.

"Leresy Cadigus," he said.

The young prince, twin to Kaelyn, looked haggard and nearly mad. The gilt on his horns, a sign of nobility, was peeling. Grime clung to his scales. But worse were his eyes; they were a madman's eyes. Something inside them had broken like snapped springs inside a doll. The red dragon cackled and leered.

"Hello, dragons!" he said. "You will kneel too. But first you will fall, yes. Fall!"

He raised his claws, holding up a cylinder of leather and glass.

Rune wasn't sure what the contraption was, and he had no time to contemplate it. He soared with Tilla, and they blasted fire again, shooting the jets up at the prince.

Red light shot down.

At first Rune thought it a stream of fire. Then he realized--red light was streaming from the cylinder like a sunbeam. Rune roared, tried to fly higher, and gasped.

An unseen claw tugged at his magic.

He growled, trying to cling to it, but the magic was jerked away like sleep vanishing under shaking hands.

Among the clouds, he resumed human form.

He tumbled.

At his side, he saw Tilla falling too. They pierced the clouds. They fell through open sky. The black fields below spun, racing up toward them. The red light still bathed them.

"I can't fly!" he shouted.

Even as she plummeted, Tilla managed to glare. "I noticed!"

He grimaced and tried to summon his magic again. Its tendrils coiled inside him, but whenever he reached for them, they slipped from his mind. It felt like trying to remember a fading dream. Leresy still flew as a dragon. He cackled and dived, aiming the cylinder down. The red light still bathed Rune and Tilla.

"It's that damn light of his!" Rune shouted. "It's canceling out our magic."

Tilla shouted in frustration. "Yes, Rune, I can see that! Thank you, Sir Obvious."

The ground grew closer. Rune winced. He had only seconds to live.

"Damn it, Leresy!" he shouted up. "We're not your enemies. It's Rune and Tilla. You know us! Take that light off!"

But the red dragon seemed fully mad. He laughed, head tossed back, and blasted fire across the sky. His chest rose and fell, and smoke sputtered from him. He seemed like some cracked, leaky cauldron about to shatter.

"Rune and Tilla, Rune and Tilla!" he chanted. "I know you. Yes, I know you! Rune the silly boy my father wants. Tilla the tall woman with the nice, pale skin to kiss, yes." He howled with laughter. "I craved you both once, one to kill and one to bed, but which was which?"

The air howled around them. The ground loomed so close, they could count the boulders and trees. They had only a breath or two left.

"Leresy, stars damn you!" Tilla screamed. "Stop shining the light!"

"Take it off, Leresy!" Rune shouted, panic thudding through him. "We're not your enemies! We're your friends!"

The wind roared.

The ground reached toward them.

Rune winced and knew: *This is it.*

He reached out and held Tilla's hand.

He held his breath.

Leresy laughed and soared, and the red light vanished.

Treetops skimmed Rune's boots.

Roaring, he shifted into a dragon.

His wings bent the trees below. He blasted fire and sucked in air and his eyes watered.

I'm alive, stars, I'm alive.

Tilla soared at his side, howling.

Still laughing, Leresy made a lazy arc in the air, turning back toward them.

"Tilla, fly down and land!" Rune shouted.

They swooped.

They crashed between the treetops.

Several feet above the forest floor, the red light bathed them again. They lost their magic and thumped into the snow in human forms.

Rune moaned. The fall wasn't high enough to break his bones, but he would bruise. He raised his head, coughed, and struggled to rise. Tilla moaned at his side and pushed herself up onto her elbows.

Before they could stand, the red dragon crashed down through the trees. His claws thrust out. One dragon foot slammed against Rune, shoving him down. Snow filled his mouth and he moaned. The second foot slammed against Tilla and pinned her down.

"So, Rune and Tilla, Rune and Tilla," said the dragon. "Or should I say... Relesar Aeternum and the famous Lanse Tilla Siren?" He cackled and spat fire. "Oh yes, I've heard of your ascension, girl." He thrust down his head, reached out a tongue the size of a human arm, and licked Tilla's head. "Oh my, but you taste delightful. You taste like honey and moonlight. I've wanted to taste you for a long while."

She spat and her face twisted in disgust. "Go lick gutter shite, Leresy. Get off me."

She struggled and kicked but couldn't free herself. Rune squirmed too. The cylinder's light no longer shone upon him, but Leresy's foot pressed down too mightily. Whenever he grasped his magic and tried to shift, the weight squeezed it away like juice from a fruit, leaving Rune in human form.

"What do you want?" he demanded, twisting his head to stare up at the dragon.

Leresy laughed. "What do I want? Oh, silly child of the woods. What do I want?" He lowered his scaly head, and his smoke fluttered across the forest floor. "I want to kill all my enemies. I want to bed every woman in the world. I want power and money and booze. I want to forget the blood, the screams, the fire. What do I want, lost children?" His voice strained, shoving out each word through a clenched jaw. "I want the *throne*."

The claws dug into the soil beneath Rune, then tightened, coiling around his torso like a steel cage. Rune grimaced, his arms pinned to his sides, and glared up at Leresy.

"Go take your damn throne then," he said. "Go fight your madman of a father. Or if you want to face me, face me like a man, or let me shift and face you as a dragon. Or are you a coward?"

Leresy laughed and lifted Rune from the ground. In his other foot, he held Tilla, squeezing and pinning her arms to her sides. The red dragon bucked and tossed his head, blasting smoke across the forest.

"A coward?" he said. "Am I a coward? I slew Beras the Brute. I found the Genesis Shards. I will kill my father. I will kill my sister Shari. I will--"

"Your damn sister is already dead," Tilla spat out, squirming in the claws. "I killed her myself. Stabbed my blade right into her chest."

Leresy froze.

He panted, not moving, holding Rune and Tilla still in his claws. His eyes widened.

"My sister... Shari... dead?"

Rune nodded. "I saw her die. Tilla is speaking truth. You've been away from the capital for too long."

For a moment Leresy stood frozen. Fire crackled in his maw. Then, with a howl, he reared. He tossed back his head and blasted fire, igniting the treetops. He laughed. His tail lashed, slamming into trees. Flaming branches fell and sparks showered. The grass kindled.

"Shari is dead!" Leresy howled and laughed, sounding like a demonic child overcome with joy. "Dead, dead, dead! Shari is dead!"

He bounced around with glee, tail knocking down trees, still clutching Rune and Tilla. Smoke filled the forest. Trees blazed.

Rune coughed, blinded. Before the flames could burn him, Leresy leaped up and soared, rising into the night sky, still clutching his prizes.

"Dead, dead! Shari is dead! Happy night, happy night, Shari is dead!"

Rune coughed and squirmed, trying to free an arm, trying to shift, but the claws clutched him so tightly he could barely breathe.

"Stars damn you, Leresy, I thought we were fighting together. You helped us in Lynport. Now free me!"

Leresy laughed and began flying back west, back toward the capital. The clouds streamed by, the forest below burned, and the wind roared.

"Shari is dead!" he cried into the night. "I am heir. I am heir to Requiem!"

Tilla kicked wildly.

"Leresy, you bloody fool," she shouted into the wind. "Your father banished you. He will kill you if you return. You're no heir, damn you."

But the red dragon kept flying, clutching them, and roared fire over their heads. He beat his wings, flying faster, streaming over the forests.

"Banished me?" He laughed. "Yes, yes, that he did. But now I return. Now I bear his greatest prizes--Relesar, the lost whelp of a miserable dynasty, and Tilla Siren, the traitor who murdered his daughter. Frey Cadigus will name me heir now. I will be his golden child." Leresy howled and his fire bathed the sky. "It is Leresy's turn to rise. Requiem is mine."

Rune and Tilla cursed and shouted and squirmed. The red dragon tightened his claws, grinned, and flew through the night.

KAELYN

A thousand dragons, their scales chipped and charred. A thousand riders on their backs, bandaged and burnt and bearing their guns. A ragtag force of refugees and rebels. A whisper in the night. A single flicker in a storm. They flew through the night and beheld the capital of Requiem ahead, rising from the dark forest like a crown of fire.

"Nova Vita," Kaelyn whispered, flying ahead of her people.

The capital had many names. Jewel of Requiem. Gloriae's City. Light of Aeternum. Yet to Kaelyn it was more than that. It was her home, her haunting pain, and her glittering prize. It was all that mattered in the world.

"Nova Vita." Her voice shook in the wind. "City of our ancestors. City of my pain and hope. Today I liberate you, Nova Vita, or I die upon your walls."

The city still lay miles away. From here it seemed no larger than a ring she could slip onto her finger. Fires blazed upon its walls, countless torches to light the night. More fire crackled within the ring--dragons flying over the roofs in patrol, blasting their flames. All around the capital, the land slept in darkness, a black sea.

Kaelyn took deep breaths, narrowed her eyes, and flew faster. The others flew at her sides: Valien, her guiding light; Erry Docker, a coppery dragon with flames in her nostrils; and two thousand more of her comrades, the dearest souls she knew.

"And you wait for me there, Rune," she whispered. "I will find you and I will free you. Be strong, my friend."

At her side, Valien raised his head, and his eyes shone in the night. He gazed upon his city and began to sing. His voice was a low rumble, a thunder rolling in a distant storm. Kaelyn knew the song. He sang Old Requiem Woods, an ancient tune, a song the Vir Requis would sing before they had a kingdom, before marble columns stood, before books were written and myths were told. It was a song of days before gunpowder, before walls of stone, before bloodshed and swords and a land that was torn, a song of the Vir Requis living in this forest below, wild children of the woods.

Kaelyn joined her voice to his. He sang in a rumble, but her voice was soft and pure as summer wine. Behind her, the others joined. A thousand dragons raised their voice in song.

"Old Requiem Woods, where do thy harpists play, in Old Requiem Woods, where do thy dragons fly..."

They flew closer. The city blazed ahead, a disk of light in the darkness, the beacon of her heart. With every mile they crossed, more details emerged, and Kaelyn could soon see dark towers and battlements. The streets stretched out, lit with palisades of lamps, shaped like a wagon wheel. In the wheel's center, like an axle, rose the black tower of Tarath Imperium, a thousand feet tall.

A rumble sounded ahead, a distant chant.

The Resistance flew onward, singing their song.

Ahead, the walls of Nova Vita blazed with torchlight. Specks upon the walls grew larger, revealing themselves to be dragons, tens of thousands of them. Smoke plumed from their nostrils, and flames blasted from their maws. A thousand cannons rose between them, small as matches from here but growing larger with every flap of wings. The rumble upon the walls grew louder, becoming a battle cry, a howl for blood.

"Hail the red spiral!" rose thousands of distant voices. "For the glory of Cadigus! Purification!"

Kaelyn snarled. Her heart twisted. Fear pounded through her. But she flew on and she kept singing. She raised her voice, letting her song ring out. All around, the other dragons sang with her. Their voices rose in hope, in light, in memory.

The Legions howled ahead upon the walls.

"Slay the Resistance!"

"We will break them upon the wheel!"

"We will drink their blood!"

"Leave none alive!"

Kaelyn shivered as she flew. Her heart pounded in her throat. Ice seemed to wrap around her spine. Myriads roared for her death ahead--hundreds of thousands. Half a million troops or more waited here, each bred and broken into a machine of perfect hatred, a killer who longed for her blood. Half a million demons... flaming and screaming for her death.

She flew among two thousand.

The miles blurred below. The walls grew ahead. The Legions screamed and blasted flames. The Resistance sang their old song, voices clear and deep, a psalm of old.

In darkness and firelight, with song and with prayer, after two decades of fighting in shadows, the Resistance flew toward the ancient walls of Nova Vita, capital of Requiem.

"Old Requiem Woods, where do thy harpists play, in Old Requiem Woods, where do thy dragons--"

A thousand fuses burned. Upon the walls, a thousand cannons blasted.

Fire ripped across the sky. Smoke blasted upward. Cannonballs blazed through the night, streaked like comets, and slammed into the Resistance.

Blood sprayed. Iron tore through dragons. In death they lost their magic; they scattered in a shower of blood and human limbs.

Their song rose louder.

Kaelyn sang out the old words. Her comrades sang with her. They flew on. Their flames lit the night. They sang and they flew and though fear filled her, Kaelyn felt the light of Requiem guide her onward and glow within her.

"Cannons!" rose howls from officers ahead. "Fire!"

The Resistance sang as they flew.

Matches burned. Explosions rocked the walls, blasting smoke and flame.

A thousand more cannonballs flew through the night.

The rounds ripped into the Resistance. Hundreds of dragons howled, lost their magic, and fell dead as ravaged men and women.

Kaelyn kept singing, staring ahead.

The others flew around her.

The walls loomed closer.

Cannons fired. Smoke and blood filled the sky.

They flew over the last fields, and Kaelyn tossed back her head and blasted a jet of flame.

"Arquebuses!" she cried.

At her side, Valien roared. "Tirans, fire your guns!"

The dragons of the Resistance swooped toward the city walls.

The cannons blasted and smoke blinded them.

Hundreds of arquebuses blasted. With an explosion of smoke and flame, with a thousand *cracks* of gunpowder blasting, the iron rounds pummeled the city battlements.

Legionaries fell.

Iron rounds tore through armor, more powerful than any sword or arrow, cutting into steel like knives into butter. Blood sprayed in a mist. Men and women tumbled from the walls.

"Dragonfire!" Kaelyn shouted. She dived toward the battlements and rained her flames.

Around her, a thousand dragons of the Resistance swooped and blew fire. The walls rose in flame. Barrels of gunpowder burst, and smoke and fire covered the sky. Stone cracked. Kaelyn roared and beat her wings, churning ash and smoke. Below, she beheld a wall crumbling. Bricks rained and cannons tumbled, disappearing into clouds of dust.

"Fly, Resistance!" she shouted through the inferno. "Fly to Tarath Imperium. Crush the tower!"

She could no longer see the city, only a storm of gray and red. Cannonballs flew through dust and smoke and ash. Dragons screamed around her, lost their magic, and collapsed into bits of flesh. Kaelyn screamed and kept flying.

"Forward, Resistance!" Valien howled somewhere ahead. "Fire your guns. Blow your fire!"

Kaelyn couldn't see. She could barely hear beyond the ringing in her ears. A cannonball blasted ahead of her, missing her by inches. A second round flew behind her; it banged against her tail, knocking off a spike, and she screamed. Yet she flew on. Through the dust and smoke, she could still hear the Resistance singing their song.

"To the tower!" she cried. "Fly on, Resistance. For Requiem!"

They flew over the walls. Through the smoke, Kaelyn glimpsed the city roofs and streets. Nova Vita sprawled below her, a labyrinth of shadows and firelight.

Shrieks tore through the sky ahead.

Flames blasted toward her.

Through the thinning smoke, she saw them swarm: countless dragons of the Legions, beasts clad in steel, death in their eyes, fire in their jaws.

"Miya, are you still there?" Kaelyn shouted above her shoulder.

Upon her back, the young woman shouted back. "I'm here!"

"Fire your beam!"

Kaelyn snarled and flew toward the Legions ahead, a mass of scales and metal and smoke. They covered the sky.

"Miya!" she screamed.

The Legions howled and charged toward her, their fire blasted, and Kaelyn winced.

Red light blazed above her head and slammed into the horde.

They lost their magic.

They fell as men and women, clad in armor and bearing swords, and crashed onto the roofs and streets below.

Ahead, she saw a second red beam pierce the smoke and fire. Valien flew there, her lord, the man she loved. The silver dragon flew through fire and blood, roaring his cry. The Legions fell before him and his fire rained.

For Requiem, Kaelyn thought. *For Rune. And for Valien Eleison, the greatest man I know.*

Their guns blasted. Their beams blazed. Their fire lit the night. The Legions surrounded them, darting between the beams to burn them down. Cannonballs flew from every tower, crashing into their ranks, felling them from the sky.

The Resistance flew over the city, and they died. They died by the hundreds. Their corpses covered the roofs and walls below.

And yet the survivors flew. And they sang. They fought on, and even as their ranks crumbled, and their comrades fell dead around them, they shot forward. They plowed through the Legions, an arrow driving through a giant's flesh.

Tears in her eyes, her scales cut and burnt, Kaelyn saw it ahead, rising from smoke and fire.

Tarath Imperium soared in the night, the tower of Requiem, the pillar of Cadigus, the heart of the empire.

My childhood home.

Smoke and light filled the night. The city burned and crumbled, and thousands fell dead all around. It was the greatest battle of her life, the last battle she would fight. It was the end of the war.

With song and blood and blazing light, the remains of the Resistance, only a few hundred strong, dived over the last streets toward the dark tower.

LERESY

Leresy flew high above the city, watching it burn.

The capital blazed and crumbled, a painting in red and black. A chunk of eastern wall had fallen, and scattered fires burned around it. Cannons and arquebuses rang out, dragonfire blazed, and smoke filled the sky. Corpses lay upon roofs and towers, and blood painted the streets. The Legions covered the sky, hundreds of thousands of dragons roaring. The Resistance drove through them, shining their two remaining Genesis Scopes, cutting down thousands of dragons, sending men crashing against roofs, walls, and cobblestones.

Leresy had fought in battles before. He had defended Castra Luna. He had fought in the great Battle of Lynport. He had slain legionaries upon the beaches. Yet he had never seen such death, thousands falling from the sky, a rain of corpses. For every resistor killed, the beams sent a hundred imperial dragons falling, yet the Legions kept swarming.

"Fly at them!" their officers shouted, voices ringing across the sky. "Fly and slay them, fly around their light, fly and die for the red spiral."

As Leresy flew above, watching the carnage, a chill gripped his heart. His father was willing to send thousands to die in the Genesis Beams, all to slay only a handful of rebels. Was the death of a resistor so worthy, the life of a legionary so expendable?

"Leresy, damn you!" Tilla shouted, clutched in his left claws, still in human form.

"You're going to die here with us, Leresy!" shouted Rune, also in human form, clutched in his right claws. "The Resistance is slaying your father's troops, and they will slay you too."

Leresy snorted fire. He tightened his claws, almost snapping his prisoners' ribs; they grunted and fell silent. He shook his head wildly, clearing it of morbid thoughts. He could not contemplate morality now. He had to deliver his gifts, claim his inheritance, and save his city.

"Oh, but you are wrong, little ones," he said. "The Resistance will fail. I will save this city in its hour of need. I will deliver you to my father." He tossed his scaly neck, allowing his Genesis Scope to swing on its rope like an amulet on a chain. "Then, with my scope, I will cut down your feeble Resistance and save my empire."

He grinned. With Shari dead and his newfound glory, everything was finally falling into place.

You will finally see my worth, Father. You will finally name me your heir.

Below him, the Resistance had crossed the city center. They were attacking the palace of Tarath Imperium, the great axle of the wheel. Cannons were blazing from its walls, ripping into resistors. Imperial dragons were leaping from its tower, only to crash into the Genesis Beams and tumble a thousand feet to the ground. Dragonfire bathed the tower, smoke unfurled, and the walls shook.

Leresy laughed. "Now, Father... now as you huddle in the darkness, waiting to die, it is I--Leresy, the son you outcast and shamed--who will save you."

He cackled, almost tempted to let the Resistance swarm the palace and kill the bastard. But no. Valien would only seize the throne for himself, one despot replacing another. Leresy did not crave to see this rabble rule his empire.

"So I will save you, Father, though you disgust me," he said. "In return, I will watch you age and wither until the throne is mine."

He blasted fire, narrowed his eyes, and dived.

Smoke raced around him. Flames exploded like fireworks. A stray cannonball whistled by his side. Still he swooped, snarling, his captives clutched in his claws. Rune and Tilla screamed--human bodies were so frail, the skulls so small, squeezing under a fast descent. Yet Leresy would not slow his flight, and he sprayed fire, crashing down like a comet.

A Genesis Beam blazed his way, red and humming.

Leresy banked sharply, skirted around the beam, and kept diving. The beam shone upon a battalion of imperial dragons to his north, scattering a rain of armored men.

The steeple of Tarath Imperium reached up from a sea of smoke and fire. Black spikes crowned the tower like the claws of a giant. In the inferno of war, the tower seemed like the charred hand of a corpse. Cannons fired from its battlements, and a hundred men in black robes stood upon its roof, warriors of the Axehand Order, awaiting the resistors.

Valien and his mob swarmed from the east. The Legions surrounded the tower and covered the city. Here above the tower's crest, Leresy flew alone. Laughing, he dived toward the outreached claw of battlements. Several feet above the tower roof, he stretched his wings wide. They caught the smoky air, billowing like sails, slowing his descent. He reared in the air and shot a blazing inferno skyward.

"I am Leresy Cadigus!" he howled, beating his wings, a beast of wrath and glory. "I bear Relesar Aeternum and his whore in my claws. Open the tower doors, axehands!"

Shrieks sounded behind him.

Leresy spun to see a dozen resistors shooting toward him, rabid dragons bearing riders. Guns blazed from their saddles.

Their fire crackled. An iron round slammed into Leresy's shoulder, digging through scales into flesh, and he howled.

He landed upon the tower, pinning Rune and Tilla down under his feet. He twisted his neck, grabbed his Genesis Scope between his teeth, and popped off the lid with his tongue. More guns fired, and another round slammed into his flesh. Grimacing, holding the scope in his mouth, Leresy aimed the beam.

Red light blasted forward, lighting the resistors.

A dozen dragons, only feet away and howling for his death, lost their magic.

They resumed human forms--wild, long-haired men and women clad in leather and rags. They tumbled. Most crashed down beyond the tower and into the night. Three, the closest to Leresy, crashed against the tower roof. The Axehand Order swept forward, black robes swaying, and swung the blades strapped to their stumps. Resistors screamed and died.

Leresy panted and mewled. Two iron rounds dug into his flesh. Each was small, only the size of a marble, but crackled with agony.

He limped across the tower roof. With every step, he pressed his captives down against the floor, all but crushing them. He had to beat his wings to keep moving. The battlements towered around him, fifty feet tall, their obsidian reflecting the firelight. Across the roof, axehands chanted prayers, blades swung, and dragons roared. Fire crackled and cannons blasted, their booms deafening. Leresy's ears rang. His blood dripped. Yet he gritted his teeth and kept moving, his claws wrapped around his prisoners.

The tower trapdoor lay ahead. Fifty axehands surrounded it, blades raised. The firelight pierced their hoods, painting their iron masks a demonic red.

"Let me through," Leresy demanded, limping forward, slamming Rune and Tilla down with each step. "I've caught the escaped heir. Let me pass!"

As the battle raged beyond the battlements, the axehands stood in the firelight and smoke, hissing. One spoke, his voice ghostly, a sound like steam fleeing a kettle.

"You are Leresy the Outcast. Our lord, the God of Dragons, has banished you. Leave this place, or we will feast upon your organs for the glory of the red spiral."

Leresy hissed and blasted smoke their way. "The city is burning. I have the heir of Aeternum in my claws. I have the traitor Tilla Siren, the killer of Shari Cadigus. I have a Genesis Scope, the only weapon that can stop the Resistance now." He spat flames at their feet. "Let me pass or watch this tower fall."

The axehands stared, silent. Jets of dragonfire crisscrossed overhead. Arquebus rounds blazed; one slammed into an axehand, knocking the man down. Dragons screamed and flew above and corpses showered down. The tower shook. But Leresy only stared at the axehands, smoke rising from his nostrils, his claws gripping his prizes.

Finally, after what seemed an eternity, the axehands parted, clearing the way to the trapdoor.

Leresy barked a laugh and stepped between them, still in dragon form.

"Now grab these prisoners!" he said. "Chain them up. Drag them behind me, and we will present them to the emperor."

He tossed Rune and Tilla down, then shone his scope upon them. They were bloodied, bruised, and weak; he wondered if he'd snapped their bones. The wretches tried to escape. They could not shift under the light, but they crawled across the tower, coughing and struggling to rise.

Pathetic, Leresy thought. And yet... he found his blood heating. The boy Rune was a maggot, but Tilla... even as she crawled and gasped for breath, her skin bloody and ashy, Tilla was more intoxicating than wine. Her clothes were tattered, revealing her shapely flesh. Her eyes blazed with fury, shining like two black gems. Leresy watched her struggle and licked his lips.

I've craved you since I first saw you at Luna, he thought, and his drool dripped between his teeth. *I will bed you yet. You will be my prisoner and my concubine.*

The two struggled to their feet, pitiful lovers. Before they could take a step, the axehands swarmed around them. The robed warrior-priests grabbed them, shoved them down, and pulled chains from their cloaks. The two traitors screamed and kicked and punched. Rune managed to knock an axehand down. But they were too weak, and the axehands were too many. Within moments, the prisoners were chained, and the axehands were dragging them into the tower.

"Wait!" Leresy said. "I will lead the way. Drag the prisoners behind me."

He shifted into human form. His wounds blazed with new agony, and blood soaked his clothes, but he ignored the pain; soon all his pain would end. As the sky burned and bled, he stepped toward the prisoners. Rune and Tilla stood before him, struggling in their chains, screaming for his blood.

"My sweetness," Leresy said, approaching Tilla. Her wrists were bound, and four axehands held her still.

Leresy caressed her cheek, then pulled his hand back as she tried to bite. She spat at him but missed his face, and her spit landed at his feet. Iron rounds and fire crashed all around them, and dragons fought overhead. Blood pattered down. Chipped scales clattered around them like hail.

"I will kill you, Leresy Cadigus, you gutter worm," Tilla said, her cheeks red with fury.

He licked his lips. "Good. You're still feisty. I like that. I want you to struggle tonight as I make you mine." He snapped his fingers. "Axehands! Follow."

Grinning, he stepped through the trapdoor and into the tower.

He walked down a coiling staircase. Torches lined the walls, and the axehands walked behind him, dragging the kicking prisoners. Guards stood every few steps, armed with halberds and swords and shields, clad in black steel.

Soon they will serve me, Leresy thought. *Soon these soldiers will hail Leresy as their god.*

He laughed as he descended the steps. Finally, after all this blood and fire and pain, glory was his. Finally Shari was dead. Finally *finally* after all the agony, he--Leresy Cadigus--had emerged triumphant.

"Tonight you will see, Father," he said to the shadows as he descended. "You will see that Shari was weak, that she died like a dog. You will see that Kaelyn is a mere worm. You will see that I, your outcast son, am the strong one, the glorious one, the heir to your crown." Tears burned in his eyes, but Leresy forced himself to grin. "And you, Erry... you betrayed me. You will watch me rise to glory, and I will hunt you down, and I will force you to kneel. And I will force you to kneel too, Tilla. I will force this whole damn world to kneel and worship my glory."

He reached a corridor and marched across its black tiles. Guards stood alongside, swords drawn, waiting for battle. Within moments, Leresy knew, the Resistance could swarm down these halls like poison through the arteries of a giant. By then it would be too late for them; Leresy would have claimed his domain.

"Leresy, fight us like a man!" Tilla screamed behind, but hands muffled her cry.

Leresy's grin widened and he kept marching. When he reached a tall, bronze door, he paused and inhaled deeply.

Father's door.

The tower of Tarath Imperium rose from a sprawling palace, a complex of halls and courtyards. The throne room, far below this place, loomed so large a hundred dragons could fly within it. Intricate mosaics covered its floors, gold shone upon its columns, and paintings of dragons bedecked its ceiling. The Ivory Throne rose there, resplendent... and usually empty.

Lowborn Frey Cadigus was a soldier at heart, disdainful of pomp. Once or twice a year, he entertained guests in his throne room, putting on a show of majesty. The rest of the time, he lurked here in this tower, in the austere chamber of a soldier, a place where he could butcher his animals, torture his prisoners, and--so many times--beat his children.

Standing before this door, Leresy's knees shook, and he clenched his fists. He closed his eyes.

No, Father! cried a small voice within him. *Don't hit her. You're killing her, Father! It's I who stole the fruit. Beat me instead.*

He had stood shaking outside this door so often as a child. Beyond this door, he had screamed, bled, and hurt so much. The throne room was a place of glory, but here... here beyond this door lurked blackness, pain, and terror.

He sucked in breath.

I must not fear the shadows today, he told himself. *I suffered here as a child. But now, as a man, my glory will blaze within this darkness.*

He opened his eyes, grabbed the doorknob, and pushed the door open.

Shadows greeted him. He entered the wolf's lair.

The place looked less like the chamber of an emperor and more like a butcher shop. The bricks were rough and gray. Meat hooks hung from the ceiling, holding animal carcasses. One poor lamb was still kicking as it bled out. Some slabs of meat, those in the shadowy back, looked oddly human, skinned and red. The stench of blood and offal filled the place. Leresy swallowed, feeling ready to gag.

Emperor Frey Cadigus stood before a table laden with cleavers. Despite the battle raging outside, he hadn't donned his armor, perhaps too proud to admit any danger. Instead, he wore his bloodstained butcher's apron. In recent years, Frey spent less time governing and more time with his passion, cutting and dissecting beasts and men. The meat was never eaten. Frey Cadigus never ate meat; he only craved to cut it.

"Father!" Leresy said, marching toward him over the bloodstained floor. "I've returned."

Frey stared at him across his table. His eyes were cold chips of obsidian.

"My son," he said, lips curling in disgust. "Have I not banished you? You return now as battle rages?"

"I return now to win your battle!" he said and tossed the Genesis Scope forward. It thumped against the table. "Have you wondered how the Resistance has been felling your dragons from the sky? They're using these weapons. Here is yours--a gift worthy of an emperor. And I bring further gifts, my lord." Leresy snapped his fingers and raised his voice. "Axehand! Bring forth my prisoners."

The robed priests entered the chamber, dragging the bound Rune and Tilla. Leresy pointed at the floor, and the axehands shoved the prisoners down. Smirking, Leresy placed a boot against Tilla's neck, shoving her face against the tiles. He drew his sword and held the blade against Rune's neck, keeping the boy too pinned down.

"Behold!" Leresy said. "I've brought you imperial gifts: Lanse Tilla Siren, the traitor who slew your daughter, and Relesar, the heir of Aeternum. It is I, your son, who captured them. They are yours, Father. Accept my gifts. All I ask is that you return me to your good graces. Name me your heir, and these prizes are yours."

His heart thumped and his chest rose and fell. He had rehearsed this speech all day. His fingers trembled, and he took a shaky breath, expecting his father to beam, to embrace him, to shower him with love and approval.

But Frey only stared silently, no emotion on his face.

Leresy hissed. His breath rose to a pant. He pushed down with his foot, pressing Tilla's face hard against the tiles. The axehands knelt around him, holding the prisoners still. Frey only stared, eyes cold, saying nothing.

"Well, Father?" Leresy demanded, able to wait no longer. "Here is your key to victory! Here is your vengeance, the prize you have sought for years. I brought you victory, I brought you Shari's killer, and I brought you Relesar. I brought you all that you've ever desired. Will you not speak?"

Frey reached across the table. Leresy thought he'd grab the Genesis Scope, but instead, his hand clutched a meat cleaver. Finally he spoke.

"Is that so, Leresy?" he said, his voice dripping the same old disgust. "Did you bring me all I've ever desired? What of my desire for a worthy son, a noble heir of my own blood?"

Leresy pounded his chest. "I am here, Father! I've proven myself worthy. Reward me!"

Frey lifted the meat cleaver and turned the blade, letting the torchlight glimmer against it. "Is that all you seek, Leresy? Rewards? A treat for a begging dog? You have spoken here of yourself, of your own vainglory, of the gifts you demand. Not once have you mentioned the glory of Requiem, the honor and strength of our empire. Even now, as the Resistance smashes against our walls, as blood and fire purifies our empire... even now, you only care for your own power."

Leresy realized his error and his eyes watered. He screamed hoarsely, already knowing it was too late.

"I care for you, Father!" His voice sounded too young to him, no longer the voice of a hero, but the voice of frightened child. "I brought these for you, for--"

"For me?" Frey snorted. "I am a soldier. I fight for the eternal glory of Requiem. It is Requiem I serve, not my own hubris. It seems you've learned nothing from me. Still, after all the times I've disciplined you, you care only for yourself." He turned to stare at the axehands. "Men! Take the girl to the Red Tower. Chain her but do not torture her; that will be my pleasure. Take the boy down into my bedchambers. Chain him there; should Valien reach my halls, I would have him gaze upon the boy."

The axehands bowed and hissed.

"Yes, God of Dragons, Lord of Spiral."

They retreated from the chamber, robes swaying, clutching the screaming and kicking prisoners.

Leresy stood alone before his father.

"Well, Father?" he demanded, tears in his eyes. "Will you say no more?"

Frey fixed him with a glare. "What would you have me say?"

Leresy snorted a laugh, but it sounded more like as a sob. "Thank you, son! You saved the empire! You made me proud!" Tears ran down Leresy's cheeks and his lips shook. "I love you, son. Welcome back to my court." He hated himself, but he couldn't stop his tears, and he couldn't stop his knees from shaking. "Any of those thing would do splendidly, Father. But you have no emotion in that rotten, shriveled-up organ you call a heart. Even now, as I won you the war, as I brought you all your desires, you only stare at me like... like I'm some worm. Like I'm nothing but a common soldier." He screamed, tears falling. "I am your son!"

Frey stared at him silently for a long moment.

"Are you quite finished?" he finally said. "Yes. Yes, you are my son. As shameful as that is to admit, it's true. I do not know why the gods have cursed me so. I had two strong children; one now lies dead, and the other flies against me. Alas, it is my son--my *son*, who should be my greatest warrior--who snivels here before me, weeping like a child. But yes, Leresy. Yes, you are my son. And yes, you brought me gifts that I desired. For that, you shall be rewarded."

Leresy gasped. Hope sprang inside him, and he rubbed his eyes.

"I... I will receive your grace?" he whispered.

Frey lifted a whetting stone and began sharpening his cleaver. "When the battle is over, and we've crushed the Resistance, I will welcome you back into this city. I'll give you a small house to live in, somewhere... far in the shadows, out of my way. Perhaps in the slums around that brothel of yours. You would like that. And you shall be allowed to live out the rest of your days there, in the darkness, drunk and surrounded by your whores."

Leresy took a step forward and raised his fists. "I demand more! I demand to live in this palace. I demand to be named your heir, Father!"

Again Frey snorted. "My heir? I would sooner bed a peasant girl and name her whelp my heir than you." He fixed Leresy with a stare like stabbing daggers. "You will never be my heir. You will never be more than a miserable drunk. Now leave this palace. It is forbidden to you."

Leresy stood speechless.

His hands dropped to his sides.

His mouth worked silently.

Frey walked around him, heading toward the door. "And now I have a battle to win. I have a Resistance to crush. When I return with the head of this Valien, I expect to see you gone."

Leresy fell to his knees. He reached out, grabbed his father's leg, and clung.

"Father, please!" he said hoarsely. "I am your son!"

Frey grunted, kicked himself free, and shoved Leresy down.

"And so you keep reminding me," the emperor said. "It's a disgraceful truth I wish I could forget. If you have any honor, boy, fly out now against the Resistance and die in their fire. That is the greatest gift you could give me."

With that, Emperor Frey exited his chambers, leaving Leresy in darkness, tears, and old clutching pain. He lay on the floor, punched the tiles, and screamed.

VALIEN

He ran up the stairs, scales clattering, and slammed into the palace doors. They creaked and stood strong. Valien cursed, stepped down a few steps, and ran again. He was a burly dragon, yet when he slammed into the palace doors again, he groaned and thought his bones would crack.

"Valien, we can't hold them back much longer!" Sila shouted, standing upon the staircase. Ash, sweat, and lacerations covered the Tiran captain. He fired an arquebus, smoke blasted, and he spat.

The staircase led from the Square of Cadigus, a cobbled expanse larger than most towns, to the palace gates. The remains of the Resistance covered the steps, swords and guns in hand. Looking upon them, Valien felt his heart sink.

How many were left? Four hundred? Five? No more than that. Horror pounded through him. They had flown here with thousands... now only a handful remained.

These surviving resistors were firing arquebuses. The smoke hung thicker than storm clouds. Only Kaelyn and Erry held no guns; they were shining Genesis Scopes in every direction, holding back the swarms.

The Legions covered the city streets, the square below, and the sky above. Hundreds of thousands swarmed, a tightening noose, a puddle of scales and flames. Wherever the beams shone, imperial dragons fell from the sky. Wherever men charged in armor, swinging swords, arquebuses cut them down. Thousands fell. Their corpses covered the square in a demonic carpet of flesh. Yet for every legionary who died, more emerged. Cannons fired from within their ranks. Dragonfire blasted. Arrows flew. Every moment another resistor screamed and fell.

Valien slammed into the palace gates again. At his sides, two other dragons, gruff warriors of the Resistance, charged with him. Yet the doors were too thick, their oak iron-banded; even three dragons could not break them.

"Valien!" Kaelyn cried below, shining her Genesis Scope at a swooping battalion of dragons, sending them falling. "Valien, hurry!"

He looked upon his forces and could barely breathe. They were trapped here; the enemy surrounded them, miles deep, a colony of ants surrounding a piece of fruit. More resistors fell, torn apart by cannons and claws. Soon they were down to four hundred men, then only three. Valien could feel those old hands clutching his throat again.

We will all die.

He tossed back his head and roared, blowing fire.

Then we will die fighting.

He beat his wings and soared. He shouted commands at the two dragons who fought by his side.

"With me! Fly high."

They ascended along the palace walls, leaving the doors below. The palace bricks blurred. Arrows fired from slits, clattering against them, and one sank into Valien's shoulder. He grunted but kept flying.

A thousand imperial dragons howled above. Their claws reached out. Their maws opened, swaying in heat waves, smelters spilling fire.

"Kaelyn," Valien shouted, "your beam!"

He kept soaring, his warriors at his sides. The imperial dragons shot down. Fire blasted, and Valien winced and rose through the flame. One of his dragons screamed in the fire, lost his magic, and fell burning.

"Kaelyn!"

The Legions cackled above, their claws extended, their fangs bared, a shimmering cloud of steel and scale, and Valien kept soaring, flying into his death. Fire blazed, and his second warrior howled and fell.

Valien winced, seconds from slamming into the enemy.

Red light blazed.

The Genesis Beam slammed against the horde.

The imperial dragons lost their magic. Dozens tumbled down, screaming troops in steel.

Just below the beam, Valien growled and kept soaring. Upon the stairs below, Kaelyn kept raising the beam, clearing a path through the sky.

Through fire and smoke, Valien saw his target--the battlements of the palace hall. They overlooked the square, lined with cannons. Beyond them, Tarath Imperium rose from flames, but Valien did not care for that tower now. He shot toward the hall's crenellations.

Cannons blasted his way and Valien banked, dodging the missiles, and rose higher. He blew his flames.

Gunners screamed and fell ablaze. Some rolled upon the walls, clutching at their heated armor. Others tumbled off the battlements, living comets, burning and screaming before crashing onto the stairs below. Barrels of gunpowder exploded. The walls shook. Fires blasted out.

Valien shot toward a cannon that stood between two merlons. Its gunners were busy reloading; one man was pressing a ramrod down the barrel, while another was already lighting the fuse. When they saw Valien charge toward them, a howling silver dragon, they leaped back and drew their swords.

With a roar, Valien clawed them apart. They fell lacerated from the walls. Tail lashing, knocking back charging men, Valien grabbed the cannon.

He roared. The barrel was still searing hot; it burned his feet. He grunted and beat his wings, struggling to rise. The cannon must have weighed more than he did. He grimaced and lifted the gun into the air. With two great flaps of his wings, he cleared the battlements and began his descent.

Dragons howled and charged around him. Kaelyn was blazing her beam, carving him a path through the horde. Arrows flew. Two slammed into Valien's chest, and he roared and nearly dropped the cannon. He plummeted down, nearly at a free fall. The stairs rushed up toward him. Hardly three hundred resistors remained fighting; the rest lay dead upon the steps. Groaning, the searing barrel clutched in his claws, Valien stretched his wings wide. He slowed his fall and dropped the cannon onto the stairs, its muzzle pointing at the door. It came free from his grip with bits of seared flesh, cracking the stone steps.

"Clear the way!" he howled.

Between him and the door above, arquebusers moved aside, firing their weapons at the encroaching Legions. Bleeding and burnt, nearly too weary for fire, Valien managed a puff of flame, igniting the cannon's fuse.

He winced and stumbled aside.

The cannon fired.

Smoke blasted out, covering the stairs. The cannon flew backward, tumbling down the staircase, crashing into charging legionaries. Its projectile slammed into the palace gates.

With flame and a shower of splinters, the doors crashed open.

Valien bellowed and raced up the stairs.

"Charge!" he shouted, his voice a mere rasp, but loud enough to carry across the battle. "Resistance, into the palace. Death to Cadigus!"

The remains of his forces howled, three hundred scarred and burnt souls. They charged. They swung swords and screamed for blood.

"Death to Cadigus!"

Shouting, Valien ran through the smoke. Still in dragon form, he crashed through the shattered doors and into the palace hall.

Ahead in the shadows, palisades of columns held a grand, vaulted ceiling painted with scenes of flying dragons. A mosaic of aerial battles covered the floor, depicting wyverns and phoenixes. Far ahead rose the Ivory Throne, but tonight it stood barren.

Between Valien and the throne, hissing and glaring, stood a hundred dragons. Each wore an iron mask like a muzzle; the metal was bolted on to the flesh. Each was missing his front paw; instead, their legs ended with raised axe heads.

"Hail the red spiral!" the deformed beasts cried. "Hail Frey, God of Dragons!"

Valien blasted his dragonfire.

His flames filled the hall.

The axehands shrieked and charged.

With a roar, a green dragon shot into the hall, flew over Valien's head, and blazed a beam of red light.

The Genesis Beam fell upon the deformed dragons. They shrieked and ran afoot, men clad in black robes, swinging their axes.

Valien roared his flames. Behind him, dozens of resistors swarmed into the hall, running between and around his legs. Their arquebuses fired. The rounds tore into the axehands; the dark priests fell, writhed, and burned.

"Find the emperor!" Valien shouted, running into the hall. He whipped his head from side to side, blowing fire. Between the columns, dozens of guards were charging his way, swinging swords and firing arrows. His flames washed them. His gunners cut them down.

"Where's Frey?" Kaelyn shouted at his side, still in dragon form, her beam clutched in her claws.

He growled and stared at the throne. It was so close, only a hundred yards away, rising from fire. He could run over and seize it. But no; without Rune here, and without Frey's body, it was an empty prize.

"Kaelyn, climb the tower," he said. "Take half our forces with you. Seek Frey there."

She nodded. "What of you?"

Arrows and iron rounds blazed around them. Legionaries fell dead at their feet.

"I'll search the ground complex," Valien said. He swung his tail and sent a legionary flying.

As the fires roared and the blood spilled, she met his gaze, and for an instant they stood still, staring at each other. Her eyes glimmered, those hazel eyes that had guided him for years, the beacons of his soul, his starlight in the dark. He loved her, and he saw the love in her eyes, and he knew her thoughts. They were the same thoughts he himself was thinking.

I might never see you again.

He wanted to hold her, to speak of his love, to share a last embrace. But the battle raged. Soldiers fell dead all around. One arrow flew between them, and another snapped against his scales.

"Valien," she whispered.

"Go!" he said. "Climb the tower and find him."

She nodded, shifted into human form, and ran between the columns. She shouted orders, and men ran behind her, firing guns and clearing a path through the Legions.

Valien grunted, spun around, and flamed three charging men. He shifted into human form too, drew his sword, and bared his teeth. About a hundred resistors stood around him.

"Sila!" he shouted to the sailor. "Take your men and search the dungeons. Everyone else, follow me. We'll find the bastard."

Snarling, he raced between the columns, leading fifty warriors. He swung his sword, and gunners fired around him. They moved into a corridor, cutting men down, splashing the walls with blood. They fought for every step.

As he killed, Valien could not stop seeing her eyes in his mind, and the terror ignited his blood. He might die this day. He might find Rune dead in the dungeons. He might never seize the throne. But most of all he feared for Kaelyn. He roared, swung his sword, and carved a path of corpses.

KAELYN

She ran upstairs, swinging her sword and cutting men down.

Fifty resistors ran behind her. Two ran at her sides; the stairway was just wide enough for three to climb abreast. Legionaries shouted above, running down toward them, swinging longswords.

"Fire!" Kaelyn shouted.

The resistors at her sides pulled their triggers. Their arquebuses blasted; they were so loud her ears rang. Four legionaries crashed down above, pierced with the rounds. Two more raced her way, and Kaelyn swung Lemuria. Her sword crashed through one's armor, severing his arm. She parried the second man's blow, swung down, and cleaved his helm. Their bodies crumbled, and Kaelyn ran across them, climbing higher.

"Men, swap!" she cried.

The men at her sides, their guns smoking, retreated down the staircase to reload. Two more fighters, their guns loaded and ready, replaced them.

"Hail the red spiral!" cried legionaries above, swarming downstairs.

"Fire!" Kaelyn said again, and two more guns blasted. Two more men retreated to reload, and two more, their guns ready, replaced them. Kaelyn screamed and thrust her sword. She trampled corpses and climbed on.

She climbed for hours, it seemed, corkscrewing up the tower. Her men kept firing and retreating, moving in a constant cycle. Their guns cut down the legionaries, blasting through armor, killing two--sometimes three--men deep. All those legionaries who escaped the gunfire met Kaelyn's blade.

A hundred cuts covered her. A gash on her thigh bled--the same place Shari had wounded her almost two years ago, the night she had flown to Lynport, seeking Rune. She howled, driving onward, climbing floor by floor. Her limbs shook and her ears rang, but she fought on.

I will always fight on, she thought. *Until my last drop of blood. Until the last beat of my heart.*

"Father!" she shouted as she climbed. "Father, come face me! Are you a coward?"

But she heard only his Legions, the endless chants, the bloodthirsty cries of those he'd molded into killers. And she killed them. She slew them with steel and iron, and their blood covered her, stinging her lips, coppery and sweet.

You made me a killer too, Kaelyn thought, swinging her sword. *You made me a greater killer than any in your Legions. I can forgive you for killing my people. But I can never forgive you for making me kill yours.*

"Father!" she shouted. "Face me! It's me, Kaelyn. Do you hear?"

Arrows whistled down from above. The men at her sides screamed and fell, and their guns clattered down. Kaelyn ducked. An arrow flew over her head, slicing her hair. She grabbed a fallen arquebus, screamed, and fired. The gun blasted, blinding her with smoke, nearly knocking her down the steps. When the smoke dispersed, she saw two fallen legionaries above, but more stood behind them, ready to charge.

She rose to her feet. She swung her sword and cut a man down. She fought on.

When shouts rose behind her, she cursed. The Legions were charging up the stairs from below too, trapping her and her men. She fought onward, killing with every step. An arrow slammed into her left arm, and she cried out in pain. She kept climbing.

"Father, come and face me!"

She ascended another few steps. Men fell before and behind her. The stairs were slick with blood.

"Father!"

A cackle rose above, muffled behind the walls. "Kaelyn, my sweet traitor! Have you fought all this way to scream under my punisher?"

She sucked in air. It was his voice, the voice she had heard a thousand times in her nightmares.

My father.

She kept climbing. Her left arm hung uselessly, pierced with an arrow. Her leg bled. Her head spun. Yet still she killed. Cut, burnt, and pierced with arrows, her men fought around her. Ten more steps, and Kaelyn saw a red door. The cackling rose beyond it.

The sight of this door pierced her with more pain than her wounds.

"No," she whispered. "Oh stars, no, not here."

Frey Cadigus kept many chambers in this palace. His throne room, a hall of glory, lay far below. Still farther above, near the tower's crest, festered his butcher room, the place where he slaughtered both beasts and men. Yet here, Kaelyn thought, here behind this door lay the true heart of his madness.

"His trophy room," she whispered. "The center of his pride and insanity."

"Kaelyn!" he shouted, voice echoing beyond the door. "Kaelyn, my sweetest betrayer. Do you remember this place? Come inside, Kaelyn, and scream for me."

Guns fired over her shoulders. Legionaries clattered down. Kaelyn could no longer see the men battling around her. She could only stare at that door. She could only see the old nightmares.

"This is the room you are most proud of," she whispered. She grabbed the arrow in her arm, grimaced, and pulled it out with a gush of blood. "This is the room where I kill you."

She kicked the door open, barged inside, and swung her sword.

A crowd of axehands ran her way.

Kaelyn clutched her sword with both hands and ran toward them.

Behind her, her fellow resistors charged into the room. Guns blazed. Smoke filled the chamber; Kaelyn couldn't see farther than her blade's tip. She spun in circles, cutting limbs, kicking men down. All around the guns fired, steel sparked, axes flashed, and blood sprayed. The iron masks of the axehands leered at her. A blade sliced across her side.

"Father!" she shouted. "Face me alone! Call back your thugs and face me, coward."

The clanging of steel and crashing of guns rang out. Every heartbeat, more bodies thudded to the floor. Blood sluiced around her boots. When the screaming died and the dust settled, Kaelyn found herself standing alone. Corpses surrounded her, resistors and axehands alike.

All lay dead.

Kaelyn stood panting, Lemuria still clutched with both hands.

I stand alone.

She took a step farther into the chamber, sword trembling in her hands.

"Father?" she whispered.

Her head spun. She walked hesitantly, stepping over corpses. She saw nobody living. Could Frey have died among his axehands? Heart thudding, she stepped deeper. Her knees shook. Her breath shook in her lungs. Blood dripped from her wounds, but she moved on, whipping her head from side to side, seeking him. The eyes of the dead stared up at her. The stench of death flared so powerfully Kaelyn almost gagged.

Deeper into the chamber, candles glowed and she saw his trophies.

A chill ran through her.

Thousands of years ago, the first King Aeternum had raised a marble column in the forest. King's Column had stood since; ancient magic protected it. Frey had smashed the rest of the old palace, but King's Column remained, and all his cannons and dragons could not topple it. Instead, Frey had built Tarath Imperium around the pillar, a black tumor growing around a single white bone. That ancient marble rose inside Frey's tower, the stairway coiling around it like a snake coiling around a rod.

In this chamber, surrounded by black walls, Kaelyn saw the capital of Aeternum's ancient monument.

The column rose only three hundred feet tall; most of Tarath Imperium still towered above. This room was Frey's museum for Aeternum's fallen glory. The column's capital stood forlorn, pale and glimmering, carved in the shape of rearing dragons. If Frey could not smash it, he would display it like a master displaying a chained slave.

All around the marble artifact, he displayed the rest of his trophies. The severed heads of the Aeternum family floated here in jars, each standing upon an obsidian pedestal. Their faces stared at Kaelyn, still torn in anguish. Their swords lay shattered upon the floor.

A glass tank, six feet tall, stood here too. Kaelyn had never seen this trophy before. Liquid filled the container, and a woman floated there, her body naked and cut with red spiral scars. She had wavy hair the color of honey, feline features, hazel eyes, and a pale face strewn with freckles.

The woman looked exactly like Kaelyn.

"Marilion," she whispered.

A voice spoke in the shadows.

"Marilion Brewer of Cadport, that was her name. Wife to Valien. Sister of that drunkard who raised Relesar in his tavern. Such a beauty. Such a waste." Frey emerged from the shadows, placed a hand upon the glass, and admired the floating corpse. "I told Valien that she still lives in my dungeon. The fool must have believed me. He took the bait and came here. I lured him out of his hiding and into my lair." He turned toward Kaelyn. "And now he will die, my daughter. Now you will die too. You both will float here with her."

Kaelyn screamed and charged.

Frey stepped back, and Lemuria slammed against the tank, scratching the glass. The woman inside swayed and seemed to stare at Kaelyn, eyes still wide in pain, mouth open in a silent scream.

Kaelyn raced around the tank, all her weakness gone, all her pain drowning under rage. She swung Lemuria and met her father's blade.

He had drawn his sword, a monstrous hunk of black steel named Fellwair, a weapon as long as Kaelyn's entire body. She had seen him severe his enemies' heads with this steel, seen him hack into flesh and lick the blood. It was the blade he had killed the Aeternum family with, the blade that had slaughtered the last soul of Osanna, that had killed Marilion.

Now this terror swung toward her, and Kaelyn screamed as she parried.

"You've returned to me, my daughter," Frey said, and a cold smile twisted his face. "Do you remember this chamber? Do you remember how I chained you here, how I forced you to stare at the heads, how I beat you until you wept?" He snarled and swung his sword. "I will hurt you here again, my daughter, more than ever. I will hurt you here for years before I let you die."

She screamed and thrust Lemuria.

"You will never more hurt me." She could barely see him; she had lost too much blood, was too hurt, too weak, but she fought on. "You die tonight, Father. No, you are no father to me. You are nothing but a beast."

He laughed, a mirthless and cold sound.

"Is that so, daughter?" he asked. "Already you weaken. I see the blood soaking your clothes, draining from your flesh, leaving you weak and pale. You cannot best me in swordplay. Nor can your pitiful Resistance hurt me." He blocked another blow and sighed. "Oh, my dear, foolish daughter. Do you not see? I have planned all of this."

She screamed and swung her blade. It sparked against his own.

"Silence, liar! For years I suffered under your heel. For years I fought you. Tonight you die."

He parried languidly. He did not even bother attacking.

"Do you not see, my wayward child? I knew of your island all along. I let you linger there. I placed the lure and watched you come. I drew you into my trap... and now you are here. Your warriors lie dead outside. Your friend Valien seeks me in the twisting halls; his men too are dying." He shook his head in mock sadness. "Oh, my poor child. You and Valien have done exactly what I wanted. Soon you and he will scream here together. The boy Relesar will scream too. Who will scream the loudest, I wonder?"

She trembled as she fought. Her eyes stung.

"You lie!" she screamed. She slammed her sword against his breastplate, but could not pierce it. "All you do is lie."

"And yet you shiver. And yet you weep. Your Resistance is fallen; you know this. All your hope is faded like the starlight of old gods." His face hardened. "My eldest daughter proved herself weak. My son proved himself a fool. And you, Kaelyn... you are the worst among them. You are a traitor." He snarled and his eyes blazed. "Now is your time to suffer."

Finally he thrust his blade.

Fellwair, black and wide and over five feet long, swung through the air. The blade caught the firelight and burned red. Kaelyn raised her sword, her slim and short Lemuria, and the blades clashed. Sparks rose in a fountain. She wanted to thrust again, to chip at his armor, to crack the steel and slay him. But she was too slow. She had lost too much blood. It was all she could do to parry.

Frey fought with bared teeth, eyes narrowed, his face demonic. He swung his sword again and again, slamming it into Lemuria, showering sparks. With every blow, pain shot up Kaelyn's arm. She thought her shoulder would dislocate.

She panted. Sweat and blood drenched her. Fellwair swung down. With a scream, Kaelyn raised her sword and parried.

The blow knocked her to her knees.

She knelt before her father, panting, bleeding, praying. He raised his sword again.

No, she thought, *no, I can't die now. I must live. For Requiem. For Valien. For Rune and my brother and everyone else.* She took a shuddering breath.

"I am Kaelyn Cadigus," she whispered. She struggled to rise, legs shaking. "But I foreswear your name. Know this, Father. When you are dead, I will marry Valien Eleison. Your grandsons will carry his name." She stared into his eyes and raised her bloodied blade. "But they will not know of you. They will not know you are my father. Your legacy will die."

With a howl, she drove forward, exposing her left side, ready to suffer his sword for a chance to pierce his neck.

But he did not take the bait.

He could have stabbed her left arm, severing it. He could have attacked and maimed her, allowing her right arm to slay him. But he only stepped back defensively. His blade swung sideways, biting Kaelyn's fingers.

Her blood spurted.

She screamed. Her sword flew from her hand; so did two of her fingers.

She howled. She tried to grab the dagger in her boot, but her left arm was numb from the arrow. Her right hand gushed blood. And Kaelyn knew she had lost this battle.

The chamber spinning around her, she tried to retreat. She took a few steps back, her heels banged against a corpse, and she fell. She landed upon bodies. Before she could scramble up, he was upon her.

Frey's hands reached out. His one hand clutched her throat and squeezed. The other pulled her hair. He leered down, his face twisted into something between a grin and a snarl, something monstrous and insane.

Please, Father, I'm sorry I ate the fruit! Please, don't hit me.

Again she huddled under her bed, a screaming child, as his hands reached into the darkness, clutched her, pulled her into this very chamber to beat her.

"Please, Father," she whispered.

His grip on her throat tightened. Her eyes rolled back. Darkness fell into nightmare and endless screams echoed.

VALIEN

He stumbled down the corridor, bleeding and alone. With a final gasp, the last of his warriors--a young woman with flaming red hair--fell dead.

So weak he could barely see, Valien leaped forward. He swung his sword, shattering the head of her killer. The axehand, his blade dripping, crashed down.

Valien stood in place, panting. His chest rose and fell, and his breath wheezed. He looked around and saw nothing but dead. They filled the hallway, axehands and resistors alike. Their blood pooled and splashed the walls.

And so the Resistance ends, he thought. If Kaelyn and her men fell too, he was the last. The last resistor. The last hope of Requiem. And his light too was flickering. Valien wanted to fall, to lie down, to join his comrades. He would close his eyes, let his blood flow, and his soul would rise to the starlit halls of his ancestors.

He fell to his knees, head spinning, blood flowing down his arms. His sword clanged to the floor.

The dead woman stared up at him, and her face did not seem pained or frightened, but soft, welcoming, her eyes large and green. She was at peace. She sang among the white columns of their forebears, a land of eternal glory.

On his knees among the corpses, Valien looked up. The ceiling was black and bloody, but Valien imagined that he could see beyond it. The old palace of Requiem rose among the stars, celestial and shimmering.

"The true palace still shines above," Valien whispered, gazing up at the ceiling. "A reflection in the stars. You wait for me there, Marilion. You wait for me there, all those who fell."

He took a shuddering breath and reached up, almost feeling that warmth, almost seeing that glow.

A scream shattered the illusion.

Valien lowered his gaze and stared down the hall.

The scream sounded again--high, pained, and pleading.

Valien inhaled sharply.

"Kaelyn," he whispered.

With a raspy breath that burned his throat, he pushed himself to his feet. He lifted his sword and took a step forward. Grunting, he trudged on.

He wanted to shout her name but forced himself to remain silent; he would not reveal his location. He stepped over corpses, moving silently, barely daring to breathe. His hair dangled over his face, slick with blood.

The scream sounded again, then died off. Valien hissed and clutched his sword. The call had come from nearby, only a chamber or two away. He kept moving down the corridor. Torches crackled on the walls and blood trickled between the floor tiles. No more guards filled this place; he saw only bodies.

I'm coming for you, Kaelyn, he thought. His chest shook and he plowed on. He could no longer hear the scream. Had Frey killed her? Would he find her dead, Frey's sword thrust into her belly, like he'd found Marilion all those years ago?

A whimper rose down the hall.

Kaelyn. It was her; he was sure of it.

Breath shuddering, Valien trudged onward. He held his sword in bloodstained hands. As he walked down the hall, he realized that he knew this place. He had walked here before. Twenty years ago, white tiles had covered the floor, and instead of an eastern wall, a portico of marble columns had revealed forested hills. Today the hall was black and narrow but... this was the same place. Valien could feel it.

Sweat beaded on his brow and his fingers shook. A few more steps and he saw a door--a door he knew would be there.

He stepped forward. Hand slick with blood and trembling with weakness, he pulled the door open. He stared into the chamber.

His breath left him and his eyes watered. He felt like ash melting in the rain, all his hardness fading into shimmering memory.

In the past twenty years, this palace had spread and rotted like a canker, but his chambers had remained untouched. His old tapestries still hung from the walls, depicting scenes of sunset over forests and mountains. The same vases and mugs still stood upon his table; even the dried roses were still there. His bed stood by the wall, topped with the quilts Marilion had woven--the bed where he would love her, where he'd sleep holding her, where he'd found her dead.

"He kept it the same," Valien whispered. "Why?"

A voice answered him. "Because I knew you would return."

Valien growled, stepped into the chamber, and turned to his right.

His world seemed to burn and his heart froze.

"Let them go," he rasped and raised his sword. His heart unlocked and burst into a gallop. His fist shook around his hilt. "Let them go, Frey."

The emperor smiled thinly. "Welcome to my bedchamber, Valien Eleison. Welcome to your old home."

Frey Cadigus stood clad in his imperial armor, a suit of black plates that covered him from toe to neck. His pauldrons flared out, and motifs of golden dragons coiled across his breastplate. His sword hung across his back. He held an arquebus, the gun bloody. The fuse was crackling like a pipe, the flashpan full of powder.

Before the emperor, in sight of his muzzle, Rune and Kaelyn sat tied to chairs.

Valien struggled for breath. He took a step closer, reaching out to them, but Frey pulled the trigger back a hair's width. The gun creaked. Valien froze.

"Rune," he whispered. "Kaelyn."

They were wounded; they looked within a few breaths of death. Burns and welts rose across Rune's flesh, peeking from the tatters of his clothes, and he was thin, thinner than he'd ever been. His cheeks were ashen, his eyes sunken. He met Valien's gaze. His mouth was gagged, but in his eyes, Valien saw relief mingling with fear.

Heart wrenching, Valien turned to look at Kaelyn. Blood seeped between the ropes that bound her to the chair. More blood dripped down a wound in her arm; it looked like the hole of an arrow. A gash ran across her thigh, and two fingers were missing from her right hand; the stumps bled. She too was gagged. She too looked at him, her eyes wide and fearful but loving.

"It's all right," Valien whispered to them. "I'm going to get you out of here. This ends now."

Frey grinned, gun in hands. "Yes... you can save one of them." He licked his lips, turned his eyes away from his prisoners, and looked at Valien. Mockery filled his eyes. "I have only one round for this crude contraption I stole off one of your warriors. I can slay only one of your little friends."

Valien took another step forward, but Frey *tsk*ed and hefted his gun. Valien froze.

"Frey, enough of this," he rasped. "Put the gun down and draw your sword. Face me like a man, not a coward."

"Oh, but I will face you," said Frey. "We will duel with swords, the duel we should have had years ago, the duel you fled from. But first... first, my old friend, I will slay one of these two wretches. And I will let you choose." His licked his lips. "Choose, old friend."

Valien snarled and raised his sword. "Enough of these games. I've not come here to play, but to fight you. Place down your gun. Do not toy with me."

Frey only laughed, a sickly sound, and sucked in air between his teeth. "Will you have me choose then? Perhaps the boy?" He turned the muzzle toward Rune. "Ah... the young heir of Aeternum. The babe you saved all those years ago. The whelp you fought this war for, the hope of Requiem, the backside you hope will warm my throne." The emperor chuckled, a sound like blood bubbling from a wound. "Should I slay him with my single round?"

When Valien hissed and took another step forward, Frey shook his head and turned his muzzle toward Kaelyn.

"Or perhaps," Frey said, "I will slay my daughter. The fair, beautiful Kaelyn. The woman who betrayed me. The woman you love." He raised his eyebrows. "She has spread her legs for you, I know it. She is a whore and yet you love her. Perhaps I should fire my gun at her?"

Valien stood frozen, shaking with rage and fear, daring not take another step. "Fire your gun, and before you can draw your sword, you will die."

Frey nodded. "Perhaps. But I think I should have enough time to draw my sword, to duel you, perhaps to slay you too. Who would win a fight between us? I do not know. I know only one thing." He stared at Valien, all amusement gone from his eyes. "One of these two will die. Rune or Kaelyn. The heir or the lover. Twenty years ago, you chose Rune over the woman you loved. You saved him and let your wife die. She died in this very chamber, in this very bed where I now sleep every night. Choose again, Valien Eleison. Choose now or I will choose for you."

Valien wheezed for breath. He looked back at them. Both Rune and Kaelyn struggled in their bonds. They stared at him, eyes pleading, and he saw the words in their gazes. They each wanted him to choose the other.

"Choose!" Frey demanded. "The fuse burns low; you have only a few heartbeats left. Choose, Valien! The boy who can heal Requiem or the woman who can heal your heart. Choose!"

The fuse flickered. Frey raised his gun and bared his teeth, ready to fire.

Valien grimaced, his eyes burned, and his breath froze.

I cannot choose, he thought. *I cannot!*

Again that night returned to him, that night twenty years ago. Frey's men had swept through the halls, killing all in their path. Marilion had waited in this chamber, Rune in a nursery across the palace.

I chose Rune then, he thought. *I chose hope for Requiem.*

He looked at Rune now, a grown man, a man he could crown tonight. He looked at Kaelyn, the woman he'd flown with for so long, the woman he loved, the woman who filled his heart with so much light.

When Marilion died, he thought, *I broke. I fell into darkness, into drink, into madness.* He looked into Kaelyn's hazel eyes. *You saved me, Kaelyn. You saved me from the wreck that I was. You gave me strength to fight. You gave me something to fight for. I cannot lose you too.*

"Choose!" Frey shouted. "Choose now, Valien!"

Valien lowered his head.

All sounds faded.

He closed his eyes.

"Spare Kaelyn," he whispered.

For a moment the silence continued. Then Frey began to laugh--a dry, crackling sound like twigs breaking. His laughter grew until he was cackling.

He pointed his gun at Rune.

Tied in the chair, the young man looked up and gave Valien a last look. Rune nodded and Valien's eyes dampened. In his eyes, Rune was saying: *I understand. I accept. Goodbye.*

A scream rose outside.

A shadow darkened the window.

Frey pulled the trigger.

The arquebus blasted smoke.

A red dragon crashed through the window, roared, and shifted into human form.

"I will kill you, Father!" screamed Leresy, leaping through the air, a dagger in hand. "Die, bastard!"

The iron round slammed into Leresy's chest, spraying red mist.

Still screaming, the prince slammed against Frey and drove his dagger into the man's neck.

Father and son crashed down, screaming and struggling. Leresy howled, pulled his dagger back, and thrust it down again and again, stabbing madly and screaming. Frey gasped, blood spurting from his neck and cheeks.

"Die, you bastard!" Leresy cried. His tears poured and blood covered his arms. "Die! Die... I..."

The prince coughed blood, fell over the corpse of his father, and trembled.

Valien raced toward the shattered window. Rune and Kaelyn still sat tied to their chairs, glass shards in their hair. Valien cut through the ropes, freeing them.

They rose on shaky limbs, and Valien pulled them into an embrace, a crushing grip, and his eyes watered, and he held them and gasped and wept.

"It's over," he whispered, chest shaking, and held them close. "It's over. You're safe. You're safe."

He kissed their bloodied cheeks and tasted their tears.

KAELYN

Countless thoughts rattled in her head, vying for dominance.

We won the war.

I'm wounded and bleeding.

My father is dead.

Rune is alive.

My fingers are gone.

She trembled in Valien's embrace, and each thought howled inside her, each alone enough to overwhelm her. Yet as the voices rattled, one emerged above the rest, bringing tears to her eyes.

My brother is hurt.

She disentangled herself from Valien, limped forward, and fell to her knees above Leresy.

"Oh, Ler," she whispered.

He had fallen off their father. He lay on his back, smiling wanly. A hole gaped open in his chest. He placed a hand against the wound and coughed weakly, blood on his lips.

"Look at us, sister," he said. He coughed again but did not lose his soft smile.

She wept. She knelt over him, touched his cheek, and placed her second hand above his.

"I'm going to take care of you," she whispered. "You're going to be all right."

He laughed--a weak, choked sound. "I've got a hole in my chest a rodent could crawl through. But I killed him, Kae. I killed him for us." His smile turned into a sob. "He can't hurt you anymore. Never again."

She nodded. Her voice was so soft she could barely hear herself. "He can't hurt anyone anymore." She looked over her shoulder at Valien and Rune who stood watching. "Get bandages! Get medicine! We have to heal him, we--"

Leresy gripped her hand. "It's too late for me, sister. Look at me again. I want to die seeing your face."

She turned her eyes back toward him. "You can't die. I won't let you."

With a shaky hand, his fingers bloody, he reached up and touched her cheek. He whispered so softly she had to lean down to hear.

"Sister... make this a good kingdom. Whoever takes this throne... make sure they do a good job."

She nodded. She could no longer even whisper, only mouth the words. "I will."

"Find Erry." Leresy blinked his damp eyes. "Look after her. Give her gold and a house to live in. Make sure she has a good life. Tell her... tell her that I forgive her. No. Don't tell her that. Tell her that she was right and that I'm sorry. Tell her that I love and that I'm so sorry."

She pulled him into an embrace. "You will tell her."

He shook his head. "Goodbye, my sister, my twin, my Kaelyn." He smiled and suddenly all pain left his face; he seemed at peace, as if already floating toward the starlit halls. "And make this a good life for you, Kae. May your wings always find our sky."

He went limp in her arms.

She held him against her for a long time, whispering to him, praying as his soul rose.

TILLA

She stood atop the tower of Tarath Imperium, gazed upon the city, and closed her hand around the hilt of her sword.

It was too quiet.

Frey Cadigus was dead, but the sun rose as always. Below in the streets, people emerged to their daily routines. Merchants hawked food in distant markets. Shops opened their doors. Hammers rang on anvils, smoke rose from smelters, and saws ground in sawmills. People moved along the streets, busy selling, buying, working, and living.

Tilla shook her head. This... this was wrong. She had expected... what? The Legions still attacking, sworn to slay the Resistance even with their emperor dead? A hundred claimants to the throne, bastards or madmen or distant relatives of Cadigus? She did not know. But when hearing of Frey's death, she had expected... not anvils ringing but cannonballs blasting, not smoke pumping from chimneys but the blaze of dragonfire.

Yet here she was. Frey lay dead and the city bustled with life.

"But I cannot forget," she whispered from the tower, eyes stinging. "I cannot just go on with my life."

She raised her chin and closed her eyes. Rune had won his war. He had slain the tyrant. But Tilla still had her war to fight. She still had her vengeance to claim.

She opened her eyes and nodded. She would do what she must.

With a deep breath, she leaped off the tower.

She tumbled down, shifted into a dragon, and caught the wind. She glided toward the Square of Cadigus below--or whatever its name might be now--and landed outside the palace gates. They still stood smashed, guarded by a handful of surviving resistors. Tilla walked between them--they knew her as Relesar's ward, the woman they had unchained from the Citadel--and entered the palace hall.

She walked between the columns, boots thudding against the mosaic, and drew her sword. Ahead rose the throne.

They stood around it, the survivors of the Resistance, no more than fifty men and women, most still wearing their tattered, bloody clothes. They were bandaged, weary, and covered in grime, and they ruled the world.

As Tilla stepped closer, her eyes stung and her breath shook.

"Which one of you is him?" she called out, voice hoarse. "Who among you is Valien Eleison, leader of the Resistance?"

She did not even need to ask. As she stepped closer, she knew who it was. Only one here stood with the aura of command. He was a tall man, broad-shouldered but haggard. His shaggy hair framed a weathered face and eyes full of scars--not the scars of knives, but the deeper wounds of the soul. Tilla almost lost her step. She had expected to see a demon, a barbaric warrior leering and drinking the blood of his enemies. Yet this man seemed weary beyond reckoning, an aging, outcast knight who longed to lower his blade. He seemed almost pathetic, a man who hated battle yet whose honor forced him to fight on.

Tilla sucked in her breath, raised her head, and banished all sympathy from her heart.

He might seem weary, even kind, but he killed my brother. She stepped toward him, sword raised. *He would not have seemed so harmless that day years ago.*

"Are you Valien?" she said.

His warriors--perhaps they were no longer *resistors*, for their Resistance had triumphed--drew blades and stepped toward her. Valien raised his hand, holding them back. They froze.

"I am Valien," he said. His voice was but a rasp, the sound of a strangled man. "Will you give me the courtesy of your name?"

She took another step toward him, sword raised. She considered giving him her new surname, the noble one Shari had bestowed upon her, but decided against it. She was no longer Tilla Siren; that woman had died with Shari.

"I am Tilla Roper," she said through a tight jaw. "Does that name mean anything to you?"

She saw that it did. Understanding filled his eyes. At his side, a young archer with long, golden hair breathed deeply, and her eyes softened.

Valien's rasp dissolved into a whisper. "Rune told me about you."

Her sword wavered in her hand. "Then draw your blade! Draw it and fight me, if you wish to die like a man, or I will kill you like a dog." She spat at him, narrowly missing his boot. "Draw your steel. Fight me and I will kill you like you killed my brother."

Her eyes burned and her chest heaved. She waited for him to rage, to draw his blade, to howl and lunge at her. But he only stood still, and no bloodlust filled his eyes, only sadness.

"I won't fight you, Tilla," he said. "I have fought for too long. I have swung my sword too many times. The war is over. Let no more blood spill."

She stepped closer, sword pointed at Valien, close enough that if she just leaned forward, her blade would cut him.

"Do you confess then that you killed him?" She wanted her words to sound strong, to speak with the authority of an officer, but today her voice cracked. "Do you confess your murder? Confess now before you die."

He looked into his eyes. There was no hardness to his stare, no malice, no fear, no hate... only weariness.

"I confess," he said, and Tilla snarled and prepared to thrust her blade, but he continued speaking. "I confess to killing many. I killed dozens with my own hands, Tilla Roper of Lynport, maybe hundreds. I sent tens of thousands to die; their blood stains my hands too. If you kill me now, you would be justified in doing so, perhaps. Thousands across Requiem grieve for brothers, sons, daughters, fathers... people I killed. Their deaths still haunt me. I will grieve for every soul I had to extinguish. Did I kill your brother too? Perhaps. You might find me heartless to say this, but the truth is, I don't know. I killed too many; I don't know their names. But know this: If your brother fell to my sword, his death too weighs upon my soul."

Her tears fell and her sword wavered in her grip. "Do you think contrition can save you now? Do you think some convoluted apology, if that's what this was, can save your life?"

He smiled thinly. "I don't know. But I know that I won't fight you; as I've said, I've fought too much already. And I know that Rune loves you. And I know that you saved his life. If you are a person he loves, I don't think you will slay me here."

Tilla's nostrils flared, her tears fell, and she panted.

You are wrong, coward, she thought, barely able to see, and readied her sword to strike.

"Wait!" rose a voice.

Tilla froze, her sword an inch from Valien's neck. She turned to see the young, golden-haired archer reaching out toward her. Tilla noticed that the woman was missing two fingers on her right hand; the stubs were bandaged.

"Wait," the young woman repeated. She heaved a sigh. "Valien did not kill your brother."

"How do you know?" Tilla demanded, teeth bared.

"Because I killed him." The archer lowered her head. "I am Kaelyn Cadigus, daughter of Frey, fighter of the Resistance." She looked back up at Tilla, and her eyes were damp. "I don't know the names of all my kills either, but I know some. I know the first one. I'm sorry, Tilla. I'm so sorry."

Tilla could barely stay standing. She hated herself for it, but her tears kept falling. She howled, the howl of a wounded animal, and spun her sword toward Kaelyn.

"Why?" she said. "Why did you kill him? He was only a ropemaker. Oh, stars. He was good."

Kaelyn nodded. "I know. Many who are good fight for evil men. He fought for Frey, same as you did, same as almost every youth in Requiem did. He flew against me. He fought well. We fought as dragons over the eastern skies. He was the first man I killed." She closed her eyes. "I was only sixteen, only a child, but... even a young dragon's fire burns bright. I still see him dying in my dreams."

Tilla closed her eyes too.

And I still see my first kill, she thought. She saw him now too, the quarryman in the hut. *I burned him. I sliced open his belly and let him bleed out. And every night, I still hear his screams.*

Tilla heard a clang and realized she had dropped her sword.

"I wasn't meant to be this person," she whispered. "I wasn't meant to hold a sword, to fight, to kill, to torture." She opened her eyes and looked at Kaelyn through her tears, not knowing why she spoke these words to this stranger, but unable to stop. "I'm just a ropemaker, but he made me a soldier. He made me kill so many. And I obeyed him. I murdered for him. I killed hundreds. And I still hear their screams." She took a step toward Kaelyn. "How do you forget? How do you wash the blood from your hands?"

Kaelyn smiled, a sad smile like a single ray of light breaking through clouds. "I don't think you can forget. I think you just keep living, and you try to do good. You try to build with your hands that once swung a sword or fired a gun. You try to bring life to a world you burned."

A voice spoke behind them from across the hall, and footfalls echoed.

"And now is the time to bring life. Now is the time for laying down swords, the time to lift sickle and loom and hammer. It's time to rebuild this world."

Tilla turned around and saw him there across the hall, walking toward her.

Rune.

His dark hair fell across his brow. His scars were fading. He wore a new doublet and cloak, and his eyes were somber.

My Rune, she thought. *The boy I grew up with. My best friend. My lover. My future king... a man I no longer know. A man named Relesar. A stranger.*

"And will you rebuild this realm as king?" she asked, and a new sadness filled her. He had his throne. He had an empire to rule. And she... what did she have?

He reached her. He took her hands and squeezed them, his grip warm, and his eyes stared into hers.

"We will rebuild it together," he said.

She scoffed and her eyes still stung. "You would have me be your queen? Do you think that's what I want?" She shook her head. "You are mistaken. I don't belong in this place. I don't belong up here in this capital anymore. And nor do you, Rune Brewer." She shook her head, cursing her damn eyes that would not stay dry. "You're just a damn brewer's boy."

He smiled and nodded. "That's all I want to be. Queen? Tilla Roper, if you were queen of Requiem, the realm would just suffer under another tyrant." He winked.

She growled and tried to pull her hands free, but he held them tight. "Why do you mock me? Will you marry Kaelyn then?" Her jealousy flared, and she hated herself for that too.

He shook his head. "I will marry you."

She growled. "Damn you, Rune! I told you. I'm not going to be your damn queen."

"Oh stars, Tilla! You are dense." He rolled his eyes. "I don't want you to be my queen, I told you that. And I don't want this throne." He squeezed her hands. "I want us to go back home--together. I want you to rebuild Lynport with me."

A stunned silence fell... and then the throne room erupted.

Everyone began shouting at once.

Kaelyn grabbed Rune's collar and shook him, yelling that he was the heir, that he had to sit upon this throne. Valien was emitting that rasp of his, insisting that they had fought this war for Rune, to return Requiem to his line, to restore the ancient dynasty of Aeternum. Other resistors all crowded around, some red with rage, others pale and shaking their heads.

"Friends, please!" Rune said, tugging himself free from their grasp. "Listen to me."

Kaelyn was snarling, her eyes flashing, and she twisted his collar tighter. "You listen to me, you stupid boy. We fought this war for you. Your forebears have sat upon this throne for four thousand years--since the days of the first king. How can you just... just walk away from it?" She released his collar and covered her eyes.

Again everyone started shouting, tugging at his clothes, gesturing at the throne, and filling the hall with echoes.

Only Tilla stood silently throughout the ruckus. She looked at Rune through the crowd that came between them. He met her eyes.

There he is, she thought and breathed deeply. *There is Rune Brewer. There is the boy I grew up with. There is the man I love.*

As the others tugged at his arms, his collar, and his shoulders, Tilla stepped forward, reached out, and held his hand. She smiled tremulously, and she was with him again on the beach. They no longer stood here in this throne room, this place that was foreign to them, this place of gold and marble and ghosts. In her mind and in his eyes, they were already back home.

She nodded.

"Yes," she whispered. She turned to Valien, who was still railing about ancient dynasties, and touched his arm.

He turned toward her, face red. "The boy is a fool!" he said, teeth grinding. "Tilla, will you talk sense into him?"

She sighed. "For the first time since I've known him, he is making perfect sense. Look around you, Valien Eleison. We don't belong here. I'm not a soldier. Rune isn't a king." Seeing him open his mouth to protest, she held up her hand. "Oh, I know all about his lineage. You've spoken of it enough. But those are old lines. Look at that throne, Valien. Is that the throne his father ruled? The Oak Throne of Requiem? No. Frey burned that ancestral seat. I see only an ivory mockery that Frey sat upon. Dynasties change. Requiem is reborn, and she is ready for a new line." She looked back at Rune and she smiled. For the first time in years, she smiled a warm smile, the sort of smile that filled one's entire body, that tickled like spring dawn after winter. "Let him return south with me. You needed him to rally hearts and win this war. You don't need his silly little backside to polish some seat." She returned her eyes to Valien and winked. "That backside of his now belongs to me."

Valien gaped at her, eyes wide, mouth open, and then something happened that caught Tilla by surprise.

Valien, the gruff and grizzled leader of the Resistance, laughed.

It was a creaky laugh, sort of like a tree thawing after a long frost. Tilla guessed that like her smile, his laugh was reemerging after long years of slumber. It started awkwardly, scraping and crackling, then became a deep, joyous sound. And Tilla laughed too.

She pulled Rune into an embrace. She held him close and would not release him, and she kissed his cheek, and she kept laughing. When finally she could laugh no more, she touched his hair and whispered softly.

"Can we do this, Rune? Can we rebuild our home?" She lowered her gaze. "Not much is left."

He held her in his arms. "*We* are left. And we are together. We can rebuild the whole damn world."

She pinched his cheek and mussed his hair. For the first time in many years, she had laughed this day. For the first time in many years, she was happy.

ERRY

She stood in the crowd, watching Valien and Kaelyn's wedding. Or was this their coronation? Erry couldn't tell and she fidgeted, hopping on her tiptoes and twisting her fingers behind her back.

"Damn ceremonies," she muttered under her breath. "Who in the Abyss gets married *and* crowned on the same day? Too much pomp and too much damn--"

"Shh!" Miya said, standing at her side. Her younger, taller sister glared down at her. "Valien is being crowned now, so hush."

Erry grumbled, frowned at the girl, and grudgingly bit down on her words.

She stood among a crowd of... stars, it must have been a hundred people. They covered the palace walls all around her--resistors, city elders, and whatever other dignitaries Valien had deemed important enough to stand here with him. And below the walls--maggoty toe juice! Erry's head spun to see it. A great square spread below; Erry thought it larger than all of Lynport. Hundreds of thousands crowded down there, maybe a million. All of Nova Vita had come to see the coronation, it seemed, filling the square.

Upon these walls where Erry stood, no more banners of Cadigus hung, nor did they fly from the tower that rose above. Tarath Imperium had been rededicated. New banners hung here now. They were deep green, and the silver stars of Requiem appeared upon them, shaped like a dragon--the Draco constellation, the forbidden gods now worshiped again.

Miya elbowed her and whispered from the corner of her mouth. "Erry! You're not watching the coronation. This is a historical event. Stop gawping at the clouds and look at Valien."

Erry growled. "You're a pushy little sister. Remember that you're younger than me, and I can beat you up."

The young Tiran's eyes flashed. "You might be older, but I'm taller. Now hush and *watch*."

With another grumble, Erry looked up toward Valien. He stood upon the walls perhaps a hundred yards away, looking down at the crowds. Erry had always seen him wearing only furs and leathers, but now he wore his old knight's armor, the steel plates polished to a bright silver. Birch leaves were engraved on his breastplate, and he bore a new sword, abandoning his old hunk of steel for a kingly blade. For the first time since Erry had known him, his beard was trimmed, his hair brushed and neat, and his eyes bright.

By the stars, he's actually handsome, Erry thought and felt her blood heat. *Who knew?*

She turned to look at Kaelyn, who stood at Valien's side. The young princess had always been beautiful, even when covered with grime. But now, dressed in an azure gown, her hair braided and strewn with flowers, Kaelyn looked fairer than ever, so much that Erry's blood heated further. With her short hair and scrawny limbs, Erry wasn't sure if she felt jealous of or awed by Kaelyn's beauty.

Valien is a lucky bastard, she thought.

The coronation began.

Rune stepped forth, clad in green and silver, and he too looked more clean and handsome than Erry had ever seen him. The last Aeternum approached the newlyweds, bearing two crowns. When he reached Valien and Kaelyn, they knelt before him.

He spoke some words; they flitted into Erry's ears and out again. She did not understand court-speak. Rune recited some fancy talk about abdi-something the throne, passing on the torch, and naming Valien Eleison the new king. He placed the crown upon the man's head, then turned to Kaelyn and crowned her too, and then spoke some more. He prayed to the Draco Stars and blessed them.

Erry rolled her eyes and rocked on her heels. Rune had just memorized the words yesterday. He was no priest or ruler; he was just the boy from the boardwalk, the boy she would play mancala with, the boy who brought her food sometimes. And she was just a dock rat, and Tilla was just a ropemaker. They were just southern beach children. They didn't belong here. They didn't need any of this pomp and ceremony.

She sighed.

But maybe we're no longer those things, she thought and lowered her head. *Maybe we did change. Maybe we did grow. Maybe... maybe Rune is wise now, and Tilla is a warrior, and I... what am I?*

She looked at Miya who stood at her side. The young woman's eyes gleamed as she watched the coronation. Erry looked past Miya at the tall, golden-skinned man who stood farther back, a captain of the southern seas.

No, I'm no longer a dock rat, she thought. *I'm a sister. And I'm a daughter.*

Her eyes stung and her chest constricted. The urge to flee welled inside her. She had to escape this place, to run, to get away, to stop those damn tears from burning.

She tightened her lips, clenched her fists, and began to shove back through the crowd. Miya gasped at her and people muttered, but Erry didn't care. She had to get out. She couldn't... couldn't bear this anymore, couldn't bear these feelings that stung her, that felt so warm in her chest.

Let them have their celebrations, she thought, worming her way between the people. Trumpets began to play and singers to sing, but Erry ignored them. She had never needed anyone. She had always been a lone wolf--on the docks and here in this city.

She found a staircase and descended toward a small courtyard, moving away from the music, the crowds, the flowers, and all those things that still stung, that still frightened a child grown up in shadows. She walked upon cobblestones, walls and towers at her sides, finally able to breathe, to calm her heart. She had always felt most calm in solitude, and though she had often felt unfortunate as a child, she found herself missing the beach, the sound of waves, and the company of her animals. Perhaps that was the only life she truly knew how to live.

She walked along paths and porticoes. Finally she found a small garden between brick walls. Several oak trees grew here, surrounding a statue of Frey Cadigus. Thousands of his statues filled the city; many had been toppled already, but some still stood, tucked away in small gardens or courtyards, still watching the city and awaiting their felling.

Erry was about to sit under a tree when she noticed a figure standing ahead, watching the statue.

Tilla.

Erry froze, not sure how to proceed. Tilla had once been her dearest friend, but last time she had seen the woman, Tilla had worn the armor of a legionary, and she had burned Erry with her punisher; Erry still carried a faded scar from the attack. Today Tilla wore no armor and bore no weapon. She stood in a white tunic, a string of seashells around her neck. A breeze rustled the trees and billowed Tilla's black, chin-length hair.

She's staring at the tyrant, Erry thought. *Does she still worship him? She has removed her armor, but is her heart still dark?*

She had begun to tiptoe away when Tilla spoke, not turning toward her.

"It's a funny thing, isn't it?"

Erry paused in mid-step, turned back, and saw Tilla still staring at the statue.

"I've heard folk call Frey a god or a monster," Erry said, "but funny is a new one."

Tilla nodded, face blank. "I think most saw him as both, a monstrous god to worship not from love but from fear. That's why I served him."

When Tilla turned toward her, Erry took a step back.

No, her face isn't blank, she thought. *There is deep pain there, a horror she hides under her cold mask.*

"Well, he's dead now," Erry said, still hesitant, not sure that she wanted to be here, and the old scar on her chest burned. "So to the Abyss with his rotten carcass, and may they dump this statue in a cesspool."

She turned to leave, but Tilla called out.

"Erry, wait."

With a huff, Erry spun around and glared. "What?" Rage flared within her. "What do you want with me? You have your statue here. Go make love to it, or worship it, or spit on it. I don't care. I'm looking for a quiet place of my own."

When she turned to leave again, Tilla raced toward her, held her shoulders, and wouldn't let go.

"Erry, please. Just... wait a moment."

"Don't touch me!" Erry said and shoved her off.

Tilla took a step back and nodded. "Erry, I'm sorry, all right?"

She snorted a laugh. "Easy to be sorry now with your lord dead."

"You served in the Legions too. We both served him." Tilla lowered her head. "That doesn't mean he's my lord."

"Oh, we both served him, did we?" Erry's voice rose, torn with anger. "I never killed for him. I never collaborated with his daughter. I never..." Her eyes burned with tears, and Erry hated herself for it. "I never betrayed a friend."

"And I did," Tilla said. "I did all those things. I know it. And I'm sorry. I was... how would you say it? A horse's arse."

Erry snorted. "You were a particularly big, smelly horse's arse."

Tilla nodded. "Fair enough."

"With fleas."

"All right."

"And with an infected, maggoty red spiral brand right on it. And with some ticks and--"

"All right, Erry, I get it."

Erry sighed, knuckled her stinging eyes, and looked at her feet. She spoke in a low whisper. "You're my best friend, Tilla. You're my *only* friend. You and Wobble Lips." Now her own damn lips wobbled. "I never had any other friends." She looked up through damp eyes. "I love you, you stinky horse's bottom."

Tilla smiled, laughed, and pulled her into an embrace. "Love you too, you little shrimp."

Erry held her friend and felt warm and safe. She closed her eyes, leaned her cheek against Tilla, and thought this better than all the crowds, weddings, and coronations in the world.

Leresy would hold me too, she thought. A hundred men before him would hold her like this, but they hadn't loved her. They had all wanted her sex, or they had wanted her to heal their souls. But this felt right. This felt good.

"I'm moving back to Lynport," Tilla said. "Rune is going too. A few hundred townsfolk survived, and we're going to rebuild. Rune and I will rebuild the Old Wheel and run it together." She held Erry at arm's length. "Come with us. Brew ale with us or serve tables or cook meals... just be with us. We'll run the place together, us three."

To live with Tilla and Rune? To have a roof over her head, regular meals, a home of her own? Warmth filled Erry, spreading through her like sunrise over a rolling landscape. And yet she shook her head.

"Nah, it's called the Old Wheel, not the Third Wheel. It's not a place for me. Go and make it a great place, Tilla. You and Rune. I know that you will. But me... it's not a place for me."

Tilla's eyes softened. "So where will you go? Do you have a place? Are you sure you don't want to stay with us?"

A hesitant smile tingled Erry's lips, soon turning into a grin. "I have a place now. I have a home. I have a family."

The spring sun warmed the land, leaves budded on the trees, and new light shone across Requiem. Masons bustled in cities and villages, building new temples to the stars. Statues of Frey fell. Knives scratched red spirals off armor, swords, and shields. A new dawn rose for Requiem, and King Valien ruled with light, justice, and wisdom.

"I helped save Requiem," Erry whispered, flying over the forests and mountains of the kingdom, the sun bright above. "But not for me. It will never be a warm, safe place for me."

She had suffered here too much. Her body and soul bore too many scars. The beaches, the forests, the city walls... they all carried too many memories, too much pain.

How do you cleanse your memories of blood? she thought as she flew on the wind, the forests rolling below her, the capital vanishing far behind. *How do you find light when so much darkness still fills you?*

Erry didn't know. For so many years, she had run from pain. She had run to her docks, into forests, or into men's arms. Today too she was fleeing.

Yet now... now she had a good place to fly to. Now she had somebody to fly with.

"Hey, Erry!" Miya cried from her back, seated in a saddle. "Can't you fly any faster?"

Erry growled over her shoulder. Her little sister's hair flapped in the wind, and her cheeks were pink, yet still she pointed forward, demanding more speed. Their father sat upon the saddle too, smiling, his hard face showing rare peace.

"Do you want to fly instead, Miya?" Erry said.

"Not fair. I'm a Tiran. You know Tirans can't fly. Tirans *sail*."

"So be quiet and let the half-dragon do her work."

Tirans sail. And Erry too had Tiran blood. She too would sail. She inhaled, already smelling the salty air.

They flew across Requiem for days. They left the birch forests behind, and they flew over the great plains of Osanna. They traveled over hills, woods, and mountains. At nights, they slept in taverns or simply under the stars. They flew until they saw the eastern sea, the blue border of the empire.

In a clear dawn, they descended toward the port of Altus Mare, an ancient city. Once a place of docks and shipyards, a great hub of merchants, the city had fallen in the wars, its original inhabitants slain. Today a small fishing village rose upon the ruins, home to several hundred Vir Requis, a tanned people clothed in canvas, their faces weathered with the sea winds.

Erry walked onto the docks, stared out into the sea, and tapped her chin.

"Now what do we do?" she asked her father and sister. "The islands with our ships are a three-day flight away. I can't fly for three days straight, not without a place to rest at night."

Her father stared into the sea, inhaled deeply, and smiled.

"We fly back the way we flew here," he said. "You take turns. Every few hours, you return to human form and sleep upon another dragon. We just need to find that other dragon."

And so they spent the night in Altus Mare, and in the morning, they paid a young fisherman three silver coins to fly with them. At first Erry didn't want him riding her. His grin was too wide, his eyes too green, his curly hair too wild. She had fallen for too many pretty boys to let another into her life.

"Not this one," she said, pointing at him upon the docks. "He's too young."

The boy flashed a grin. "I'm twenty years old. I can't be much older than you." He winked. "And I bet I can fly faster."

"You keep pretending that," Erry said. She turned back toward her father. "This one is trouble. You should never have paid him silver. I would never agree to him, had he not already pocketed the coins." She grumbled. "I fly first. And I fly fast, so hold on to your saddle."

She shifted into dragon form. They climbed onto her back. And she flew.

The sea rolled below them, blue patched with green, and he would not stop taunting her, that rude boy with the green eyes. When finally it was his turn to fly, and she rode upon his back with Sila and Miya, she wanted to taunt him too. But she was too tired. So she only leaned back in the saddle, closed her eyes, and slept.

They flew for three days and nights, and finally they saw Maiden Island ahead, a woman rising from the sea, her hair formed of a waterfall, her hip and waist crowned with trees. In the cove between her curves, it waited--the *Golden Crane*, its masts tall, its hull emblazoned with golden sunbursts. When Erry saw it, her eyes dampened.

My new home.

"You're wobbling again," said the boy on her back. He jabbed her with his heel. "You wobble too much when you fly."

She glared over her shoulder at him. He was smiling his same mocking smile.

"Be quiet or I'll wobble so much you'll fall off."

Upon the *Golden Crane*, dear old Bantis--he had stayed to watch over the ship--danced a jig and waved and whooped.

My crazy grandfather, Erry thought and laughed.

She flew down and landed on the deck. When her riders dismounted, she returned to human form, placed her hands upon the railing, and inhaled the sea air. In her mind, she could already imagine the sails wide, the ship cutting through the water. She could fly faster than a ship could sail, and yet... flying was lonely. This ship was not merely a vessel; it was family and it was home.

Her father smiled and held her hand. Her sister and grandfather embraced her. They stood together on the deck and Erry smiled too. This was right.

"Well," said the green-eyed boy and stretched. "I suppose now it's back to the village with me. Back to fishing and lying around on the beach." He sighed theatrically. "I reckon you don't need me here, so if you could just take me a few miles back, I'll fly the rest of the way."

Erry groaned, jabbed his chest with her finger, and glared at him. "If you want a job here, pretty boy, just spit it out. Don't play your little games."

He grinned and mussed her hair. When she shoved his hand back, he only grinned wider.

"So you want me to stay! You'd love me to. I can see it in your eyes, little one."

They left Maiden Island, the wind in their sails, only five souls heading into the open sea. He was right, of course. She had wanted him to stay, that rude boy with the taunting smile and green eyes. And their first night on the waters, when her family slept, Erry was tempted again. It would be so easy! She could sneak into his hammock, doff her clothes, and let him bed her. She would look into his eyes, press her body against his, and she would feel warm, feel a respite from the chill that always filled her.

But no. Not this time. She let him sleep, climbed onto the deck, and watched the moonlight glimmer on the sea. This time she would be a different Erry. She had to be different now, not the same old dock rat, not even with this very rude, very pretty sailor. She could wait a little longer with this one.

The *Golden Crane* sailed on into the night. The wind filled her hair, the good scent of water and salt filled her nostrils, and Erry smiled softly. In the darkness, she thought of Mae Baker, and she thought of Leresy, and she thought of all those she had lost. She remembered the pain of her childhood and the wars of her youth, and she knew those memories would always fill her, that her scars would always burn. Yet standing here upon the deck, she could smile, for Erry knew that while darkness stretched behind her, light shone ahead. And that was all right. That was enough for her.

A gleam upon the sea caught her eye. She leaned over the railing and frowned. Something was floating in the water, small and bright in the moonlight.

Erry leaped and shifted into a dragon. She dived down to the water, gripped the sparkling item in her claws, and flew back onto the deck. When she shifted back into human form, she found a silver amulet in her palm, shaped like a sun.

It was her father's amulet, the amulet that had been hers for so long, that had brought her here. She slung it around her neck and stood for a long time, watching the sea.

RUNE

They walked along the beach, watching sunset gild the waves. The cliffs of Ralora rose behind them, and the sand caressed their bare feet. Seashells glimmered in the light, countless jewels hiding and emerging with every wave. The wind from the sea blew their hair, scented of home.

"Do you know why I love the sea?" Tilla said, voice soft.

Rune looked at her. She was staring into the water, her high cheeks, normally so pale, golden in the light. A smile touched her lips, but a sadness filled her eyes, a good sadness like memories that were too special, too important, for joy alone.

"Because it's always different," Rune answered.

She looked at him. "Yes. Have I told you before?"

He smiled. "Only a hundred and one times."

She looked back at the waves. "This evening the sunlight breaks through the thin clouds, rays fall upon the water, and a path of gold trails into the horizon. Yesterday birds sang here, and the water glimmered with white mottles. Sometimes the water is blue and sometimes it's green. Sometimes the sky is a single, uniform azure, and sometimes it's a patchwork of a hundred colors." She reached out and held his hand, still watching the waves. "And sometimes, standing here, we are young and scared. And sometimes we are older and scarred. And sometimes... sometimes we're just two people in the sand, a story of pain and triumph, and we too are a patchwork like the sky, a dappled painting of hurt and joy. And some days, like today, when the wind is warm and the waves whisper, when the light falls on seashells and sand, and when the sky fades into purple and indigo... I don't know who I am. But I'm happy with that. And I'm happy here with you."

Rune placed a hand around her waist, and she leaned against him. This was the same place, here under these cliffs, where they would wrestle and laugh as children. This was the place where they'd stand before the wars, watching the merchant ships rise from the horizon. This was the place where they had said goodbye two years ago, the first place they had kissed. He smoothed her hair now, and he kissed her again. Two years ago, it had been a kiss of farewell, a kiss that tasted of her tears. This one was better; it was a kiss of hope, of a future, of many more ahead.

They walked along the sand, hand in hand, heading back toward the town. Lynport rose ahead, nestled between forest and sea. Much of the city still lay fallen, but new buildings now rose here like saplings rising from the ash of an old forest fire. A few hundred survivors were finding a new life. A flame kindled in the lighthouse, the first time it had shone in twenty years. A distant figure stood fishing on the docks--Tilla's father, one of the few survivors of the slaughter. Rising farther back, Rune could see the tiled roof of the rebuilt Old Wheel. A warm meal, a welcoming dog, and a soft bed awaited them there.

He began to walk toward the town when Tilla gasped. She squeezed his hand and held him fast.

"Look!" she said.

He turned back toward the sea and squinted.

A small white square rose from the horizon, caught the sun, and blazed gold. It grew taller, blooming from the water, revealing masts and a hull. Five more ships appeared behind it, sails wide.

"They're returning to Lynport," Rune whispered. "Like they did years ago."

Tilla nodded and smiled, and a distant scent of spice wafted on the wind. Rune held her hand in the sunset, and they stood together on the sand, watching the ships sail in.

THE END

NOVELS BY DANIEL ARENSON

Standalones:
Firefly Island (2007)
The Gods of Dream (2010)
Flaming Dove (2010)

Misfit Heroes:
Eye of the Wizard (2011)
Wand of the Witch (2012)

Song of Dragons:
Blood of Requiem (2011)
Tears of Requiem (2011)
Light of Requiem (2011)

Dragonlore:
A Dawn of Dragonfire (2012)
A Day of Dragon Blood (2012)
A Night of Dragon Wings (2013)

The Dragon War
A Legacy of Light (2013)
A Birthright of Blood (2013)
A Memory of Blood (2013)

KEEP IN TOUCH

www.DanielArenson.com
Daniel@DanielArenson.com
Facebook.com/DanielArenson
Twitter.com/DanielArenson

www.ingramcontent.com/pod-product-compliance
Lightning Source LLC
Chambersburg PA
CBHW031710170626
46808CB00005B/1682

* 9 7 8 1 9 2 7 6 0 1 1 1 2 *